Novemb

Brian & Michael Turner

Best Wishes

Michael Turner

New Generation **Publishing**

Acknowledgements

We would like to say a very big thank you to Sophie Jackson, an accomplished authoress who painstakingly edited this manuscript.

In addition, she happily shared her years of experience, giving invaluable advice that we have tried to emulate, in the writing of November Keys.

Also a thank you to the New Generation Publishing team for their ongoing help and dedicated services, in the production of this book.

November Keys

We are both very proud to introduce our début novel November Keys. Having spent many happy hours creating the various characters and interweaving the intricate story line, we hope that you the reader will find it enjoyable and an exciting experience.

Happy Reading.

Brian & Michael.

Chapter One
Nearly The End

Anxious fans swarmed noisily through brightly lit turnstiles, their agitated demeanour giving the appearance of angry locusts. The majority, not relishing the battle ahead and its possible consequences, pulled their scarves tightly around their mouths as though trying to protect their identities. Many became silent, gazing intently at small blue keys dancing enticingly across the vast glass windows of the stadium's dome. Each key, boasting of past victories, darted haphazardly, tantalizingly linking together, glowing defiantly in the fading light. This boastful spectacle chronicled past successes. Triumphs that gloriously embossed the magical history of November Keys Football Club.

Recalling their victories invigorated the brooding fans, who now proceeded with a renewed optimism. Some dithered, crossing their fingers in a strange ritual, whispering half-audible oaths, others silently praying, willing their team to rediscover it's form, dispatching the opposition, as in months past, with their tails between their legs. The faint-hearted nodded their heads dejectedly, not deeming it possible that in such a short space of time, their beloved team could be in such a desperate situation.

The cold November wind interrupted their thoughts, prompting even the hardiest to tighten their jackets. Shivering uncontrollably some reflected on how cold a struggling team's stadium could be. Not feeling able to take their seats, for what they saw as a forthcoming torture, some stopped first at the chilli bar, desperate to get warm and be cheered up. The bar, a favourite, especially on a cold day, always attracted a habitual clientele. The proprietors offering a menu they claimed could melt icebergs. Friends teased each other, urging compatriots to consume dishes that scorched their throats. Others drank honey ale noisily in the large bars, nervously clutching glossy programmes. None willing to read warnings of the miserable consequences if Keys failed to win.

Those who had made the journey, optimistically, without tickets, stood forlornly outside the stadium. Frantically checking their cash, their eyes searching for ticket touts from whom they could purchase a cherished ticket at an inflated price.

Inside the stadium, older fans concealed their gloom, laughing half-heartedly at the youngsters donning their brightly coloured masks. The children with no knowledge of the possible disasters that awaited chuckled happily, revelling in the carnival atmosphere. Listening to their parents earlier, discussing huge parties, they had excitedly made their plans. Secret meeting places were appointed, to meet with friends. Their parents, had agreed unanimously, win or lose, they would keep a stiff upper lip, celebrating their Harvesting Leaf celebrations in true November Keys fashion. After all, they reasoned, their rituals dated back hundreds of years. The older locals stubbornly maintained that not even two World Wars could curtail the celebrations, let alone a football match.

Many of the teenagers however, brazenly threatened to boycott the parties if Keys failed to qualify for the next rounds. The Mississippi Bards (the visiting opposition) having finished, what the German bombs could not, they argued that there would be nothing to celebrate anyway. A few of the cheekier teenagers demanded to be told, how Harvesting Leaf was celebrated in war times, during the black outs.

The older ones retaliated, waving copies of The Echo at their tormentors. Their local newspaper had earlier conducted a poll amongst the real villagers. An important question was asked. What was deemed more important, a football match or Harvesting Leaf Day? To the rest of the country's surprise, Harvesting Leaf Day won by a large margin.

The arguing was brought to a halt, thoughts distracted by numerous wide-screen televisions bursting rudely into life. Suddenly, cameras swooped around the magnificent stadium prying at embarrassed spectators. Some waved shyly whilst others chose to hide behind their papers and programmes. The youngsters however, happily posed for the cameras, waving good-heartedly, jostling for attention. Dressed in regulatory green and white uniform, some placed Wilfred masks on to their faces, their hands making scratching movements, which they considered an imitation of the club mascot's strange behaviour.

Lionel Bains, already having taken his seat, allowed his eyes to wander around the vast arena. Gingerly pulling at his greying moustache he prayed for a Keys win, while also contemplating the possible demise of November Keys and guiltily considering his involvement with it. He had spent the best part of a week interviewing desolate fans and worried locals about their futures. Many had stressed they would have strenuously prevented the Americans getting involved. His own face had flushed with embarrassment, recalling the powers he had sold so cheaply.

Despondently, he sadly watched numerous flags dancing in the wind. Each flag represented a Keys win against various overseas opponents. For a short while he tried to count them, soon getting bored, he allowed his eyes to rest on the lavish glass domes of the stadium. Newspapers and magazines across the world had used inches of print to expound its amazing architecture.

Maysoni might have committed just about every conceivable crime, he thought wearily. However, one thing he had done that was right, he had given the fans a stadium the envy of the world.

Tom Doulby reeled from one building to another. He was enjoying himself. In addition, he did not have to worry about Vera either. When his nephew had spectacularly handed him a ticket, he had slyly glanced at his long-suffering wife, expecting numerous objections. Unbelievably, she had smiled, telling him to enjoy his game. She had insisted he wear a pair of her tights to combat the weather, in between nagging about his drinking. Nevertheless, he considered that a small price to pay for his forthcoming enjoyment. Patting his hip flask, he made his way in to one of the noisy bars, cheerfully demanding more honey ale.

The Caterpillar Express whined moodily, grinding to a stand-still. Vast numbers trudging on to busy platforms. Ticket collectors, not enthusiastic about trying to delay the embarking passengers, attempted to form a human barrier. They had been instructed to show diligence regarding possible fare dodgers.

However, the stream of bodies hurrying towards the exit was in no mood for trivial confrontations. Many, having travelled considerable distances had minds set on the coming game, rather than arguments about fares. The relieved collectors watched them disappear towards the ground.

Mike Matthews, from Moon Television, watched the crowds of fans, reflecting how they curiously resembled an army of angry ants. He surmised the damage that could be caused if they were agitated. He half smiled, watching them unashamedly jumping clumsily, attempting to catch leaves floating in the wind. Aware of their superstitions, he reflected on what use a handful of leaves would be on such an important day. Shrugging his shoulders, he whistled silently, astounded by people's faith in ridiculous old customs.

"Better enjoy yourselves while you can." He mouthed his words to himself. Later, he thought gloomily, he might be reminding millions of listeners, that Keys next challenge, was to fight off liquidation, although that in itself was not unique with many other clubs suffering similar fates. The fact that if it disappeared, it would tow the village of November Keys with it was indeed rare.

Pressing his mouth close to a microphone, he voiced his concerns about a seemingly abundance of leaves with no road sweepers to hand. His words, as he expected were met with a torrent of boos. Smiling broadly, he was pleased to hear his audience was paying attention.

John Goldsmith, apprehensively trying to spot any sign of Decesso and his cronies, squirmed uncomfortably in his undersized chair. Despite the cold weather beads of sweat trickled down his face, tiny drops splashing onto his well-pressed jacket. Ignoring the noise and activities around him, he forced his mind to concentrate on the dangers that possibly lay ahead. Straining his thick neck, he continuously commanded his eyes to investigate the crowds. Anxious to sight early, anyone who seemed out of place. He did not believe for one minute, that the gangster or his henchmen were not concealed in the stadium somewhere. He had to hand it to the American, he thought wistfully, he was the master of disguise.

Goldsmith himself, dressed conspicuously, in trademark gold suit and red tie, waved cheerfully to the roving cameras. Although the police had advised him not to appear too conspicuous, he had no wish to resort to camouflage. If Decesso thought he was going to hide, then the fat hooligan had him all wrong, he thought gravely. He was not the sort to hide away.

He recalled his meeting with the police officers, wishing they had listened and postponed the game. Everyone would have been so much safer when the American was apprehended, or at least reported to be back in the States. A thin police inspector with a hawk-like face had recoiled in horror when Goldsmith had reluctantly fed him the full facts. Studying Goldsmith's face and his own thumb disbelievingly, he had mumbled about ratepayers and taxes.

A superintendent was summoned. A huge man with a broken nose, who behaved as though he was attending a party. Waving away Goldsmith's objections, he maintained steadfastly that the game should be allowed to continue. Excited at the prospect of arresting such a prominent gangster as Decesso, the young superintendent urged Goldsmith to attend the match as well. Goldsmith, he had exclaimed excitedly, would be the bait. Goldsmith's ears ringing with well wishes, he left the police station with assurances that Operation America would be successful. His co-operation would ensure that Decesso would be back where he belonged, behind bars. Goldsmith, had shook his head sadly, convinced the police, despite their bravado, had no idea who they were dealing with.

Dabbing his face with a gold coloured handkerchief, his thoughts quickly turned to the young woman sitting opposite in his VIP box. Although she was already getting in the swing of things, shouting her own version of insults at the visiting team, he could not help feeling how vulnerable she seemed. She had already had enough of an ordeal for one so young, and he was concerned not just for her physical safety, but for her state of mind as well. When she had insisted in her customary way of rolling her eyes and stamping her feet, he had conceded that she could attend the match. Although he would have preferred her to stay away, he took satisfaction in being aware of her whereabouts.

The superintendent had been overjoyed at his second piece of bait, promising wildly the girl would be as safe as houses. Nevertheless, Goldsmith made certain he, himself, never took his eyes off her for very long.

As the vast clock sited at the end of the stadium ticked away to nearly three O 'clock, straggling fans, prompted by a desperate voice echoing through large loudspeakers, hurriedly made their way to their seats. Those who had failed to purchase tickets eyed the stadium enviously, resigned to only listening to the game outside. Squatting at the base of an old oak, radios and mobile phones pinned to their ears, they complained to each other about the abundance of leaves.

The big clock pointed its gold hands, indicating the match was about to commence. A few hearts missed a beat, the Keys' players trundled out onto the pitch, waving merrily. If they had any nerves they certainly did not intend to let it show. Listening to the loud speakers blasting out their theme song, some jigged to the music, whilst others blew kisses to the crowd.

The Keys' supporters voiced their approval, cheering loudly, analysing the players chosen to play. Some, disagreeing with the manager's selections, moodily changed their cheers to jeers. Van de Groot, dressed in customary immaculate blue suit, appeared. Jeers changed back to cheers. Staring straight ahead, he seemed to ignore the many voices screaming his name. The fans adored their manager. Putting their apprehensions to one side they chanted his name, whilst jangling whatever keys they could lay their hands on.

A voice, verging on the hysterical, announced the players' names, enthusing the whole stadium until it was drowned in frenzied cheering.

Soon a reluctant Wilfred, the club's adopted mascot, joined the players and their manager. Urged on to the pitch by his adoring fans, he could do no more than glare at his perceived tormentors. Rolling himself in a ball he laid by a goalpost, unconcernedly falling to sleep. It mattered nothing to him that he had captured the hearts of the nation. It mattered nothing to him that this was the most important game in Keys' history. He was not feeling his best and wanted some peace and quiet.

Wilfred was testimony to the fact that anyone or anything can improve their circumstances, given the right attitude. Born in a barn with little future, other than foraging for food, the stray had materialized at just the right time.

When the beloved Van de Groot had taken over his role

as club manager, the unfortunate feline, turning up from apparently nowhere, had followed him incessantly. Van de Groot, although not disliking animals, had called for the far from pretty cat to be ejected from the ground. It worried him that the scruffy feline might be carrying some terrible disease that could be transmitted to the players, or worse, himself! After twelve, sometimes noisy, ejections Wilfred would lovingly return to his adopted master. It was after one such reappearance that Van de Groot, for the benefit of all, had decided to take matters into his own hands by putting the strange animal out of it's misery and dispatching it to the nearest cat's home. The pen, being mightier than the sword saved the cat's day. Some enterprising reporter had written a story about Van de Groot's love of stray animals. Very quickly, Wilfred had been installed into every heart of every die-hard supporter. The scruffy cat had become a celebrity overnight, often appearing in newspapers across the globe. When he decided to accompany the players onto the pitch the press were ecstatic. He was duly rewarded with his own twitter page. Further, when at half-time he mingled with the crowd, sniffing their bags and pockets, his antics were discussed jovially on several back pages.

The referee at last blew his silver whistle, peering apprehensively into the crowd. Signalling for one of the most talked about games of football to proceed, his hands trembled violently. The gangsters had made it clear, that Keys were not to go through. If the Keys' supporters knew what he had to do, he thought miserably, his life would not be worth living.

Mike Matthews spoke excitedly, enjoying the deafening noise from the fans. He reluctantly reminded everyone worldwide, for the umpteenth time, that if Keys were to draw or lose they would be eliminated from the prestigious World Super League, which would subsequently cause their demise from English football.

Alphonso Decesso lounged in his car, sneering at the noise

blaring from his radio. Turning his head, he muttered to the man sitting behind him. Happy that his wishes had been obeyed, he sat back, allowing himself a rare smile. He was assured the referee had been approached, guaranteeing the hicks would lose their game. In addition, he had arranged a little farewell party.

Despite a large police presence, he had had little trouble planting bombs strategically placed around the vast stadium. After the match, when he had the girl and Goldsmith apprehended, he intended to blow the football club to pieces.

His smile turning into a snarl, he recalled how Maysoni had transformed what was a dirt track into one of the most prestigious stadiums in the world. For his troubles he had been confined to prison for the rest of his days, being turned into a gibbering lunatic.

Slamming his podgy hands onto the car's steering wheel, he smiled broadly. In a short while, the stadium would end as it started, a dirt track. That was going to be in revenge for his pal. Then he was going to have great pleasure torturing Goldsmith, but not before his aggressor witnessed the life ebb painfully from the girl. Rubbing his hands with glee, he relished the coming events. It had taken him much longer then he had expected to reach his goal and he intended to savour every moment. Scowling at his passengers, his angry eyes silently commanded that there would be no mistakes. This was his party and there would be no excuses.

Predictably, The Bards defended well, intent on not letting their rivals score. Some of the fans, becoming distracted, glanced at flashing electronic advertising boards urging sales of various products. At one time busy executives had queued on busy phone lines, desperate to place their advertisements. Now, the same executives waited with baited breath for the outcome of the day's showdown. A dead club was not a place to be brandishing your wares.

Van de Groot, continuously barking instructions, willed

the white football past the Bards' goal post. However, despite a few near misses, no goals were forthcoming. Impatient fans groaned incessantly. Checking their watches, many considered their half-time snacks, waiting for the whistle to conclude a very dull, first half. The referee, relieved at the stalemate, placed his whistle slowly into his mouth.

Jimmy Evans, wearing the number seven shirt, increased the noise of the fans' groans. Squandering a rare opportunity, he lamely kicked the ball straight into the hands of the Bards' goalkeeper. The goalkeeper, to the amazement and delight of the home fans, promptly dispatched the ball back to the boot of Jimmy Evans. The pint-sized striker, hardly believing his good fortune, smashed the ball into the back of the net.

The ground descended into darkness, before being suddenly illuminated by the glow of hundreds of gold keys dancing around the interior glass walls. A large key, glowing blue, appeared on the crown of the dome encouraging the fans to roar their approval. It's bright light reminding everyone that Keys had scored. For those in doubt, the electronic scoreboard confirmed their joy, proclaiming the score to be one – nil. An image of the goal scorer, resplendent in his team's colours, appeared to run around the dome in a lap of honour.

The referee, solemnly staring at the vast crowd, had tried to disallow the goal, however the linesman had other ideas. Waving his flag enthusiastically, the goal stood.

Trying to be heard over the loud speakers jovially blasting out the Keys' victory song, the Keys' fans sang as loud as their lungs allowed. Cheering happily, while gesturing rudely towards stunned opposition fans. For much of the first half the opposing fan's crude songs had tormented them. Now it was their turn to chant. They unleashed their frustration and relief with gusto, rattling their keys, gesturing with their hands.

During the interval, many again descended to the bars

and eating-houses. However, the atmosphere was now more jovial. Keys had scored a vital goal and in another forty-five minutes, they acknowledged happily, their homes and livelihoods would be safe again.

In a triumphant dressing room, Van de Groot congratulated his players quietly. Feeling he had no right to be present at any celebrations, he recalled Goldsmith's words urging him to act as he had done before. In a short while, he knew he could possibly be starting a lengthy prison sentence, his name splashed across every front page, of every newspaper. However, despite his own circumstances, he had a job to do. Reminding each player that they still had another intensive forty-five minutes to endure, he shook their hands and led them back out on to the pitch.

The fans, waiting impatiently, shouted at Wilfred, who remained prostrate. They wanted the sleeping feline to wake up and join in the fun. Singing happily and cheering wildly, they eagerly waited for the whistle to start the second half.

Mike Matthews ordered his cameras to zoom in on relived faces, each telling a different story. Some overjoyed at their marginal lead, others biting their nails, looking apprehensively at the big clock.

Lionel Bains sitting deep in thought mentally summarised the next edition of The Echo. An unexpected guest had arrived during the interval. If he had heard right, the afternoon was going to be very busy. News which would be shouted from newspapers around the world. He wanted some of those headlines in his own paper. Now, however, he forced his mind to concentrate on the football. Aware that Van de Groot would have summoned his players to play deep and protect their narrow lead, he guessed the game would finish with just the one goal. Nevertheless, that goal would be enough. Tugging happily at his moustache he joyfully anticipated his next headlines.

Decesso, outraged, repeatedly smashed his podgy hands on

to the leather steering wheel, screaming as many oaths as he could remember. Saliva dribbling from the corners of his mouth, he angrily blustered incoherently what he intended to do to the unfortunate referee. His frightened crew sat silently, watching his large face redden, eyeballs protruding like golf balls. His one dying wish, he ranted in frustration, was to witness every hick die in poverty. It was out of respect for his dear friend. Nevertheless, despite, the large salaries he was expected to churn out on a regular basis, his motley crew could not even perform a small task like that. Looking angrily at his watch, he screamed that there were fifteen minutes left for the opposing team to score. Wondering why everyone sharing his car was rendered speechless, he violently grabbed a mobile phone, dialling earnestly.

Mike Matthews shrilled into his microphone. Although worried about the defence tactics that the Keys were following, he commentated on the game in a positive voice. Aware that it would only take an opposition goal to turn the game on its head, he tried to remain optimistic. Forgetting his neutrality, he pleaded, along with thousands of others, for the huge clock to turn its hands quicker.

The fans sitting near to the manager's dugout heard the whinnying of Van de Groot's mobile phone. With only eight minutes remaining they were in jubilant mood, singing noisily for him to answer. Most of the world witnessed the perplexed manager eventually lift the phone to his ear. Not many observed his face take on the hue of fresh milk.

Watching him rush from his dugout, Mike Matthews quipped about him drinking honey ale. The fans merrily reminded him to come back, as he was halfway through a football match.

Neither Mike Matthews nor the fans were very merry on his return. He immediately made two unbelievable substitutions. To the world's disbelief, he was substituting his only striker and even worse, his goalkeeper. The stadium at first was stunned in to an eerie silence, then it found its voice, echoing obscenities aimed at the usually beloved manager.

The irate broadcaster, in the Moon control room, vented his own rage and frustration, angrily inquiring what Van de Groot thought in blazes he was doing. His interest soon turned to the Keys' goalkeeper, who it appeared was sitting in his goal, refusing to leave the pitch.

Mickey Gum had played his heart out. Often sneaking a glimpse at the big clock. He knew that now the Keys had scored, the only villain of the piece would be him if he were to let the ball between his posts. He had spent the entire game shouting and assembling his defence. Now with just a few minutes left to play he could feel a rush of relief drain through his body. All the team had to do was pass the ball around and the game was theirs. When his manager had indicated two substitutions, he had thought kindly that two of the non-stop-running mid-fielders were going to be changed for fresh legs. When it finally dawned on him that he was the one being substituted he laughed at the cameras, sitting defiantly down in his goal. His manager must be going mad, he thought sadly.

Optimistic fans mused that Van de Groot must be playing a clever trick, attempting to waste time. The referee, with a far different opinion constantly tapped his watch, warning that every wasted second was going to be added on.

Goldsmith, taking advantage of the confusion, rushed down to the dugout, furiously venting his rage at the Keys' manager, his eyes swivelled around the ground for any sighting of Decesso. As Van de Groot quietly informed him what was occurring, he frantically nodded his head in approval. Ready to console the ashen faced manager he heard the disturbing tones of his own mobile. Listening to a harsh voice his eyes quickly searched for the girl's seat. He could feel the bile rising from his stomach up to his throat. Her seat was empty!

On the pitch the players were remonstrating with their goalie to leave the pitch. The referee had made overtures that he intended to stop the game, at best being a replay, at worst a forfeit of all the points. Eventually, realising he was outnumbered, the large goalkeeper reluctantly stood up and marched towards the dugout, muttering every conceivable oath he could remember.

The game recommenced to a strained silence. While many of the fans felt Van de Groot knew what he was doing, many did not, and sat silently pleading with the clock to move its large hands to the final whistle.

Goldsmith stared impassively at a large car, slowly proceeding towards him. Screwing his eyes, he recognised Bridget sitting awkwardly in the rear of the vehicle. Angrily asking himself where all the supposed police were he straightened his shoulders. It had crossed his mind to disappear. He would have to admit he was frightened. However, he knew he could not abandon the girl. The car stopped, a gruff voice ordering him to get inside.

The Keys' players regrouped, determined to defend their solitary goal. Having looked to the side-lines for guidance that had not been forthcoming, Steve Brown, the club's captain had taken matters into his own hands, barking out orders. Fortunately, despite the earlier pantomime only four minutes of added time had been allowed. Breathless, he screamed at his players to concentrate, emphasising that in four minutes they would have won their prize.

Two minutes into extra time, the ball was cleverly dispatched to a Bards' player who flicked it down deftly, inching it dangerously towards the goal. Brown, reading the danger calmly arrested the ball, orchestrating a brilliant tackle. Uncertain of any lurking players, he kicked it out of danger, conceding a throw in to the now frantic opposition.

The wild cheering from the stands soon turned to booing and jeers. The fans could not believe they were witnessing their beloved captain being shown a red card, the referee pointing to the dreaded spot and awarding a penalty.

Mike Matthews vented his frustration loudly, shouting obscenities at his back-room staff. He wanted to show a replay of the incident leading up to the penalty, showing what a buffoon the referee was. On being told countless times, by a now timid stream of employees, that they could not retrieve the picture, he screamed desperately into his microphone, hoping that at least half the world, could still hear him.

On the pitch, despite the players manhandling of the referee, the penalty stood. Matthews, not believing his eyes, bellowed into his microphone, as each of the Bards' players in turn refused bluntly to take the awarded kick.

He screamed even louder, demanding at whatever cost to get the picture back. A large man, resplendent in a smart blue suit, strode onto the pitch. Grabbing one of the players by his neck, he frogmarched him to the penalty spot, thrusting a note into his hand.

Pushing away bewildered officials, who had now decided to take some action, he looked menacingly at the startled player, pointing towards the goal. The player, face drained of any colour, stood rooted to the spot, his eyes pleading for some assistance. Slowly opening the note he shook his head disapprovingly and acknowledged he was ready to take the ill-awarded shot.

The Keys' fans, hissing their disapproval, were stunned into silence, watching the ball float into the corner of the net.

Decesso chuckled approvingly. Swivelling his fat neck, he glared at Goldsmith and the terrified girl, insisting that they listen to the remaining two minutes of the match. He happily reminded them that he was about to blow up half the inhabitants of November Keys, while the other half would survive to live in despair and poverty. However, he stressed loudly, the fate of his prisoners was going to be far worse. Rubbing his podgy hands with glee, he burst into song.

The Echo
News to follow.

Chapter Two
Once Upon A Time In November Keys
(Ten Years Ago)

Why the American gangsters initially chose the village of November Keys to launch their offensives, would be debated in crime chronicles for many years to come. Had they not wanted to waste their ink and time, however, they could not have done any better than to ask a certain Alphonso Decesso. Decesso, although persuading his peers otherwise, had no real need of a fortress in a remote village in the countryside of England. However, nursing a well-guarded secret he knew the prize that awaited him there. Amazed that no one had stumbled on his lucrative treasure, he finalised his plans, using the full might of his misguided bosses. His secret, he was certain, was going to make him the wealthiest and most powerful man in the world.

Maysoni made quite an impact when he first appeared in Keys. Many bowled over by his rich American dialogue. Promising great riches and fame, he soon had the residents of Keys seduced by his charms, ready to sell their village to the Devil. He eloquently offered what every self-respecting red-blooded Englander desired. A football club equipped to win every honour in sight. The income that would be made from these successes would establish a thriving community that would become abundant with well-paid labour. No one ever really questioned why he had chosen November Keys and he never really cared to explain. He was indeed baffled himself why he had been pulled half-way round the world, to a place that had as much in common with his native New York as the moon.

The village never hinted a suggestion of closet gangsters or offered likely conspirators for the bosses' crimes. Indeed, although the inhabitants were guilty of the usual failings of petty jealousies, greed and gossiping, the village police officer was hardly bogged down with unsolved crimes.

Much of the world could not understand why hard-working Americans would want to deposit hard-earned cash in such a strange place either. To many outsiders November Keys was a place to give a wide berth. Rumours abounded how the residents were quirky with ingrained strange superstitions. Those who resided outside the village prompted their young children to eat their vegetables at teatime, or risk emulating the creepy residents of Keys. This caused the children to imagine a strange assembly of misfits, who failed to eat their greens, resulting in them indulging in some very strange pastimes. However, despite continuous warnings and threats, many a lass brought worry to her parents by fraternising with the boys from the village. These liaisons were hotly discouraged by irate fathers.

The geography and layout of Keys, again, allowed no clue as to why the gangsters would pursue it as a fortress. The only routes into the village were by two narrow lanes. Often blocked by numerous tractors, their owners unhurriedly pursuing their daily chores. During the spring and summer, the lanes would light up with various wild flowers growing on the hedgerows. Hardly a place befitting those capable of committing heinous crimes and murder.

Those approaching the village from the north would be greeted by the building that was going to eventually make worldwide headlines. Keys Football Club. Erected during Queen Victoria's reign, it still boasted the same drab colours and uncomfortable iron seats. Although ugly and basic, it had once been the pride of the village. The building's purpose was to entertain residents to the skill of football, although many had several other uses for its muddy pitch and decaying seating area. Having given up on any hope of honours, they utilised the facilities the best they could. On a bright day, it was considered a reasonable place to walk the family dog. This hobby could coincide with spreading gossip with other pooch lovers.

So popular was this pastime, it was said that opposing

teams nicknamed the ground the officer's mess, often stipulating that the playing area was cleansed before they would walk on to the pitch.

Many of the younger residents, when sunlight finally dwindled, found its secluded area perfect for night-time dalliances. Many romances commenced and concluded on the playing field. Many of the participants often returning home, red-faced and caked in mud.

Some of the locals did take the club seriously though. JJ, Jack Carpet's son, found great pleasure coaching some of the village youngsters. Despite goal posts that would topple at the softest touch coupled with nets with holes the size of cannonballs, JJ enjoyed his responsibilities. He maintained that sport led to a healthier life and kept bored youths out of trouble.

Simon Potts, who had taken over as chairperson fourteen years previously, repeatedly attempted to instigate some pride and love for the old building. Indeed, during his leadership, Keys were to win their first competition in Club history. At one time he had contemplated ripping out the ancient seating and replacing it with modern décor. However, when the villagers learnt that these alterations would incur an entrance fee, he was soon persuaded to abandon his lofty ideas.

Often on a Saturday afternoon, young Bridget Bluestone could be seen with her tea stall, providing lukewarm tea for those brave enough to turnout in the harsh winds. Her stall proved to be very popular among the younger teenagers, who would queue optimistically, jostling each other to attract her attention, while the older boys would practise their chat up lines on Bridget hoping to secure a date for later in the evening.

Standing at five foot two with bright blue eyes and hair the colour of straw, she was considered a prize to fight for among the village's youth. A cheerful, hard-working girl, she was fully aware of her inherited assets, but resisted the youth's charms. Her energies, she insisted, were concentrated on trying to raise necessary funds to continue her education. Although she loved the village, her mind was set further afield. After university, she continuously claimed, she would set up her own business and travel the world.

If she were not selling beverages from her dubious stall, she could be seen toiling at one of the farms. Although grateful for any paid work, she regarded farm work boring. More than once she could be heard complaining loudly about the menial tasks she was expected to do. Having lost her parents at a young age, many of the older residents felt a responsibility towards Bridget, which induced them to ignore her unfounded complaints. Regular work was always available for her.

Jack Carpet and his wife April viewed their duties towards Bridget very seriously. Often inviting her over for meals, April would supervise her laundry. Taking on a maternal role she also gave advice about young women's requirements.

Jack would find work for her, tending his beloved chickens. Or painstakingly showing her how to collect honey from his numerous beehives. Ignoring Bridget's continuous gripes, he kept a careful eye on her.

Bridget regarded the Carpets as uncle and aunt, often taking April into her confidence where boys were concerned. Although she often stated steadfastly that the opposite sex were of no interest to her (much to the amusement of April) that did not stop her blushing bright red when JJ made his entrance. The young man delighted in teasing his parent's guest. Quite often the two would noisily argue. Bridget pouting and stamping her feet. She often proclaimed her eternal dislike for the only youth (although she would never admit it) who was able to make her heart jump.

Jack and April would look on smiling, never contemplating that the American coming to save the village football club would nearly destroy their son's mind.

The main end of the high street, near the oak, was just a small stroll from Jack Carpet's farm aptly named Honey Bee. Jack, born and bred in Keys, was one of many generations of Carpets that had farmed in the area through the years. Along with his wife April and son JJ, he could be seen in the fields from dusk to dawn. He would be the first to admit that if farming paid an hourly wage, he would have been quite wealthy. However, he was content and like most farmers ate well on his produce.

Residing on the farm was Rose, a black and white border collie. Rose had been with the Carpets as long as anyone could remember. No one, other than Jack, could quite work out why she was there. Predominantly, she was meant to supervise Jack's chickens. However, if her mother or father had taught her the basics of being a farm dog, she had either long forgotten them or given up any intentions of using them. Prone to scratching, she would lumber around the farm making sure her beloved master was always in sight. On a warm day, rather than tend chickens, she would prefer to lie in the sun. If she seldom felt energetic awake, she would chase imaginary foes in her dreams, emitting a strange barking, that resembled the cry of a young girl.

Jack was very tolerant of his dog's eccentric ways. However, he did insist she perform one specific task. Rose would reluctantly oblige, usually turning her chore into a cabaret. Indeed, many of the villagers would often stroll over to Jack's farm at about the time the chickens needed bedding down. Jack kept hundreds of fowls. Rose's job was to supervise them into their coups to bed down for the night. Nearly always the obstinate fowls would have different ideas, providing an evening's entertainment for the locals. Watching the ill-equipped canine chasing the reluctant hens made them laugh with delight. Listening to her strange bark echoing through the fields made their evening complete. Even better was when the angry hens turned the tables and chased Rose, clucking angrily with the indignity of it all.

Although no one would accuse Jack of being eccentric, they often discussed his peculiar habit of taking his prized fowls for daily walks. Knowing every chicken by name, he would amuse his neighbours by talking incessantly to the birds whilst chaperoning them along the high street. Every so often the dubious posse, with Rose lumbering behind, would stop to look in shop windows. Jack excitedly pointing to wares on sale to his feathered guests.

In addition to his chickens, Jack also kept bees, of which he was extremely proud. Every morning he could be seen collecting his honey, which would eventually be used to make special ale. A recipe, Jack claimed, was hundreds of years old. It was a widely known fact he fed his livestock on his honey ale and that his chickens lay the largest eggs for miles around. At one time a news programme had discussed his eggs, suggesting they might qualify for an entry into The Guinness Book of Records. As a result customers, having travelled a considerable distance, would often queue just to boast they had eaten one.

Any surplus ale would be meticulously placed into brown bottles with labels boasting of an old age recipe, and sold in the village pub. Jack named his brew after an old monk who had lived in the village during its construction. He swore the original recipe, devised by the monk, not only tasted delicious but contained life-saving properties. Regardless if his stories were true, the ale was very popular. Jack was often advised to invest in the appropriate machinery, setting up a distillery to manufacture his ale on a larger scale. Jack would chuckle, reminding his well-wishers that he was a farmer and content to remain a farmer. He had no idea of his fate when Maysoni came riding into town.

Further along the high street stood the pride of the village, The Black Cat Inn, proving to be more popular than the football ground for whiling away the time. The inn dated back hundreds of years with architecture that was once the pride of England. Sporting oak beams and a large open fire it was idyllic for the locals to play their often heated games of dominoes or sit and talk the evening away.

Cheryl, along with her long-suffering husband, had resided as proprietor of The Black Cat as long as anyone cared to remember. Certainly there were few who would dare to argue with the way she chose to run her establishment. Being a stickler for the routine of three meals a day, she transformed one of the bars into an eating area. Here, those with strong stomachs could indulge in Cheryl's home-made cooking.

She would often boast that people travelled many miles to sample her cuisine. She always omitted to tell that few returned. Although the jovial host was enthusiastic about providing food, she had forgotten one basic rule and that was to learn to cook. It was not uncommon for those who had mistakenly eaten at the Black Cat to be grumbling well into the night. Some having to rummage for medication.

Further up, stood the old church. An imposing building that dated back hundreds of years. The locals loved to boast of its sinister connections. Even the shyest inhabitant of Keys would happily relate the story of Isobel, a supposed witch, being imprisoned in the church to await a grisly death. Speaking through the corners of their mouths, eyes bulging with excitement, they would be eager to finish their tale.

Isobel apparently evaded going to Hell, taking up residence in the dense woods adjoining the church. Her moans and whining were testimony to that evidently, numerous villagers had heard Isobel's screechy voice, promising to destroy the village that had sent her to such a grisly death.

Such was the fear of the supernatural that many of the locals would refuse directly to go anywhere near the woods after dark. Indeed, stories abounded how superstitious farmers would abandon their search for a lost sheep near the woods. When the sun had died, darkness forbid anyone's presence among the dense trees.

Leading a somewhat depleted congregation was the Rev Peter Handlin. Born and bred in a village himself, he understood the superstitions among his flock. However, he attempted to quell rumours regarding things that went bump in the night. In some respects the teenagers that refused to attend his services helped his cause. Not sharing the superstitions of their elders, they were often reported to be disappearing into the woods, hours later reappearing with the broadest of smiles. Many of his sermons would be on the subject of unfounded fear. His loud voice rationalising that the supposed spooky noises were tricks of the wind or the cries of wild animals and crows that were abundant in such areas. However, the few ears that his loud voice managed to penetrate remained deaf, and the woods, after dark, remained a no go area.

Some parents even prohibited their children to swing their legs into the clear stream that ran through the woods. It was wildly acclaimed that Alfred the monk had drowned himself in the same stream, and no self-respecting parent wanted their heirs abducted by a ghost in flowing robes.

Coming back along the high street was the home of The Echo. Proprietor Lionel Bains, after many barren years, now found himself kept busy broadcasting the news of an American interest in the football club. Never before had his newspaper had such a big story. Often he could be seen out and about, notebook and pen in his hand. Anyone silly enough to stand still for a moment would be pounced on, the enthusiastic editor demanding their views for his paper.

Walking past the village shop and back towards the Honey Bee farm sat the old oak. Stories were rife in the village of how it had grown from a small acorn. Legend had it that Isobel, while being led to her execution, threw the acorn there. Those who wanted to mingle a little romance in their story recalled the supposed dalliances of Isobel and

Alfred.

Apparently, Alfred the village monk fell in love with Isobel whilst she was incarcerated. He provided the hapless woman with the acorn, as a token of his love. Villagers would relate with trembling voices that Isobel and Alfred had promised a fate worse than death on those who stunted the tree's growth or interfered with it in any way.

Fantasy lovers maintained that a large brown owl, who noisily resided in the tree, was a creature from the depths. It was sent by the Devil to protect leaf monsters that hid between the large branches.

Not many would deny believing in the strange yellow-eyed creatures that resided at the peak of the oak. Although no one actually saw them, their presence was taken for granted, with many an argument developing should outsiders rubbish their existence. Endless stories abounded how the mysterious leaf creatures had saved countless lives and properties. Although supposedly equipped with razor sharp teeth and hideous faces it seemed their purpose was one of benevolence. Nevertheless, as most of the stories were conjectured after a long night in the Black Cat, and no one actually admitted to seeing the creatures, they were discounted as quickly as they were told.

By whatever means the tree flourished, it was regarded with reverence by everyone in the village. Its heritage was taken very seriously and no one was allowed near its massive branches. The tree was regarded as a protected species. Even children knew when to draw the line, not one attempting the tantalising climb to its summit. Possibly many were genuinely frightened by the grown-up's stories of how they might end up as dinner for the owl or that they might be imprisoned by the monsters that resided up there.

Superstitions were rife in the village and no one would ever consider missing Harvesting Leaf Day. To outsiders this was considered a ridiculous ritual when on November 13th the whole village would chase any floating leaves which fell from the trees. Nevertheless it was a festival the village had celebrated for hundreds of years and residents would throw themselves into the fun with great gusto. This was an important day of the year.

The creatures living in the oak discarded their unwanted neighbours into the world. Each one camouflaged as a leaf. It was widely believed that if the leaves were caught before they reached the ground they would bestow great wealth and happiness on their captors. While the ones that evaded out stretched hands and fell to the floor, were secretly some type of evil spirit. Not wanting evil spirits spoiling their party, the village would not rest until the offending leaves were ceremonially dumped onto one of many bonfires. When everyone was sufficiently happy that they had repelled their evil invaders, they would continue through the night with a huge party.

Very often the villagers would perform their own entertainment and April, helped considerably by her husband's honey ale, would delight many with her melodious voice. Sometimes during these celebrations a tribute would be paid to a certain Mr John Goldsmith. Goldsmith, having been born in the village, had become somewhat of a celebrity by opening a chain of restaurants across the globe. Very eccentric with a passion for wearing gold coloured suits, his name was known all around the world. To the villagers, his success was the pinnacle of hard work and dedication. Such was his fame and reverence, a plaque was installed on the front of the village hall in his honour. Most, stringently objected that the reason they clinked glasses to the great man, was the several crates of wine he regularly donated on Harvesting Leaf Day.

As the villagers braced themselves for the arrival of the American, newspapers up and down the country debated the consequences that might follow. Some saw Maysoni as a saviour, destined to save English football, while others, given his dubious past, urged the people of Key's to ignore his hair-brained boasts and send him packing.

Rev Handlin was much opposed to the selling of the club, making known his opposition continuously. As things stood he was not comfortable with some of the celebrations the village held, notably Harvesting Leaf Day, which he felt bordered on blasphemy.

Try as he may, he could not fathom out why fully-grown adults could believe in such tripe. However, he was inclined to over-look the village's passion of superstition, if they attended church on a regular basis. Here, he thought optimistically, he could gently remind them of the folly of their ways.

To witness the village surrender part of its heritage to gangsters from overseas, was something completely different. As the guardian of the people, he felt it his duty to prevent them mingling with the very people he preached about.

Joined by an unlikely ally, John Purdy a prominent sports journalist, they both campaigned heavily against the American setting foot in Keys in the first place.

Although few of the villagers were particularly religious, they had a liking for Rev Handlin and many listened to what he had to say. Standing at six foot four with a body weight of sixteen stone, he was the perfect anchor when the neighbouring villages held their tug of war contests. He could also bowl a wicked ball at cricket, often helping Keys to victory against their rival neighbours. The Key's committee were desperate to keep his services as vicar, since before his arrival Keys had hardly won anything at all. So consequently, when he called an impromptu meeting at the village hall, it was unusually packed to the rafters.

Taking the opportunity to address many that he did not often see in the old church, Rev Handlin passionately preached of far-reaching consequences if the village allowed a pistol-packing gangster into their domain. He warned about the love of money, urging them to consider their important heritage.

Whilst some nodded their heads in agreement, many

others, especially the younger adults, argued that it would be perfect to have a top quality football team within their mist. One teenager, over stepping the line of cheekiness, reminded that the church preached the act of forgiveness. According to the press, the American who was going to visit Keys had paid his dues and was reformed. He continued that the American should be forgiven and allowed to have his say, especially if he was going to bring wealth and fame.

After much debate and arguing, it was finally agreed that Simon Potts would meet the American and would be free to discuss terms. However, the final decision would rest with the committee.

Rev Handlin was not dismayed by the decision. Certain that the committee were hardly likely to sanction the sale. He also doubted that Simon Potts would get involved either. The man cherished his leadership of the club, protecting it as a mother nurses her first baby.

However, those that were in favour were delighted, convinced that the sale would now go through and optimistic about all the wonderful things that were going to follow. Their village, they reasoned, needed to be dragged into the new twenty first century. If it was a gangster from overseas who achieved that task, so be it. Both parties, for and against, were reasonably happy with the evening's proceedings and there were no objections when the meeting was declared closed.

As a glowing moon emerged, it was considered a good time to retire to the comfort of The Black Cat. Exchanging normal pleasantries, they set off noisily on the short walk to the inn. They did not get very far. The old oak, its branches swaying freely in the night's wind, emitted sounds the group swore, resembled that of an old crone laughing raucously. Superstition soon taking over, the older ones in the party muttered about witches, creatures with yellow eyes and everything else that was embedded in their troubled minds. The younger ones laughed at their distress, attributing the noise to creaky branches and wind.

Nevertheless, even they quickened their step upon hearing the noise of laughter followed by a strange sound that resembled someone giggling nervously.

The nervous party, having considered the short walk not so appropriate, rushed back into the village hall, to be met by a disconcerted reverend who could only shake his head in dismay. Deciding the only way to clear the hall was through his own involvement, he generously offered to accompany the group to the sanctuary of the Black Cat.

Realising he would be on neutral ground having to listen to their superstitions, did not put him in the best frame of mind. However, the thought of a few complimentary whiskies made him feel better.

The short journey, nevertheless, was curtailed when echoing through the hall came the noise of what seemed like a tortuous giggling noise. Watching some of his flock take on a white hue whilst trembling violently, caused him to shake his head angrily. He was in no mood to explain again about countryside noise. Ready to lament the group about their apparent lack of courage, his words were not uttered.

The lights, in the hall, at first flickered gently. Then, as though someone were playing with a light switch, continuously darkened and brightened, stopping abruptly before plunging the hall into darkness. An exasperated Rev Handlin quickly fetched some candles from the nearby church, gently explaining that power cuts were common across the country. He eyed the quivering bodies staring at him earnestly, with sympathy. At least he had something to work on for his Sunday sermon, he thought wistfully.

The Echo
American confirms his interest in purchasing football club.
The Reverend Handlin warns of possible consequences.
Fuse box in village hall being investigated.

Chapter Three
The Offer

Alberto Maysoni reclined in his luxury car seat, grunting angrily. Drawing heavily on his Cuban cigar, he flicked smouldering ash through a half-closed window, screwing up his eyes. The sun's heat produced small beads of sweat, nesting on his brow, trickling along his receding hairline. Wiping his forehead with a silk handkerchief, he squinted at the offending sun, grunting again.

"Reuccio, what on earth are we doing in a place like this?" Without waiting for an answer he heaved his eighteen stone bulk out of the chair, violently pushing his car door and stepping heavily onto the pavement. "I think Alphonso must be going mad." He looked angrily at his sidekick, who was grateful to be wearing dark sunglasses to shield his fox-like eyes. "He sends me halfway round the world to a place that has only got dust tracks for roads." Breathing heavily, Maysoni kicked the dust from the pavement. Watching the dust spray haphazardly he pointed accusingly at the small man sitting in the car. "Are you sure this is the place?" While speaking his face reddened, the veins on his neck starting to protrude. Reuccio, despite his protective glasses, looked away nervously.

"This is the place boss, I saw a sign." Reuccio, despite his nervousness, tried to speak confidently. Nevertheless his voice emitted a nervous squeaky tone when he realised his boss was kicking out angrily at their car. "It said November Keys." The small American looked anxiously at his peer. "And I don't think you should kick the car." He spoke again quickly before Maysoni could reply, "These English love their Rolls Royce's, and we had to leave a deposit."

Maysoni eyed the hired car disconcertingly. "And I am supposed to be buying a soccer club here?"

"Yes boss that's what Mr Decesso said." Reuccio descended from the car, breathing in the warm sunshine.

"Anyway, it seems a nice place to play football, they call it football here." The two men stood silently looking across yellow fields. Maysoni shook his head angrily and drew heavily on his cigar. Pointing it at Reuccio, he gestured to the cigar.

"You know what, I bet this cigar is worth more than this whole crazy place put together." Throwing the cigar to the ground, he killed the last glowing embers with a gleaming Cuban boot and pulled a grey fedora hat onto his head. "Anyway let's get this over with, I want to get back to the States."

As he spoke, he looked aimlessly ahead eyeing a lone figure wandering along with two chickens. Rubbing his eyes, he squinted, watching the figure shuffling along the dusty pavement. Following was a strange looking dog, barking at their every move. Maysoni stared for a moment, to his disgust, the stranger bent down and spoke to the hens.

"Do you see that?" Maysoni shook his head in disbelief. "There is some guy taking his chickens for a walk." He rammed his fist into his clenched hand, staring menacingly at his insubordinate. "And he is talking to them." Shaking his head, he strained his eyes, wanting to be sure they were not deceiving him. "What on earth do you say to chickens?"

"Perhaps he is asking them what they want on the plate with them, fries or wedges." Reuccio's eyes were laughing behind his shades but he made sure his face did not give his merriment away. He was very much aware of his boss's temper and had no wish to be on the receiving end. Maysoni stared straight through his employee's glasses, stamping his Cuban boot angrily on to the sun-drenched pavement.

"So you are amused?"

Realising his thin disguise had not worked, Reuccio jumped back in a panic.

"Reuccio, you and Alphonso are as bad as each other. I swear you will both regret the day you make a fool out of me."

"Boss, relax." Reuccio sensed his employers' increasing

anger. However, sure that he was safe whilst on English ground he tried to reason with the large American. "This place is going to make you millions." He nodded at the lone figure. "It's probably their way of taking their animals to the market." He grinned at the approaching figure, beckoning him over. "Hi, good afternoon, can you show us the way to a Mr Simon Potts' office please?"

The man stopped, peering at the two Americans, his dog barking furiously. "You must be the multi-millionaire tycoon who is going to buy the club?" Without waiting for an answer, he bent down and patted his dog's head. "We have heard all about you, haven't we Rose?" Leaning over he picked up one of his chickens, pointing it at the now agitated American. "Look Millie, here's that tycoon person I was telling you about."

Reuccio, sensing his boss's anger, strategically placed himself between the two men. Not wishing to see the stranger's brains splattered all over the sidewalk, he smiled at each man, as though they were lost brothers. He weighed the stranger up, through his dark glasses. It was not a good idea to wave chickens at the most notorious boss in America's underworld. Relieved that his boss, who was standing, mouth open, had not sprang into action, he quickly got their directions and strode off.

Maysoni followed, shaking his head in astonishment. This place he had been summoned to was like a nightmare in some shanty-town south of the States. He had often read what those people did to their animals and found it hard to believe that England harboured the same type of person. He had always associated the strange country with buildings like Big Ben and the Houses of Parliament, not a place in the wilderness, full of hicks.

Shaking any bad thoughts from his head, he quickened his pace intending to get the deal done and head back home. Back to proper people. He was aware he had to complete his assignment without any excuses. Knowing full well what failure meant, even to someone as high ranking as himself.

If people wanted to talk to chickens, he reasoned, that was fine as long as they spent well in his clubs and casinos.

Suddenly he stopped dead in his tracks. It dawned on him that they had walked past an old lump of wood with the words 'Keys' painted on it. The artwork appeared to be the work of a ten-year-old. He suddenly realised this was supposed to be the football club's sign. The wood swinging gently in the afternoon breeze was cheap and nasty, giving no confidence to any indecisive punter. Stepping back abruptly, he decided to have a second look. First appearances were important.

"What the blazes," he looked at the swinging timber angrily, "that's supposed to be a sign?" He foraged for his cigar case, quickly pushing one of his large Cuban cigars between his teeth. Lighting the tip, he inhaled the thick smoke angrily. "Reuccio, if that is their sign what in the blazes is the rest going to be like?" He asked the question not expecting an answer.

Allowing his eyes to wander further ahead, they rested on to a mass of decaying metal seats. Hardly believing that any sane person would try to use them for their intended purpose, he drew on his cigar heavily. His gaze now took in a mass of yellow grass, sprouting reluctantly in what appeared to be a swamp. "Next they will be telling us that, *that* is the playing area." He pointed at the uninviting field, sucking on his cigar thoughtfully. "Luckily they don't have gators over here, otherwise I guess most of the players would end up as dinner guests."

Thinking his remark funny, he faced his comrade expecting him to laugh. When Maysoni, cracked a funny everyone laughed. Reuccio, aware what was expected, duly obliged, feigning laughter while pointing at the overgrown grass.

"Boss that's probably where that guy takes his chickens for a night out." The two men thinking this remark quite funny, collapsed into laughter.

Simon Potts had been sitting nervously at his desk for over three hours. Watching the second hand on his clock drift slowly around, he tried to will the time away. As always, when he was apprehensive his lip quivered involuntarily and he tried to still it with the end of a broken pencil.

Peering around his office, he was suddenly alarmed at the clutter, wishing that he had had the sense to do some tidying when he had time. Having convinced himself that Americans did not do tidy, he had spent an idle hour daydreaming of his soon to come riches. Eventually however, his mind had started playing tricks, warning him of all the things that might go wrong.

Trying to push his uninvited thoughts aside, he reminded himself of his business acumen. He had bought Keys for next to nothing and now he was about to make a fortune. All he had to do was put on a good show for his guests and hey presto. Well there was also the not so small task of persuading the committee and Rev Handlin. Nevertheless, he was optimistic his sales expertise would win the day.

Everyone expected him to refuse any offers for his supposedly cherished football club. Secretly he could not wait to get out, having had enough of November Keys and its strange inhabitants.

Suddenly his thoughts turned to coffee, and the recollection that he had no milk. Pressing his quivering lip hard with the pencil, he hoped that Americans drank their coffee black. Trying to stop his thoughts from tormenting him, he was rudely brought back to earth by the noise of laughter coming from outside. Peering through torn net curtains he spotted two men stylishly dressed, collapsed into a heap of laughter.

He brushed down the lapels of his best suit, just recently retrieved from the dry cleaners and took a deep breath, walking out into the sunlight to greet his overseas benefactors.

"Hello, I am Simon Potts." He uttered his words as confidently as his confused mind would allow. "I am the chairman of Keys."

"Ah, Mr Potts." Maysoni stood up abruptly, offering his hand. "It's nice to make your acquaintance."

After the three men had gone through the normal pleasantries, Simon nodded at his office, gesturing as politely as he could with a sweating hand. "Shall we talk in my office Mr Maysoni? I am sure you could use some coffee."

"Yeah, that would be fine." Maysoni looked at Simon expectantly. "Where is your office Mr Potts?"

Simon nodded at the small wooden building he had just vacated, smiling at his two guests. Maysoni looked at the small hut and then at Reuccio. He could feel his face reddening and decided to take deep breaths.

He had flown thousands of miles to conclude a million-dollar deal and this guy wanted him to go into a mop and broom room. Reminding himself to speak to Alphonso at the earliest opportunity, he reluctantly followed his host through the ageing door.

Entering the sparse building, his nose was met by the odour of freshly made coffee, which cheered him up a little. His eyes roaming around the cluttered room, he wondered what it was like to be poor in England. If this person Potts was a successful chairman, how did unsuccessful people survive? The guy could not even afford any furniture.

Substituting for a table was a pasteboard lined with years of different paints. Balancing precariously on four uneven legs it looked like it might give way at any minute. In the corner of the room were four cardboard boxes crammed high with yellowing papers.

He had seen better conditions in Sing Sing, New York's maximum-security prison. Maysoni shrugged his shoulders, glancing back through the open door. He was pleased to see that Reuccio had positioned himself, alert to any trouble. Content that business should commence, he settled himself onto a battered cane chair.

"How do you take your coffee?" Simon asked the

question pleasantly trying to put Maysoni at ease.

"Black, three sugars and strong." Maysoni allowed his grey eyes to scan the shabby room, finally resting on a faded photograph. He recognised a young Potts. Bending his head forward he tried to decipher some faded writing scribbled at the bottom.

"Fourteen years ago, when I took over as chairman." Potts pre-empted his question, offering his guest a battered mug full of steaming coffee.

"Yes very good, must have been a special occasion?" Maysoni spoke slowly looking suspiciously at the cracked mug he had been handed. Gee, he is trying to give me typhoid, he thought angrily. Glancing up at the ceiling, covered in cobwebs, he realised why England had suffered from plagues so many times. He shrugged his large shoulders deciding to swallow the bullet and get on with it. Tomorrow, he thought smugly, he would be back in the States with the deal completed.

"Shall we get on with our business Mr Potts?" He gestured with his hand, indicating that he did not require an answer. "As you know myself and my, er, syndicate wish to buy this quaint soccer, I means football ground of yours."

He rose to his feet, studying various certificates pinned onto the wall before turning to face Potts. "Mr Potts we are willing to offer one million dollars for complete purchase."

Potts tried to get up from his seat but felt his legs buckle. Sitting back heavily he pressed his quivering lip with his pencil. "One million dollars!" He heard the words whistling from his mouth but felt they were from another planet. After the American had first contacted him, his mind had accumulated various figures that he might be offered. Yet even his greedy mind had not been able to pass fifty thousand.

"Yes Mr Potts, and although that is not a great deal of money, before you decide, think about your village."

"Not a great deal, think about my village?" Potts was starting to feel sick with excitement.

Maysoni grinned to himself. He knew when he had his prey cornered. "Mr Potts, we are going to take this club to heights you could never dream of." He walked over and tapped a fading photograph of Potts, resplendent in dinner suit and bow tie. "You Mr Potts are going to go down in history as the man who put November Keys onto the world platform."

"World platform?" Potts tried to concentrate but could only visualise a bank account stuffed with a million American dollars. "I am sorry, what do you mean?"

Maysoni peered through the open door, clicking his fingers. Reuccio, knowing it was time for his cue, entered the office as casually as he could.

"Cigar Mr Potts?" Maysoni offered a black leather case with his finest Cuban cigars. Simon, taking one, placed it nervously between his teeth. His lip was quivering furiously and he hoped the luxurious cigar would conceal his nervousness. Accepting a light from a diamond studded lighter he slumped back into his chair watching the man called Reuccio spread a pile of neat papers onto the dubious pasteboard desk.

Reuccio, having completed his duties, gave a slight bow and wandered back out into the sunlight. Simon tried to take an interest in the papers but could not take his eyes from the lighter gripped in Maysoni's large hand. It was as though the gems embedded into the gold were hypnotising him. Maysoni chuckled, throwing the lighter to Potts who fumbled to catch it.

"Just call it a little present Mr Potts. A gesture from the USA. Now if you please, l will outline our proposals."

Potts thought he might have to pinch himself. He must be dreaming he thought sadly. This sort of thing did not happen in real life, people didn't just offer you gold lighters and a million dollars.

"Mr Potts, if you please." Maysoni's deep American twang bought him back to earth. "I will leave these papers for your own use, but as you see we intend to increase the size of the stadium to seat one hundred thousand spectators."

Potts tried to answer but his words stuck deep in his throat, unable to form a sensible statement.

"Obviously," Maysoni carried on, "we need to fill the stadium to capacity. It is essential we steer your club into top-flight football." Maysoni pulled deeply on his cigar. "That I believe is what you call your Monster League."

Simon drew on his cigar, cherishing the luxury he was being afforded. He tried to find words that would not offend his benefactor. "Mr Maysoni, this all sounds wonderful but do you realise the investment you would have to make?" He pulled hard on his cigar again, hoping the blue smoke would help him choose the right words. "The cost would run to millions of dollars." Inhaling too much smoke, coughing violently, Potts spluttered his next sentence. "I think what you are proposing is unachievable."

Maysoni felt his face redden, wanting to smash his fist down onto the fragile paste table. Correcting himself, he smiled sickly at Potts. "Mr Potts, nothing in this life is unachievable, nothing." He pointed to a picture tacked onto the wall. "Is that not the team that triumphed in your cup thing?"

"The Local Football Club Knock-out Trophy." Simon spoke softly fearing he had upset the American.

"Did they use the words unachievable?" Maysoni walked over to the makeshift table, picking up the neatly piled papers. "Mr Potts, have you heard of the Chicago Flies?" Without waiting for an answer, he waved the papers in the air. "When I came across them they were playing in dirt. Now over a billion people worldwide watch them." He drew heavily on his cigar, tossing the burning remains through the open door and stared at his host menacingly. "Mr Potts, leave success to me, now do we have a deal?"

Simon looked up nervously, sucking heavily on the remains of his cigar. He wanted to smoke it for as long as possible, but thought he had better follow his guest's behaviour and discard the glowing embers through the door. Trying to find somewhere to rest his eyes other than on the large American, he glanced at the papers Maysoni had handed him. Absorbing the mass of print, he nearly fell out of his chair.

"Thank you for your consideration Mr Maysoni." He stuttered on his words aware that his guest was studying him intently. "I am sure once I have put your offer before the committee we can reach a conclusion to suit us all." He hoped that his benevolent guest could not sense that he was lying.

"Committee," Maysoni almost bellowed, "Who owns this place, you, or some committee?"

"Well it is really just a formality." Potts lied again, aware that his guest was angry. "As long as the old oak will be all right."

"Oak," Maysoni could not believe his ears, "are you talking about a tree?"

"Yes, it has an owl." Simon shuffled in his seat. "It would have to be protected." He fidgeted uncomfortably. "Your plans suggest it might have to be felled."

"An owl?" Maysoni had been nearly convinced that these people were close to mad, now he was very sure. First, some lunatic walking along talking to chickens and now this guy hedging over the best deal he had been offered in his life because of an owl. "Mr Potts are you serious or are you having some kind of joke at my expense?"

Maysoni felt his face reddening, the veins on his neck starting to bulge. The last time he had felt this mad, he thought sourly, he had wiped most of the Canoloti mob off the face of the earth.

Simon, sensing his million dollars starting to vanish before his eyes, tried to pacify the angry man standing in front of him. "It's sort of protected." He rose to his feet nervously. "It's been in the village for hundreds of years." He tried to sound as apologetic as he could.

"Mr Potts, we are offering you a small fortune, the best

soccer team in the world, and you are worrying about a tree?" He glared at his strange host, grabbing his pile of papers. "I am sure that we can find another club just like yours." He strode angrily through the open door of Potts' hut, summoning Reuccio to follow him. "Good day Mr Potts."

Potts stared forlornly after him as his million dollars disappeared as quickly as it had arrived. Looking dejectedly around his sparse office, he wondered how he was going to lure the rich American back into his lair. Noticing a small case covered in dust he jumped to his feet quickly and chased after his angry guest. "Mr Maysoni," he shouted anxiously hoping the American would return, "here is a present, it's from the UK." Relieved that the big American paused for a moment he rushed up to him, proudly placing the case into his large hand. "And Mr Maysoni." Potts' lies spilled from his mouth, as he pleaded with the American. "Just give me a day to smooth talk the committee and November Keys will be yours."

Maysoni looking bemused at his strange gift, shrugged his broad shoulders. "Mr Potts you have twenty-four hours and then I leave for New York."

Maysoni sat on his bed glaring at his telephone. He was angry and wished to calm down a little before he rang Decesso to voice his complaints. The meal that had been provided by room service had been adequate but had not subdued his temper. Consequently, he was resorting to an old-fashioned trick his mother had taught him.

"Breathe deeply and pretend you are in your favourite place." Her words echoed in his mind. Well he was not in his favourite place. He had expected to be on a plane back to New York and now he was delayed because of an owl and some committee.

When Decesso had suggested moving some of his operations to England, he had been hesitant. Now he was downright certain he wanted nothing to do with the place.

Why, he thought angrily, did he have to deal with a bunch of hill-billies in some hick town when he had more than enough to do back home? For a while he studied his battle-worn face in a mirror beside his bed, wondering what his friend was thinking of. Why did the bosses want to be involved with a depleted football ground situated in the depths of human depravity? Glancing over at the strange case that Potts had given to him earlier confirmed his suspicions that these people were really off their heads.

Sitting in the case was a decaying leaf. What sort of present was that, he thought grimly? He had given the guy a gold lighter studded with jewels from all over the world and what did he get back? A leaf in a cheap case. In normal circumstances, he would have shoved it somewhere unpleasant, but the strange Potts genuinely seemed to think it was some type of heirloom. He had blabbered incessantly about fossils and English history.

Picking up the case, Maysoni studied its contents. It made him shudder involuntarily. If he had not known any better, he could have sworn the decaying leaf appeared to have some type of face. Allowing his mind to wander back to the mop room, he recalled how the guy Potts had become so excited. Thrusting a library book into the American's face he had rambled on about witches and the like.

Maysoni shook his head, promising himself if the deal went through he would summon the strange English guy to New York. They could jaunt around Central Park where Potts could find as many leaves as he wanted.

Before ringing Decesso, he decided greedily, he would sample some more of that Scotch whisky. Now that was something that was worth flying out of America for! He sat for a while savouring its satisfying mellow taste. After having sunk a few glasses he felt a lot less agitated and picked up his phone.

Simon Potts slumped in his seat staring at the ceiling for sympathy. Life was indeed precarious he thought sadly. Just a few hours earlier he had been destined to be a rich man and now he was back to square one. When the American had shown him the plans, he knew there would be a huge mountain to climb. The paperwork illustrated the ambitious plans that the American intended to pursue. Within a few years November Keys would progress from being a small village into an illustrious town.

Unfortunately, if the plans proceeded, it would mean parts of Keys being completely demolished, since masses of space would be needed to accommodate the new stadium flanked by shopping complexes. If that was not bad enough, the American intended to build a railway. Its consequent construction would necessitate the destruction of Jack Carpet's farm.

Despite, the overwhelming odds against having the plans accepted he had battled every inch of the way. He had vainly tried to influence the proceedings by reminding anyone who would listen of the high unemployment in the area. The American's offer would alleviate that problem overnight.

The committee, as he suspected, had dismissed the venture out of sight. The lure of American dollars ringing in his ears, he had continued to argue his case. Eventually, the whole village turned against him. Making it abundantly clear that the oak was not moving nor was Jack's farm.

Squirming into Lionel Bains' office he had requested the back-up of the Echo. Bains' answer had been unprintable. Staring at the papers spread on his desk he shrugged his shoulders resignedly. If the American truly wanted to buy Keys, then he was going to have to reconsider the whole project.

To Potts surprise and Rev Handlin's disgust, the committee had granted another twenty-four hours for new plans to be drawn up. Hopefully allowing for the tree and surrounding lands to be left unscathed. This would ultimately mean a much smaller stadium and certainly no railway. Remembering the American's anger earlier, Simon

Potts stood up slowly, deciding to visit the Black Cat and drown his sorrows.

The Echo
DO NOT LOSE YOUR KEYS!

Keys Football Club has been the centre of much debate. American millionaire Alberto Maysoni is believed to have made a substantial offer for the club, stating he intends to drag it into the future as one of the most successful clubs of all time.

However, the proposition made by the American would necessitate the preposterous removal of the old oak and much of the adjoining lands.

Whilst Keys committee were grateful for the American's interest, they voted unanimously to reject his offer.

However, they have given the proposed buyer twenty-four hours to revise the plans to the suitability of all concerned.

Another vote, on sight of the revised plans is expected to be made within the next twenty-four hours.

Chapter Four
The Takeover

Maysoni glared at Reuccio wondering how such a small human being could devour so much food at one sitting. Being in a foul mood, he had no wish to exchange pleasantries over a breakfast table with a human gannet. The small man sitting opposite, stuffing food into his mouth, was making his mood worse.

The previous day he had fully expected to be flying back to New York, instead he was sitting in some crummy hotel watching his sidekick stuff food into his mouth as if he was going to the electric chair soon. In addition, his head ached. Scotch liquor was not good for ensuring a clear head the next day, he thought grimly. Especially if that day was going to be shared with English hill-billies.

He rubbed his head, staring sombrely out into the bright sunlight. His dark eyes flinched from the dancing sunlight warning that this was not a good idea. Frustrated, he stretched rudely over the table and grabbed a white pot, now half-empty, containing coffee. Pouring the lukewarm drink violently into his cup he thought back angrily to his earlier conversation with Decesso.

At first, despite his mood, he had been very polite and diplomatic. Going into detail, he had explained about the tree, the strange chicken farmer and countless other obstructions. Stubbornly, he had emphasised that buying a soccer club, in the hill-billy town he was expected to stay in, was a no go. He was amazed when his boss had started to rant and rave down the phone at him, he gruffly reminded Decesso that his businesses in New York did not run themselves and expected to return back quite soon. Adding that if the hicks did want to sell the club, which was highly improbable, it was useless for the bosses' requirements anyway.

Before slamming the receiver down he added for good

measure that if the sale did go through, he did not intend to stay in England and Decesso should find someone else to amuse the English hill-billies. Assuming that finalised matters, he set about vacating his room and heading back to New York. A sharp shrilling from his phone changed his mind.

Anglico Busanani shouted oaths at him down the line, stressing that life could be very short and that if Maysoni returned home with his mission incomplete his life would be very short indeed. Maysoni, disturbed that he might have offended one of the bosses, resigned himself to a longer stay and dragged his large frame and thumping head to the hotel restaurant for breakfast.

Now watching Reuccio cram his mouth full of what looked like indigestible food, he rapped loudly on the table.

"Are you eating for America? Anyone would think you just come out the can."

Reuccio smiled to himself. He knew his boss was not happy but was not unduly concerned. He was enjoying his vacation and was in no hurry to cut it short. When Maysoni had sworn and ranted telling him that they might have to stay a few more days, he had feigned his discontent but inwardly felt pleased. A few days away from taking passengers for their last ride suited him fine. "Got to keep our strength up boss." He forced another piece of toast into his mouth. Sensing Maysoni was becoming more agitated he wiped his face and rose to his feet.

Simon Potts stared silently at the black clouds hovering above his makeshift office. He considered that if he had to choose a place to reside, it would be in one of those black clouds. He could not believe how close he had come to being a millionaire. Even if it was in American dollars. Now it seemed he was destined to a life of near poverty all because of a tree and its occupants.

He had spent many years in Keys but even so could never get used to the villagers' eccentric ways. Here was a run-down village that had a chance of putting itself on the world map and its inhabitants were refusing the chance – because of a tree.

His thoughts turned towards the irate American, pondering why such wealthy people would want to invest in such a dilapidated club in the first place. Not thinking of any conceivable answer, he shrugged his slim shoulders, staring miserably at the black clouds again.

Placing his hands onto his head, he quietly mused over this disaster. When he had called a meeting of the committee, he had expected at least a small amount of support. Amazing, he thought grimly, how short people's memories were. When he had taken over as chairman of Keys they could not thank him enough. For fourteen, unappreciated years he had nurtured the wretched club like a new born baby. Pouring vast amounts of cash from his dwindling bank account, into the village's half-baked team. Now he had a chance of becoming a little wealthier and getting a small return on his investment he could not find a friend in sight.

Just for the sake of some old tree they were spurning his kindness along with the chance of a successful football club. Well, it was not just the tree, he thought sadly, Jack Carpet would have to vacate his farm. However, that was the cost of advancement. Not only that, he was going to get a fair price.

He stood up clumsily, rummaging through an old cardboard box. If his memory served him correctly somewhere among the clutter was a bottle of the finest whisky. Although it was early he needed a drink. Searching fruitlessly, he slumped back into his chair. It suddenly dawned on him that whisky would mar his concentration. Not wishing to appear intoxicated when the American returned, he decided to cease his search.

Having rung Maysoni earlier at his hotel, he had been alarmed at the American's anger. He had tried to explain how committees worked and that it was not his choice to abort the sale. However, he knew he had failed to convince his benefactor. Stressing that the committee had not yet reached a final decision he reminded the American of his importance as chairman. It was he, Simon, who had demanded an adjournment, to allow more time for further plans to be submitted. Nevertheless, Maysoni had not taken kindly to his news. Cursing underneath his breath, he demanded the names and addresses of those opposed to the takeover. It had taken a long time to reel them off.

Lionel Bains sat marvelling at his piece of master-work. It had taken a large amount of his time to put the headlines together, nevertheless, he was impressed with his handy work.

Do not lose your Keys.

Very subtle he thought proudly but then that was the art of a true journalist. He rubbed his hands together smugly. At last, his prowess as a journalist was going to be allowed to shine.
For twenty years he had edited the Echo and mostly all he had to write about were christenings and weddings. Well there was the time Geoff Dean's barn caught fire but that was different, it had not affected every resident in Keys. He had never intended to allow the club to be sold without a fight. Backing Rev Handlin with the might of his newspaper had been invigorating and he was relishing the next round.
    His mind wandered back a few hours, when Simon Potts had summoned the committee. The majority had nearly fallen out of their seats when they had studied the plans. The project would necessitate much of Keys land being built over. Jack Carpet would lose his farm and worse, if that were possible, the old oak would be cut down. Cutting that oak, he thought grimly, would be like severing one of Keys' limbs. No way, he mused angrily, would any American cut down that tree. The pen is mightier than the sword he thought proudly and he would use his pen to protect the residents of Keys at all costs.

When Potts had called, whining about his money, he had told him where to get off as well. Using words he would dare not print in his newspaper, he had told the weedy chairman to get lost, that he, Bains, intended to stand by his friends. Trembling at the indignity of it all his thoughts were interrupted by a tapping on his glass door. Glancing up he was surprised to see two very smartly dressed men gazing into his office.

"Good morning," Maysoni tried to smile pleasantly, "you must be Mr Bains?" Without waiting for a reply he introduced himself and Reuccio. "I understand that we will be doing business together?" Maysoni peered happily around the room. "And seeing what a professional I would be working with, I must say I could not be more pleased." Again, without waiting for a reply he tapped Bains' light-heartedly on his shoulder. "Yes Mr Bains, I can see your newspaper now, leading the way for all those second rate news sheets in London."

"You mean?" Bains stuttered on his words.

"Yes I do mean Mr Bains, Keys Football Club and the Echo, partners." Maysoni stared at the headlines his host intended to print, turning to him menacingly. "I assume you are going to vote for the takeover?" He handed a cigar to the surprised man. "Or are you going to have to be persuaded?" Maysoni smiled pleasantly while Reuccio lit the man's cigar. "Fifty dollars each, very soon you will have boxes of them."

Bains sat back quietly whilst Maysoni explained he had no wish to chop trees or force chicken farmers from their land. Blowing clouds of smoke, he emphasised that his original plans had been an oversight. Adding that he, like Bains, was ambitious and wanted Keys to have only the very best. However, Maysoni, coming from a poor background himself, would never intentionally put hard-working chicken farmers out of business.

The plans would be amended, ensuring the tree and adjoining lands were safe. Studying Bains' face, he stressed the importance of voting for the new football club. The Echo, being the village's only newspaper, would be the first paper to print any news relating to the club.

As Bains' ample cheeks flushed with pride, he sucked hungrily on his proffered cigar blowing large smoke rings. For sure, he had underestimated the kind American, he thought greedily. No one yet had realised his potential and it was very flattering indeed.

Maysoni sickened by the man sitting in front of him drew a deep breath, hastening to add that there could be more stories on offer from overseas. He had connections with world famous stars who he was sure would fall over backwards to appear in such an illustrious newspaper.

After the Americans had left, Lionel Bains sat deep in thought. Closing his eyes he pictured himself interviewing the famous stars the kind American had mentioned, his illustrious newspaper vying for attention across the globe. Perhaps a new football club was what the village needed, he thought greedily. As the American had promised to revise the plans, possibly a compromise could be arranged to suit all. Surly even Rev Handlin would not disagree to that.

The next port of call for the Americans was the local store. After more cigars and promises of great wealth, the owner was left pondering where his best interest lay. After the thoughtful American had left, he sat for a while, whistling through stained teeth, contemplating the thousands of fans rushing to his door to quench their thirst and enormous appetites. It even crossed his mind to make up some special rolls on match day. Scratching his soiled vest, a large smile formed across his chubby face. Things had not been easy in such a small village, now here was this benevolent man from overseas promising to make life a lot easier. He certainly couldn't understand why the deal could not go through. Especially as the tree would be safe. He looked sadly around his empty shop, daydreaming of his till chinking incessantly. Perhaps the football club was a good idea after all.

Paul Black had served the village as undertaker for numerous years, but admitted that he had not realised how many football fans dropped dead on match days, necessitating a sympathetic coordinator to dispatch the deceased to their place of rest. When he had voted against the club, he hastily explained while smoking his luxury cigar, he had not realised the disservice he was offering to the public.

Leonard Small, Jack's oldest friend, had been adamant from the beginning. He intended to vote against any takeover. Being a historian he saw the need to try to keep November Keys' future in line with its past and could not see a big football club allowing for that. He argued the village had coped very well for many years and could not see an ugly building harbouring thousands of unruly fans being of any benefit. When Maysoni had called offering large cigars, he politely rejected his advances, quietly informing the irritated American that he felt the village was crying out for historic culture. Not an oversized building that would surely attract hooligans from miles away.

The American sat quietly nodding his head in agreement. He insisted that he, himself, was a great lover of culture and would be delighted to help educate the masses about Keys' interesting history. In fact, he had been thinking of asking the intelligent historian to set up some type of exhibition in the new stadium when it was completed. People would be entertained by the best team in the world, fed by caterers with the highest standards and educated by Leonard Small, who would be backed up by state of the art technology.

Discussing the proposals over traditional tea and crumpets, Maysoni informed Leonard of his art collections, insisting the historian must visit New York as his guest and spend time exploring its history. The historian, hardly believing his ears, shook the American's hand, promising he would reconsider.

On each visit Maysoni complained bitterly that he should have been hired for welfare work. Normally a show of force would win him his prizes. However, he was secretly pleased with his progress. It did not matter what part of the globe you resided in, greed always won the day, he thought testily. These country hicks had their strange ways, but at least they did not let them get in the way when it came to finance.

Stopping abruptly, he stared at the old church. He knew that the vicar would never become an ally. Extreme measures were called for. Reuccio kept quiet. He knew best when not to speak. His face chiselled into a much-practised scowl, with alert eyes laughing behind dark glasses, he wondered how long he would remain in England.

Watching a large Rolls Royce manoeuvre up to his door Jack Carpet grinned, winking at Rose. Shaking his head knowingly, he stepped over his prostrate pet and made his way to the large oak door that protected his farmhouse. He had heard that the American was doing the rounds, so was not surprised at the arrival of his uninvited guests. He was surprised, however, at the cocky American's cheek. He was trying to get Jack off his land and then had the audacity to turn up on his doorstep.

Maysoni feeling optimistic that he could bribe yet another committee member, stood in the welcoming sun, glaring at his insubordinate. Reuccio had done what was asked of him, but it did not hurt to let him see who was boss, Maysoni thought unkindly. He was still smarting over his confrontation with the top boss earlier and felt that his driver should learn more about the pecking order within the bosses' crime syndicate. Ready to say something unpleasant, Maysoni was stopped in his tracks by the solid door in front of him swinging open.

Staring hard at Jack Carpet he recalled their earlier meeting when the crazy man had pointed a chicken at him. For a brief moment, he considered walking away, not wishing to converse with a mad farmer he considered to be a country hick. Shrugging his huge shoulders, he recalled again the earlier conversation with his boss, forcing himself to smile at Jack pleasantly.

"Good afternoon, err Mr Carpet." Maysoni spoke, cynically eyeing up the farm kitchen, situated behind the entrance door. "I think we have some discussions." Expecting to be beckoned in, he stood clumsily awaiting an invitation. Realising that the invitation was not forthcoming he pushed past Jack, marching into the small farmhouse. "Nice place you have here." Without waiting for a reply he took out his cigar case, pushing it under Jack's nose. When Jack refused, the American eyed him irritably and shrugged his shoulders. "Shame, the best Havana's." Thrusting one into his own mouth, he gestured for his host to sit down, "Now Mr Carpet, I do not presume to beat around the bush." He eyed the farmer menacingly. "A football club in your village would benefit everybody." He put his hands up, gesturing for Jack to remain quiet. "I understand you produce your own ale?" He voiced his question without much interest. "We will sell barrels of it in our shops." He pointed at the farmer. "You out of the very many, have much to gain." Attempting to read Jack's mind, he mentioned his earlier conversation with Potts concerning the farmer's land and the tree. "Now if we leave the oak intact and bypass your farm, will we get your vote?" He uttered his words impatiently, but was dismayed to see Jack stand up, seemingly ignoring him, and walk over to a window.

"Now cut that out Jessie." Jack looked apologetically at Maysoni and raised his voice. "Or no honey ale." Again, he looked apologetically at his guests. "She has been naughty all day."

The two Americans sat dumbstruck watching the strange farmer shout at a chicken through the window. When the chicken raced around the yard making strange clucking noises they reeled back in anxiety. Maysoni had assumed from his first meeting that the farmer was not mentally stable and it appeared his chickens were mad as well. Making a mental note not to eat any eggs during his stay, he eyed the farmer apprehensively.

"Mr Carpet," Maysoni spoke irritably, "you do not seem to understand." He looked down at Rose wondering why anyone would want to have such a strange animal in his or her house. He considered stroking the unkempt animal but thought better of it. "The rest of your committee, I think will see sense." Without waiting for a reply, he gestured angrily towards the window. "Everyone has their price."

"Well you could not afford my price." Jack, who had been listening intently, stood up and opened his front door. "My father and his many grandfathers have been ploughing these fields for generations." He spoke quietly but firmly. "So if you have finished, may I wish you gentlemen good day."

Reuccio half rose from his chair. He witnessed the look of surprise and disgust etched on his boss's face and was determined to prevent any type of incident. He could not care less about the farmer but was worried about police officers and the repercussions that they could cause. He need not have worried, Maysoni calmly rose, walking towards the open door.

"Have it your way." Maysoni said, then he hesitated as a grey mare appeared just outside the door. "Well I'll be." He grinned at Reuccio. "Just what we need, a horse." Walking over to the large animal he patted it gently. He turned back to Jack, a sneer across his face. "How much for the steed?" He patted the horse again. "Name your price?"

Jack screwed up his eyes, staring intently at his unwelcome guest. It was strange he thought how certain people, considered country folk stupid. He knew exactly where the conversation was going. "Sorry not for sale." His reply was not intended to sound apologetic "Can't sell Daisy can we Rose?" He grinned at the two Americans. "My dog won't have anyone to play with."

Maysoni, sensing that he was not getting anywhere, turned huffily on his heels. Sneering at the farmer, he gestured with two fingers suggesting his thoughts had turned to firearms. "I tried to be patient." Maysoni spat out his words angrily. "I offered a fair deal." He shook his head. "But you obviously want it the hard way." Thrusting another cigar angrily into his mouth he pointed at the old farmhouse. "In a short space of time you will be begging me to take this off your hands."

Jack watched the Americans angrily drive away, not trying to stifle a chuckle. "If they had been a little politer." He put his fingers to his lips to emphasise a whisper. "I would have offered them some honey ale."

Simon Potts miserably studied the faces of his fellow committee members. Whilst showing a brave face his stomach was tied into knots. When he had informed his wife of the possible takeover and his forthcoming wealth, she had immediately set about collecting an array of travel brochures. Not understanding the takeover was hanging in the balance, she finally decided, after much deliberation, they would holiday in Cuba. Potts, never wishing to argue with his other half, had nodded in ascent not realising that the tickets were already booked. It would have been pointless trying to explain his temporary cash flow. He prayed that the vote would be unanimous in favour of the sale. He would then be able to relax and enjoy life.

Bains stared warily at Jack Carpet wondering what his old friend's reaction would be when he learnt that the editor had sanctioned the takeover. He liked Jack but he liked even more the likelihood of his newspaper being discussed in Fleet Street. An opportunity only comes along occasionally he thought coyly, so he had little choice.

Jack Carpet studied his friends' expressions, concerned that each man showed a resolution not to face him. Surely, he thought worriedly, they could not possibly submit to the Americans wishes. Most of them had ancestors dating back the same as him. He silently crossed his fingers.

At last Simon Potts rose nervously, requesting each member to submit their vote. He reminded the voters, whilst looking away from Jack, the American had now promised not to fell the oak and build over any lands. After much hurried consultation he had had new plans drawn up which would leave the oak and much of the surrounding farmland intact. He added with a wiry look that the kindly American had only the villager's welfare at heart, as he of course did also.

The vicar in his address asked the committee to apprehend what repercussions having a massive football club in the village would incur. The others sat rigid, not daring to move, as he reminded them of their roots.

Simon, aware that the American had been busy with his bribes, cautiously asked the committee to vote. If six members voted in favour of the sale he would be a rich man.

After about twenty minutes, Simon Potts called for silence. Jack Carpet could see by the smug look on the chairman's face that the club was going to be sold. Peering at his feet, he mumbled something unintelligible, twisting his fingers into a fist.

"Gentlemen," Simon looked like the cat that had got the cream, "you have decided." Waving the ballot papers, he cleared his throat. "Those in favour of the sale seven, those against two." He looked away embarrassed as Jack's eyes made contact with his own. After spending another twenty minutes expounding the wisdom of the sale he excused himself, rushing away to call the American.

The others sat happily chatting to themselves trying not to look at Jack. In a short while they would all be wealthy and for the moment that was far more important than friendship. Leonard Small already feeling like a Judas stood up to leave. He had wanted to explain to his old friend his motives for voting. However, now was not a good time he thought sadly. Yanking the door of the decaying committee room he tried to make a swift exit. Before he had time to step out into the now gloomy night he was amazed to be standing eyeball to eyeball with a furious Bridget Bluestone. Her eyes sparkling with anger she blocked his way and spat out angry words at everyone still sitting transfixed in the committee room.

"Well I hope you are all happy with your accomplishments." She looked sympathetically at Jack and pointed at the stunned men. "This kind man is most likely to lose his farm." She paused for effect. "All because of your greed."

"No my dear, you are quite wrong." Lionel Bains was the first to find his voice. "There are new plans." Trying to hide his anger at the girl's interference, he hoped his words sounded gentle. "Jack's land and the oak," he emphasised the last word, "will be quite safe."

"Have you seen these new plans, Mr Bains?" Bridget looked scornfully at the would-be journalist while Jack tried to suppress a grin. "Or you, or you?" Staring scornfully at the group of now ashamed faces, she screwed her face into the best look of disgust she could muster. "You have just all sold your heritage down the river."

Leonard Small, realising he could not progress forward without resulting in a physical confrontation with the slight girl, jerked his head towards Jack, his eyes pleading for help. Jack, his grin now disappeared, stood up and gently urged Bridget to stand aside. Whilst secretly pleased she had decided to speak on his behalf, he was quietly angry that she had interfered in his business. The committee had made their decision, despite any consequences, protocol had been maintained, that that was the end of the matter.

He had said as much to his son earlier, who had wanted to make his protests noisily heard. After quietly explaining the protocol, which was essential for any committee member, he had banned JJ, much to his anguish, from attending the final meeting. Before Jack could reach the doorway, Lionel Bains' was on his feet angrily striding towards a flustered Bridget.

"Now, with all due respect," he eyed the girl angrily, "this matter is absolutely none of your concern." Looking around the room for support, he gestured towards the street.

"Now if you do not mind, my fellow committee member wishes to leave."

Bridget aware that her adopted uncle was embarrassed at her interruption stood silently tugging the necklace gently hanging from her slim neck. She had owned the gem ever since she could remember, feeling great comfort in times of stress from stroking its cold beads.

She knew she should not have interfered but was infuriated that her best friend's land could be in jeopardy. Jack and his family had been around November Keys forever and now they might be forced to leave. Surely, she thought angrily, the committee members were not that stupid to realise the club could not be expanded without the cost of losing valuable farming land. Eyeing Leonard Small, Jack's supposed friend, with contempt she stamped her small feet and crossed her arms. "No one is leaving." She nervously caressed her beloved necklace. "Gentlemen of the committee, I am going to picket, until you revise your decision."

Jack trying to contain his mirth at Bridget's audacity stood up again, determined to guide her away from the door. Although he appreciated her support, he could see by the look on the others' faces that she had gone too far. Before he could defuse the situation Lionel Bains strode angrily towards Bridget, his normally passive eyes smouldering with anger.

"How dare you interfere with the workings of a committee that have been in place before your grandmother was born?" Without waiting for an answer, he put up his hand to push the defiant girl away. He did not intend to inflict any harm but the raising of his hand caused Bridget to duck quickly down, her necklace becoming entangled with the irate journalist's cuff. It fell with a muffled thud on to the floor. Lionel Bains froze. He had not wanted any ugly confrontations, least of all with a young female. Quickly bending down to retrieve the broken necklace, he looked up apologetically, attempting to utter his regrets. However, no words left his gaping mouth. Suddenly the whole room filled with leaves appearing to fly haphazardly around the now silent room.

If Bridget was perturbed by the mass of invading foliage, she never said. Grabbing her necklace, she hurried from the building. Peering backwards, she waved at Jack, her face etched with sympathy.

The remaining committee members slowly cleared the leaves. Talking quietly, they questioned why leaves had blown so furiously in on such a mild evening. No one cared to mention the strange noises that they had heard.

The Echo
Maysoni Opens the Lock

It was confirmed today that long-standing chairman Simon Potts has reached agreement with Mr Maysoni over the sale of Keys Football Club. Mr Potts has been chairman for Fourteen years and his departure will saddened all that have had the pleasure of dealing with him.

Mr Maysoni has pledged that Keys will be playing in The World Super League within ten years. After successful negotiations, he has further pledged to sanctify the oak tree and all adjoining land.

This is indeed exciting times as we think of the prosperity the takeover will bring to the residents of November Keys.

We are sorry to announce that The Reverend Handlin, disgusted by recent events has accepted a post in Nigeria and will be leaving the village immediately.

Chapter Five
Gold Foods And Gold Ale

If the residents of Keys had any doubts about the intentions of their football club's new owner, they were soon diminished. In his first season Maysoni orchestrated the building of a winning team that quickly found promotion to the upper league. The new ground that he had promised was under construction and the residents were finding many outsiders taking a keen interest in their once isolated village. Trade was up and so was morale.

The owner of the local store had thought up, with his wife's prompting, the lucrative idea of baking cakes in the club's colours. Just as he had visualised, his old cash till chimed merrily on match days. Negotiations were made to have his shop painted in the Keys' colours. His wife continuously collected travel brochures for far away destinations, reaping the fruits of his hard work and ingenuity. It was a shame, he thought at times, that it was an American that had come to his rescue, but then who was he to complain?

Bridget Bluestone was in on the action as well. Although she had been in total disagreement with the sale of the club, with Jack Carpet's blessings, she continued to stand outside the old ground with her dated tea stall. In just a few months she would be going to university and needed to make as much money as she could. If that necessitated siding with the American for a while, so be it. She yearned for the day that her depleted bank account would be filled to excess, bank employees acknowledging her status as a millionaire. She only had to gain her qualifications and then the whole world would learn of her genius. In the meantime she made ends meet by standing outside the old ground selling tea and coffee from her battered mobile stall. Queues at the stall were increasing each week. Youths from the village watched enviously the well-heeled young men from out of town queuing, not for a weak beverage, but for the opportunity to talk to an attractive young woman,

There were those who still doubted the new owner's intentions. Their suspicions rose, especially when dubious people with equally dubious parcels were seen at all times hovering around the new construction.

However, the American Maysoni was good at spin and with the aid of The Echo made new friends on a daily basis. Lionel Bains had started a fan club for the American, which continuously heralded his support.

Those who frequented the Black Cat Inn would often stagger home, courtesy of the American's generosity, loudly singing his praises to the detriment of the early sleepers. November Keys notoriety was blazed across every newspaper in the land. Moon Television counted the months until the team graced the Monster League. Many headlines, boasted of Maysoni's intention to build a state of the art railway. He was often quoted stating he wanted the fans to travel in style and comfort. His fan base grew daily.

Nearer home, the Echo was giving it's full backing to the new ownership and continuously praised the American for his good work, hinting to its readers that even better things were to come. People in Keys were starting to dream of a prosperous future. Their ship was coming in and Maysoni their unlikely captain, was fully in charge at the helm.

Jack Carpet sat at his breakfast table musing moodily over another of the sycophantic fan letters within his once favourite paper. He allowed his brow to tighten and then relax. Although The Echo, now full of claptrap, got on his nerves he had other things on his mind. The smell of bacon and eggs was wafting through the room and he was hungry.

"Ah, an April Supreme."

He picked up his treasured mug and gulped his tea in eagerness. "There is one thing my April can do well and that is getting my day off to a flying start." He was about to read through the paper again when interrupted by his wife placing his much-appreciated meal onto the table. Looking at it fondly, he gave his wife a tender pat, picking up his knife and fork earnestly. "You should get a job as a chef in the pub." He hurriedly forced egg and bacon into his mouth. "There would be a queue for miles."

April smiled and squeezed her husband's arm. "I do my best Sir." She stood silently watching her husband devour his meal.

"Ah," Jack ate quickly. "Those chickens have done it again." He looked at his quickly disappearing eggs. "The best eggs for miles, and the toast, it is as delicious as you."

"Are you comparing me to a slice of toast?" April chuckled, hitting Jack playfully.

"Next you will be saying I am as good as coal, when the fire needs lighting of course."

Jack laughed and continued to eat his breakfast. He had a long day in front and needed to get on. Watching April disappear through the old oak door, he ate hungrily.

"Joined the bingo club have you?" April peered around the door waving a letter "Or do all your correspondents write in gold ink?"

"What on earth?" Jack stood up rapidly, half snatching the gold envelope from his wife's hand. "I bet it has something to do with that American."

April sensing Jack was annoyed stood patiently while he read from a bright red sheet of paper, which he had moodily extracted from the strange envelope. Watching impatiently as his brow furrowed, she counted the seconds expecting an explanation.

"As if people don't have enough to do." He spoke angrily. "Without sending me a load of rubbish through the post." He thrust the red paper into April's hand. "Seems some ultra-rich tycoon wants to buy the recipe for our honey ale, says he is going to make me a household name." He looked down at Rose, who had been sitting patiently hoping for a tit bit. "Rose, there are some strange people in this world." He patted his beloved dog on the head. "And now they are sending me letters."

Rose watched him intently, unhappy about not receiving a morsel from the table. However her master was ready to leave and that meant one thing, a day in the open air. She got up wagging her over long tail, and stood excitedly by Jack's feet.

"Jack," April spoke enthusiastically, "wait a moment." She waved the strange letter at her husband. "This letter is from John Goldsmith." She talked quickly aware her husband might leave before hearing her out. "*The* John Goldsmith. You know full well, he owns a chain of restaurants around the world." She stood upright, indicating her importance in the said matter. "I saw a documentary about him. He gives all of his profits to various charities." She thrust the letter into her irate husband's face. "It said on the telly he only writes in gold when he has a serious interest."

"So what are you saying April?" Jack Carpet looked at his wife wearily. "That I should pursue this nonsense?"

"Oh Jack, don't you see?" April could not contain her excitement. "If Mr Goldsmith pays you a good price you will be able to do some much needed work to the farm." She patted Rose on the head. Surprised by her mistress's attention Rose responded by scratching herself violently, then trying to plant a kiss on April's arm. "Jack Junior will have his legacy and Rose here, will have generations of puppies." April persisted, trying to ignore the dog's amorous advances.

"Look I don't know, we went through this with the American." Jack shook his head and threw the letter on to the table. "I will have to give this some thought." Pulling his trademark cap down over his eyes, he brushed his tweed jacket roughly beckoning a confused Rose to follow him through the old oak door.

April grinning silently started to plot her husband's visit to John Goldsmith. Although the millionaire had originated from the same area and had Keys' blood running through his veins, Jack seemed very suspicious of the tycoon's intentions. April herself, mused why it had taken Goldsmith so long to recognise her husband's farming abilities but nevertheless did not intend to look a gift horse in the mouth. The following week, her husband, qualms or no qualms would be attending a meeting with the big entrepreneur, she thought stubbornly.

A week later Jack sat in his small kitchen wrapped in cling film. April had summoned Rose outside, ensuring her husband looked his best, without unwanted dog hairs. She had spent a good hour pressing her husband's suit and examining it for possible stains. The only time the suit came out of the wardrobe was for christenings and weddings. The last occasion had been a wedding where Jack had drunk too much honey ale, so she wanted to make sure he had not returned home with some of the contents down his suit. At last, contented with her labour, she had supervised Jack's dressing noisily demanding he stay wrapped up until his car came to collect him.

"Oh Jack, a Rolls Royce, who would ever think it?" Looking through a small bay window, April could not contain her excitement. Earlier she had hatched a plot with Jack Junior to blow an old hunting horn when her husband's private car appeared in sight. Hopefully, she thought, that would alert her neighbours, who would see her tycoon husband climbing not just into a gleaming Rolls Royce, but a gleaming Rolls Royce with a private number plate.

Not expecting an answer from her irritated spouse, she checked his bag for the umpteenth time. "A bottle of honey ale." She gazed at Jack worriedly. "You do think he will buy it Jack, don't you?" She took a glass of clear honey and held it up to the light. "Of course he will, he will absolutely love it." She carried on talking to herself whilst Jack sat in his cling film sulking. "Oh, and the recipe." She held up a fading piece of paper, carefully inserting it into a plastic bag.

Jack scowled, his brown eyes smouldering at his smart but ageing suit. He was now starting to regret being talked into what appeared to be utter nonsense, feeling conspicuous dressed in a suit at the busiest time of his day.

Why on earth, he thought grimly, was some multi-millionaire going to buy some old fashioned recipe from him, when he had the pick of the world?

He looked down again at his blue suit covered in rolls of cling film, his shoulders drooped wearily. He had so much to do on the farm, yet he was about to go on some jaunt so that others could laugh at his expense. Before he had a chance of vetting his discontent, his thoughts were shattered by the noise of a horn blowing. "What on earth, the chickens must be getting attacked." He got up quickly, cling film dropping on to the neat kitchen floor. Before he could utter any more anguished words, he was again interrupted by the sound of wheels crunching onto the gravel outside.

"Oh Jack your car is here, and Jack it is pure gold." April could not contain her excitement. Looking out of the window, she was disappointed to see the plush car's arrival had not alerted any spectators. "And all the seats are red leather."

Jack reluctantly got up, making his way towards the small oak door. His forlorn hope that the car might not show had just been disintegrated and he accepted that he would have to complete his mission or never hear the last of it. As he neared the door, April placed a bowler hat onto his head, kissing him gently on the cheek.

"Good luck darling," she patted the lapels on his jacket, "and you look wonderful."

Jack knowing better then to try to dislodge the unwanted hat, made his way out into the morning sunshine. On seeing his transport resplendent with chauffeur dressed in full gear, he whistled softly to himself. Hoping his driver did not think he looked stupid, he made his way warily towards the waiting car.

"Good luck dad." Jack Junior waved happily at him

whilst clinging onto the large hunting horn. Jack shook his head feigning anger while trying to suppress a smile, which despite his best efforts, was growing wider. After polite introductions Peter, his chauffeur, weaved the luxury car through the winding lanes of Keys towards a building which, unbeknown to Jack, was going to change his and his family's life forever.

Jack, pleased that his driver chose to stay silent, sat deep in thought. Watching the trees sail past through tinted windows he wondered how this unwanted jaunt was going to end up. When he had agreed to meet his benefactor, he had no idea that he would be given a Rolls Royce and driver for his journey. This Goldsmith must have more money than he could spend, he thought wearily.

For a moment he let his mind wander back to when John Goldsmith, as a boy, used to play in the village making as much noise as possible. Being older then Jack they had never been friends but would acknowledge each other with a cautious nod of the head. Even in those days the now millionaire had been rather eccentric and many chose to avoid him. However, eccentric or not, the man had a good business head. Combining his love of cooking and sound economics, he had soon been following his chosen destiny to becoming rich.

Suddenly he left November Keys, only to reappear as a regular on TV shows as he built his empire. One of his strange quirks, other than his gold suit was his constant need to change his appearance, consequently, every time he appeared on television, the public saw a different man.

Jack leaned back into his plush chair and tried to enjoy the luxury of his vintage transport. However, he had an uneasy feeling which he could not put his finger on. He was certain, despite his wife's enthusiasm, the whole episode was going to finish in disaster.

When the American had threatened to build over his farm all of his friends and the other villagers had come out in support for him. Nevertheless, they had still voted for the takeover, which had left him feeling uneasy. He was grateful for their support, they all knew it would break his heart to lose his farm. It had been in his family for generations and would eventually be handed down to Jack Junior. However, the ridiculous talk of an intended railway disturbed him greatly. If the preposterous plan proceeded, his land would once again be in danger. The American, Maysoni, was getting his feet firmly under everyone's table and Jack's friends would probably be powerless to help him.

That is why, he supposed, he was going on this stupid journey. If this Goldsmith came up with a substantial sum, it could be ploughed back into the land he owned making way for a good life for his son and family. No one in the village would want to see that threatened. Maysoni had initially offered him a good price for the farm and then on his refusal to sell made enquiries about his recipes for the honey and ale. He had made it clear though, that there would be no dealings with a man he did not trust. The American had laughed, stressing it was just a matter of time. Jack shuddered, recalling the American and his sidekick leering at him. They were both sinister and he could not think for the life of him why Simon Potts had sold them Keys' football club. You did not have to be an England international to perceive that they had neither love nor knowledge for England's favourite sport. Nevertheless, he thought reluctantly, so far they had come up with the goods they had promised.

Jack's thoughts stopped abruptly as he realised the Rolls Royce had come to a sudden halt. Peering through tinted windows, he could see they had stopped in the middle of nowhere and looked at his driver for an explanation.

"We are at our destination Mr Carpet." The driver answered Jack's question before being asked. "Featherstone cliffs."

"But this is just cliffs and grass." Jack panicked slightly, thinking of the American and what he had read about the

Mafia taking their victims for a ride. "Why have we stopped here?"

Peter descended from the car, opening Jack's door with a quiet air of respect and politeness. Sensing his passenger was dismayed, he wanted to put him at ease.

Jack vacated his luxury transport, squinting his eyes at the now glowing, morning sun. Just about to raise his objections of being abandoned in the middle of nowhere, he spotted a large luminous sign sitting within the marbled pattern of the cliff.

GOLD FOODS.

"Well I'll be." He mumbled softly to himself. "So this is where the great man resides."

"Ah Mr Carpet." A squeaky voice interrupted Jack's thoughts. "I trust you had a pleasant journey."

The sudden intrusion made Jack jump back. When he found his composure, he was amazed to be standing just feet away from a strange looking man in his early fifties. Although he did not recognise him immediately, he guessed this must be his host and quickly weighed the man up. He stood around five feet ten and sported a paunch, which suggested a grand life style. Dressed in a gold suit and bright red shirt, Jack did not have to call on his intuition to recognize the famous Mr Goldsmith.

"I saw you on the CCTV." John Goldsmith grinned like a Cheshire cat. He put out a chubby hand. "I have been looking forward to your coming." Before Jack could summon a reply, he felt his hand being shaken vigorously. "Now follow me Mr Carpet, or may I call you Jack?" He looked at his guest impatiently. "Time is money you know."

Jack followed John Goldsmith through a maze of chalk corridors wondering what had enticed him to come to such a strange place. Although he saw no danger in his eccentric host, he felt uncomfortable. He was not used to high-powered businesspersons but even he knew that this set up was excessively bizarre. Eventually, in silence, they stopped at a large oak door with a tiny sign proclaiming the office of the owner of Goldsmith's Foods.

Entering the office, Jack felt that he should say something in the way of introduction but the sight that met him rendered him speechless. The walls were of black marble decked out in every available inch, of gemstones from around the world. Jack whistled softly, attempting to count the countless diamonds, pearls and sapphires embedded in the strange man's walls.

"About three million pounds." Goldsmith chuckled loudly pointing at the vast array of precious stones. "It's my little reward for my endeavours." He beckoned Jack to be seated. "That will save you having to ask me."

Jack sat down heavily wishing that he had brought April with him. He was not used to dealing with business people and was already feeling over-awed.

"Relax Mr Carpet." As though the bespectacled millionaire had read Jack's mind he tried to put him at ease. "We have a lot to discuss." He pressed a small buzzer on his over flowing desk. "Will you partake of some coffee?"

"Yes please," Jack was relieved to find his voice, "that would be very nice."

"Velma, bring some coffee please." Goldsmith squeaked into his intercom. "Make it nice and you might get some honey ale."

Jack sat back in his chair, clenching his fists. He did not intend to assault anyone but his hands were starting to feel sweaty and he wanted to conceal the fact from his host. He was pleased to learn that Goldsmith had an assistant nearby, it made him feel a little more comfortable knowing he was not alone with this strange character.

"Mr Carpet," Goldsmith again interrupted his thoughts, "did you know that everyday is a gold day?" Goldsmith smiled and suddenly started to tap dance around the jewelled office. "Everyday is gold, everyday is a gold day." He sang the words tunelessly whilst hurling his large frame from foot to foot. "Da da da da, Te Te te da da da."

Jack sat speechless, relieved when a tapping on the door

interrupted his host.

"Ah Velma, this is Mr Carpet." Goldsmith took a tray containing the coffees and examined them carefully. He spoke breathlessly, even more squeakily. "Hope they are nice Velma, or no honey beer."

Jack studied the girl for a moment and quickly decided that she looked normal. She looked every part the secretary, smart suit, neat hair and a lovely smile that complimented her attractive features. However, what was she doing with this mad man, he thought sadly? As though reading his mind Goldsmith handed him his coffee and clapped his smiling assistant, his podgy hands echoing around the room.

"Velma has been with me about a million years now." He beamed at the pretty girl. "Is that not so Velma?"

Without answering, other than with a sweet smile, the young girl moved across the room and started to fiddle with some strange looking apparatus.

"Now Mr Carpet, Velma is going to show you a small film." Goldsmith looked over appreciably at his young assistant. "It will show you how we put gold into our days." Watching Jack pick up his coffee and reel back in astonishment sent him into a frenzy of squeaky laughter. "Gold coloured coffee, a little novelty of mine." He was still laughing when the vast screen lit up and nosily introduced The Goldsmith Destiny.

Jack sat quietly watching, trying to concentrate on the information relayed through the state of the art video equipment. This man might be mad he thought brightly, but he certainly knew how to run a food industry. He watched in amazement as Goldsmith's Empire and history revealed itself. The eccentric had inherited a goldmine, apparently belonging to a group of monks. How he had managed to be in line of succession, no one was quite sure. Nevertheless, he had made good use of his windfall. Adamant that he would not personally profit from his inheritance he formed an ingenious idea of transforming the gold minerals into a variety of drinks. He had the rich and famous all around the world queuing to buy them. Unbelievably the odd man did not make a penny for himself, apparently every shilling being donated to various charities. Jack started to wonder where he would fit into all this. After all, honey ale was not exactly for your rich and accomplished. He wondered what his father would have made of it all. The farm had been in the family for generations and his father would have defended it with his life. Nevertheless, he would have been as proud as punch knowing the family's centuries-old recipe was to be used in posh restaurants. Mesmerised by the screen in front of him Jack sat spellbound watching the film demonstrate some of the techniques used by the vast food empire.

An array of computers, manned by a mass of white coats, whirled in unison as clear water seeped through chalk walls. A high-pitched voice stressed the clarity of the water was due to it being from a well dating back hundreds of years. Jack gasped as the computers whirled again, a large funnel depositing gold minerals into the water caused it to turn the colour of pure gold.

"Interesting, Mr Carpet?" Goldsmith's words brought Jack back to reality. He smiled as Jack nodded. "Now do you think we might do business together?"

Jack sat motionless for a while, suddenly aware he was still wearing the ridiculous hat that April had earlier placed onto his head. He tried to remove the hat without attracting too much attention but realising this was fruitless concentrated on his bag conveying the samples from the farm. Fumbling in the bag, he produced the small bottle that April had insisted he take along.

"Oh Mr Carpet, you have brought us some of your delights." Without invitation, Goldsmith walked over to Jack and whisked the bottle of honey ale from his hand. "Velma, two glasses if I may." He smiled at his young assistant. "The coffee was good so you may partake of some as well."

As Velma left to fetch some glasses, Goldsmith held the

welcome bottle up to the light. "Ah, the colour of gold, pure gold."

Jack frightened that his host might go into another of his strange dance routines coughed loudly. "The honey comes from my own bees." He sounded apologetic and his face started to redden. "The bees make the honey." Jack was at a loss for any further words and was relieved when Velma returned clutching two glasses.

"Ah so the bees do all the work?" Goldsmith all but snatched the glasses from his attractive secretary and proceeded to pour the requisitioned drink. "So the bees and honey make the money." To Jack's dismay, Goldsmith rolled back his head and burst out laughing. "Oh dear, do excuse me, but that was so funny. You are a very funny man Mr Carpet."

Jack shook his head, nervously watching his host make a simple drink sampling turn into a spectacular event. John Goldsmith cradled his glass as though it was precious metal, holding it carefully up to the light. After deliberating on the drinks texture, he swallowed half of its contents and then sat in an eerie silence for two minutes. Jack felt like that two minutes was an hour and rubbed his heels together impatiently.

"Ah, pure gold." The eccentric spoke at last. "Nectar from the gods." Goldsmith smiled at Jack and hoisted his large frame upright. "Mr Carpet, ah Jack, this delicious concoction will sell around the world." He looked over to Velma who was nodding profusely. "This gold will pass the lips of every famous person who graces our planet." He pointed at the spectacular walls in his office. "Better than all the jewels in the earth. Lords, ladies and even royalty will revel in such a brew."

Jack sat mesmerised. He found it hard to conceive this great man was talking about a drink that had been in his family for generations. A drink given to the chickens to lay larger eggs and likewise to the horses for a longer day's work. Now this tycoon was talking about giving it to Kings and Queens.

"We will give it a year's trial." Goldsmith's attitude changed abruptly. "My dear Velma will sort out the necessary paperwork." He finished his drink appreciably. Looking intently into the farmers eyes, his squeaky voice took on an all but sinister tone. "Now, have you brought the recipe?"

After studying the ageing paper and carefully placing it securely along side his coveted gemstone, he closed his safe and returned merrily. "As you are about to become rich Mr Carpet I suggest you visit one of my restaurants with your good lady. You will see how we operate." He walked over to Jack and held out a podgy hand. "Nice to have you on board."

Jack realising that the deal was concluded and he had little say in the matter rose to his feet to make his long awaited departure. He was pleased to have been offered such a lucrative contract but wanted to leave the strange place as quickly as he could. As he made his way to the entrance to meet his transport, he turned for a moment to spot his host hopping from foot to foot, waving like an excited child.

"And don't forget everyday is a gold day Mr Carpet."

Jack hastened his footsteps with the tuneless voice of John Goldsmith echoing in his ears.

As his gold car disappeared out of sight, Goldsmith stopped his tuneless melody and looked apprehensively at his young assistant. His voice was not sounding as squeaky as before. He looked bemused and wiped his brow with a gold coloured handkerchief. "Well you might say we won the first round Velma." Without waiting for a reply, he looked hard at the plastic bag containing Jack's recipe, which he had retrieved from his safe. "At least Mr Carpet is safe for a little longer."

As Jack and April celebrated their new-found wealth in one of Goldsmith's swish eating-houses Alphonso Decesso happily paced the walls of his New York penthouse. Gazing at the strollers in Central Park, he allowed himself a smug smile of satisfaction.

Things were going extremely well and Maysoni, despite his initial reluctance, was doing a good job. Very soon, they could concentrate on their shipments, especially when The Caterpillar Express was up and running. In addition, very soon, he Decesso would be the most powerful man in the world. He paused to pour himself a drink. Holding the drink to the window, he toasted the shadowy figures in the park for success for his new venture. Allowing the strong alcohol to roll around his gums he smiled again, acknowledging how easy it had all been. Everything would soon be in place but first he had to pick up some important documentation.

Maysoni had mentioned about one of the villagers being stubborn. Well he was not as nice as his colleague was and the obstinate villager had something he wanted. He raised his glass again "To a Mr Jack Carpet. A man in deep trouble."

April laughed as Jack tried to sit upright. Normally he would not contemplate having his photograph taken, not unless it was obligatory, as at a wedding. Nevertheless, here he was leering like an old master. April could only presume it was the vast amount of champagne he had drunk. Unsteadily trying to adjust her make-up she snuggled nearer to her husband, smiling broadly at the camera. She had had a wonderful evening and wanted to capture just a small part to muse over in the future. Looking around the beautiful building her hazy mind took in how lucky they both were. It would be a long time before they were treated like that again. As the camera's flash lit up the dusky restaurant both the Carpet's wore their best smiles. Neither knew that would be the last photograph taken of them as a happily married couple.

The Echo

It was announced today that local farmer Jack Carpet, has signed a one year deal to provide his famous honey ale to entrepreneur John Goldsmith.
Maysoni promises state of the art transport as Keys romp up the table.
New ground construction, ahead of schedule.

Chapter Six
Chicken Trouble

It took an hour before Maysoni finally blew his top. Sweat was starting to form under his arms and his mood became more and more disgruntled. "What is the point of this?" He glared at Reuccio as though it was he that caused him all of these problems. "Sitting outside some old chicken farmer's house." He slammed his fist onto the leather dashboard and swore beneath his breath. "What does Decesso need with this guy that we can't handle?"

Reuccio, who had been silent, suddenly sat upright in his seat. For a while he had deliberated whether to open a bag of crisps but did not want to fuel his boss's anger, so decided to go without. He knew when his boss referred to Mr Decesso by his last name only, things were getting heated in his mind and he knew who would subsequently endure most of his anger. For some reason, something that Reuccio never knew why, his boss did not approve of eating and did not realise how hungry his insubordinates could become.

"Boss," he nudged Maysoni and pointed to the front of the farmhouse, "we have a visitor."

Both men sat silently watching a gold coloured Rolls Royce drawing up outside the small farmhouse. Within minutes Jack Carpet and his wife descended, climbing into the car excitedly.

"Wow, look at them two." Reuccio whistled softly. "They look like a pair of penguins."

"They must have won their English lotto." Maysoni grunted disdainfully. "At least he's not taking his chickens." The two Americans looked at each other and grinned. "It's nice of him to vacate the house." Maysoni rubbed his hands together. "Now let's get Alphonso his stuff and get out of this hick place."

Several hours later Jack and April sat in the back of their luxury limousine giggling like a couple of schoolchildren. They had both agreed that they had had a superb evening but had drunk far too much champagne. Goldsmith had left orders that they get only the best and, on their first night out in months, they had taken full advantage. The food had been excellent, the drinks even better. To April's delight, the resident band-leader had acknowledged their presence and proceeded to play her favourite song while she and her unsteady Jack had smooched together.

"Oh Jack," April cooed, slurring, "we are so lucky."

Jack pulled himself up in his seat. April was right he thought groggily. However, he was only lucky because she was his wife. He loved her and was now going to demonstrate that love by plastering a Jack Carpet kiss onto her lips. "I love you April." He hoisted himself up further, trying to reach over to his wife, the lurching of the car throwing him unsteadily back in his seat. After trying this manoeuvre three times without success he sat back sulkily. However, within minutes, he was planning to make another assault. If he wanted to kiss his wife, he thought groggily, nothing was going to stop him. He sat for a moment rethinking his actions, glancing cross-eyed out of a tinted window. Watching the stars in the black sky twinkle continuously made him feel romantic and he wanted to relay his feelings to his beautiful wife.

Before he had been able to express his undying love, he was brought rudely back to earth by an unpleasant sight that met his gaze. Rubbing his eyes furiously he hoped that the alcohol he had happily indulged in was now playing tricks with his heavy eyes. Propped up against the old oak tree was Jack Junior. Jack squinted his eyes praying that he was seeing things, but even in the dark and under the influence, he could see that it was indeed his son, and worse, he had taken a terrible beating.

"Driver stop the car." Jack uttered his voice in a pleading voice. "Please stop the car." April, who had been giggling throughout, sat upright in her chair. The urgency and panic in her husband's voice sobered her up, commanding her muddled mind to acknowledge the sudden emergency. Looking out into the dark night, she saw the spectacle that had made Jack alarmed and let out a mighty scream.

JJ lay on a settee trying to make sense of the evening's events. He knew his parents would want explanations and braced himself for the forthcoming grilling. Gently rolling his tongue around his mouth he was satisfied his teeth were intact and sat upright. His face hurt badly and he knew without consulting a mirror he looked in a bad way.

"Oh JJ, you should go to the hospital." April had fussed over him dressing his wounds certain there was something terribly wrong, like internal bleeding.

"Mum, I am fine." JJ looked at his parents apologetically. "I am sorry if I spoiled your night." He pulled his large frame further up into his make shift bed, gingerly pushing his fingers through his thick hair. Feeling a large bump, he sat back, cursing softly.

"Here, drink this," his father handed him a glass of brandy, "and tell us what happened."

JJ gulped at his drink greedily. Staring into his glass, he tried to gauge his parents' mood. He was going to have to tell them the truth and he had started to feel ashamed. "When you left," He finished the rest of his drink, "I thought I would catch up on a couple of bits of paperwork." He shook his head sadly. "But suddenly there was this awful noise from outside." He looked over to the window trying to avert his parents' worried gaze. "The chickens were going crazy." He looked at his father knowingly. "I was pretty certain there must have been a fox amongst them." He handed his glass back for a much-needed refill. "Anyway when I got outside they were running everywhere. I called Rose and we tried to round them up." Putting his hands onto his face, he paused for a moment reliving the evening's events. "I couldn't see any foxes but something had spooked them bad. Anyway, after what seemed hours trying to sort them out." He hung his head acknowledging his shame. "I lost my temper, me and poor old Rose was chasing them all over the place. So I told them they were not getting any honey, and I told it to them loudly."

Jack shook his head trying to suppress a grin. He felt sorry for his son but that had been a daft move. "Don't tell me, Lucy threw her head back, screamed like she was on fire and flew off in a temper." Jack uttered his words quickly, immediately wishing he had kept quiet. His son had suffered enough and he did not need rebuking.

"Yeah, spot on." JJ looked up apologetically. "But she flew up the oak and refused to budge."

"The oak?" Jack looked concerned.

"Dad I had to climb up there." He looked at the floor wishing the mock Persian carpet would wrap him up and fly miles away. He knew what his parents had said about the oak. Even as a child he was not allowed to go anywhere near it.

"You climbed the oak?" April looked at her husband, diverting her horrified gaze to her son. "What on earth were you thinking?"

"Anyway," JJ tried to ignore his parents' distraught faces, "I sort of got into trouble."

Jack bit his lip trying not to show his anger. "How many times have we explained about that tree?" He could feel his anger welling up and decided to dowse it with a large brandy.

"I know dad, but I was worried about Lucy."

Jack gulped his drink and went to say something. Correcting himself, he kept quiet, sitting down with an exaggerated thud. It would have been easy to say that JJ only had to offer the stupid fowl some honey and she would have been down from that tree quicker than the leaves in autumn. JJ paused and continued.

"It was getting dark by now and I was having trouble

finding my footing. Anyway about halfway up my I came into contact with the biggest pair of eyes I have ever seen."

It was now April's turn to suppress a grin. "You saw the owl?" She shook her head sympathetically and reprimanding at the same time. "Owls do live in trees you know."

"Are you saying you fell down a tree because of an owl?" Jack interrupted, worried that his son who had spent all of his life in the country had managed to be spooked by an owl.

"No, it was not the owl." JJ looked at his parents embarrassed. "I must admit it did give me a bit of a fright." He sucked in his breath, speaking in a whisper. "As I got nearer to Lucy, I could see she was shaking with fright. And then I saw this thing."

"Thing?" Jack and April spoke together, "What thing?"
JJ bit his lip, wishing that he were not conducting this three-way conversation. "It was like," he paused trying to find the right words, "like a leaf with eyes and legs." He could see his parents badly controlling their mirth and started to feel a little angry. "Anyway as I tried to get hold of Lucy, the thing made a giggling noise and sort of hopped. I lost my footing and fell down the tree." JJ winced as his bruises reminded him of the evening's events. "I think I must have been knocked out for a bit." He looked around the room for sympathy.

"But how come you missed the pond?" April muttered her words hysterically imagining her beloved son face down in a mass of water.

"Well this is the strange bit." JJ knew his father was grinning but continued anyway. "When I fell, a pile of leaves cushioned my fall."

"What in the pond?" April shook her head in amazement.

"Yeah, and then they sort of rose out of the water bundling me against the tree."

"Well I think it's time we hit our beds, we have a long

day tomorrow." Jack spoke his words towards the ceiling hoping that his son could not see the laughter in his eyes. As he wandered half drowsily up to his bedroom, he remembered the cat that had requisitioned one of the barns to have her kittens. That is what must have spooked the chickens. He made a mental note, before he fell into a deep sleep, to remove the offending feline the next day.

Jack sat silently watching the colours flash across the family's television set. He did not normally watch anything early in the morning but the American was due to broadcast and he was curious about any forthcoming events. He gulped greedily from his mug, hoping the lukewarm contents would help the constant throbbing inside his head. Champagne was great, he thought sadly, while you were drinking it. Not so good the next day though.

He registered that JJ had not yet risen, but was not unduly surprised. It would take time for those bruises to heal and even longer for his son's pride to be restored. If JJ had not been hurt so badly, the whole episode would have been laughable. What did JJ expect climbing up a tree in the middle of the night? It surprised him though that his son had spooked so easily. He was aware as anybody the tricks moonlight can play on one's eyes. Stroking his chin, he wondered what it was that his son thought he had seen. Musing over the strange events he sat silently until he was interrupted by a familiar voice coming from the television set.

Maysoni was in his element. He was used to speaking in public and enjoyed the buzz of the cameras and filming crews. He was starting to feel happy again. The day had started badly with another argument with Decesso. In truth, he thought angrily, Decesso was getting badly on his nerves. The man was never satisfied. He, Maysoni, had done everything asked of him and all his counterpart could do was moan and whine about some recipe.

Against the noise of his boss screaming down the phone, he had tried to explain a dozen times. When he and Reuccio had called at the chicken farmer's and scared the birds witless there had been more than enough time to search the shack. The half-wit son had spent ages with his demented dog chasing the birds and then he went climbing up a tree.

Anyway, he thought grimly, despite Decesso's whining they had searched the place thoroughly and there definitely was no recipe. He had gone on to ask his aggressive boss why they were looking for recipes anyway, when they were supposed to be running a football club.

The floor director indicating he was going on air disturbed Maysoni's thoughts. He folded his huge arms, anticipating the half-wits in Keys being breathless with pride when he laid out his intentions for their hick town.

In the next thirty minutes the whole country's football community shuddered with envy and a begrudged excitement, as the big American drawled out his plans. He was confident, he stated in a relaxed way, that Keys would be competing in the Monster League in just a few years. He had hired the best manager along with the best coaching staff that money could buy. At their disposal was a fund of millions of pounds to buy and then coach the best players in the world. Very soon, he had said emphatically, Keys would be playing in the World Super League. This in turn would necessitate the building of a superior stadium that would only be bettered by the players gracing the flawless pitch. The people of Keys would be richer than their wildest dreams, with new jobs and the major expansion of existing businesses. Maysoni joked around, carrying the show with an easy air. Finally, when the British public slowly started to acknowledge his gifts to their beloved sport, he casually announced that he was going to lay on a special railway, specifically for fans old and new to travel in comfort.

Caterpillar Travel was coming to the UK, courtesy of a big-hearted American. The trains were an outstanding success in the United States and Maysoni felt that his less privileged English cousins should enjoy them too. The trains, painted in dark green, were state of the art for travel and by far the fastest. Each passenger had a computer built into their seat that told them the trains speed and the estimated time of arrival at each station. Continuous updated weather forecasts allowed passengers to dress appropriately if the journey was of a long duration, each passenger could opt to watch a recently released film or an up-to-date video of their favourite recording artist.

Maysoni had puffed on his cigar, profusely defending his generosity, maintaining that he owed so much to the people of Keys and was only trying to repay a small part of his debt. He even managed some crocodile tears, which sent some of the make-up girls diving for their handkerchiefs.

Jack Carpet watched speechless. He had never trusted the American and now he was being proved right. If the proposed plans went ahead, he knew without any doubt his farm would be gobbled up. Despite having received the backing of the village committee, he decided to drive over and speak to his old friend Leonard Small. He was not sure what reception he would get, despite being born and bred in Keys Leonard had well and truly joined the Maysoni fan club. Jack was still angry at his old friend's submission but knew deep down he could trust him to tell the truth.

Jack and Leonard had grown up together. As boys they had attended the same school, indeed sat together and shared their packed lunches. In free time they had been inseparable, fishing in the stream, or climbing trees to secure the biggest conkers. Whilst Jack had eventually taken over the running of the family farm, his friend had taken the academic route and gone to university. Although they had stayed friends, their requirements had changed and they had eventually drifted apart.

Now Leonard was engaged in a project which he maintained was life changing to the people of Keys. He had spent the last five years studying the old myth that had been told countless times and although he could not see it, it had taken over his life. To make matters worse, he could not stop boasting how the American had maintained that being a lover of history himself he was prepared to fund an exhibition at the new stadium. He had puffed on one of his large cigars, assuring the historian that it was essential that the residents of Keys be educated in their histories. Since then Leonard had spent every available minute preparing for his great day.

Jack shrugged and hastily dressed. There was much to do on the farm and the fact that Goldsmith was due for a visit did not help matters. Nevertheless, Jack felt threatened and felt duty bound to abandon his duties for a while and establish exactly where he stood.

If he were right, he thought grimly, in a matter of months his farm would cease to exist. Pleased to see JJ had entered the room he beckoned his son and they both climbed into a battered Land Rover. As he manoeuvred the rusty vehicle through the swinging gate of the farm he glanced back, bringing the vehicle to a shuddering stop. If things were not bad enough, the chickens during his short absence had found a pile of manure and decided to investigate. He took in the unbelievable sight of nearly every bird caked in horse waste and slammed his fist angrily onto the dashboard. In just a few hours Goldsmith was due to visit and what a sight he was going to behold.

As they neared Leonard's old cottage Jack studied his son from the corner of his eye. Although the boy's face was heavily bruised, he seemed otherwise all right and Jack was pleased. There was far too much going on just then to have his son out of action. As his battered jeep came to a halt outside a small cottage, Jack crossed his fingers, hoping that not many would find out about JJ breaking the firm rule of not climbing the oak.

"Hello, hello."

A heavyset man dressed in a green corduroy suit rushed from the cottage, bringing a halt to Jack's thoughts. "Jack,

JJ, what a pleasure this is." Without waiting for a reply, he pointed to the oak door on his cottage and beckoned his unexpected guests to enter. "Coffee, yes coffee." Again, without waiting for a reply he fumbled with an old kettle, slowly filling it with water. "Jack it is so nice to see you." He looked at his old friend suspiciously. "But what brings you away from your farmyard duties?" Satisfied he had placed the kettle correctly on to his ancient cooker he swung around waiting for a reply.

Jack sat silently for a while taking in the walls in the dusty cottage. Everyone from head to foot was covered in posters, showing peculiar pictures and childlike scribbles. Each poster was meticulously marked in felt tip pen. Fleetingly he wondered why someone should want to spend their time on such a ridiculous endeavour. He, like everyone in the village, enjoyed the festivities that the ancient myth allowed but this obsession, he thought wearily, was not healthy. Ignoring the chaos on the walls, he looked sadly at Leonard, wanting to get straight to the point. "You saw the programme Len," He fidgeted making sure his host was listening, "if his plans go forward, I will lose the farm."

"Jack, you must not worry." Leonard Small toyed with some cups not wishing to look Jack Carpet in the eye. "Whatever happens, happens." Placing coffee and sugar into the cups, he looked straight at his old friend. "But whatever happens, because of Mr Maysoni's courtesy and generosity, Keys is going to inherit a showcase about its history which in time will shape its destiny."

Jack shook his head sadly. He knew there was no point in any further discussions. He listened half-heartedly while Leonard explained how the American intended to fund his exhibition, with state-of-the-art technology, in the new stadium. As Leonard became more excited, the more Jack's hopes dived. He decided to abandon his mission and seek out some of the committee. He needed to get some answers and his historian friend was not helping. As they rose to leave Jack became further annoyed when he realised JJ was staring as though hypnotised at one of the posters on the wall. He was aware that his son was still suffering from the previous day's activities but felt he could have said at least a few words to back him up.

"Well, we had better get moving." Jack barked his words angrily. "We have not got all day to discuss myths and exhibitions about outdated superstitions." Getting up to move he became further annoyed when he realised his son was taking no notice, instead, continuing to stare at the poster now the focus of all three men.

"It is the myth of the leaves." Leonard spoke in an assured voice. He was pleased that his array of literature was getting some welcome attention.

JJ shook his head as though coming out from a trance, "Do those things exist?" He almost whispered his words, his eyes still glued to the offending picture. Staring at him was a cartoon type figure, which normally would have produced a few laughs. However, JJ was not laughing.

"No JJ, they do not exist, but they are a very important part of Keys history." The historian studied JJ intently hoping he might have found a convert for his project. "What makes you ask a question like that?"

Jack glared at his son and Leonard in turn. He was running miles behind his schedule and was becoming increasingly annoyed that he was being detained by a discussion over a picture of leaves that appeared to have arms and legs.

"It's just that I thought I saw one last night, I climbed up a tree." JJ looked down to the floor embarrassed. "I was chasing a chicken."

Leonard studied JJ for a moment, sucking in his breath. "I hope you are not going to say it was the oak." The historian's face paled and he looked over to his old school friend for a denial on behalf of his son. "Anyway," Leonard grinned mischievously, "you would not have encountered any of these little beauties." He nodded over to the poster that held JJ's attention. "They went out of existence many years ago. He looked sympathetically at his young visitor. He now knew why he was in such a bruised state. The young man had climbed a tree and been spooked. "JJ, toads climb up trees, but it is an easy mistake." Leonard chuckled softly to himself. "Come to my exhibition and you will see the difference."

Decesso stared hard into Central Park, glaring at the many temporary inhabitants. He had just watched Maysoni give an excellent television interview and was impressed with his number two's slick presentation. However, he was angry that his own plans had not proceeded and further angry that he had had a confrontation with Maysoni. He knew Maysoni back to front and was under no illusions if he kept mentioning the recipe, he would become suspicious. If he were to find out Decesso's intentions, he would definitely expect some of the proceeds.

Further to that, he had been informed the document that was going to make him wealthy was tucked up securely in the safe of a certain John Goldsmith. He shook his head, glaring at the strollers in the park. Goldsmith, of all the people in the world. Why him, he thought angrily? Anyone else and he would have taken it with his own hands. However, that was not going to happen with Goldsmith. The man and his restaurants were a legend in New York frequented by the mobs of the highest order.

Decesso shuddered as he recalled the night some troublemakers had caused a disturbance while the hierarchy of the mob was dining in one of Goldsmith's restaurants. Horrified at the rude outburst, the top boss had apologised to Goldsmith, the wrongdoers ended up in concrete overcoats.

Picking up his phone he fleetingly wondered why a man with Goldsmith's wealth would want to put his life on the line for something that did not concern him. Shrugging his broad shoulders, he barked down the phone for his administrator to book four tickets to the United Kingdom.

He was going to get his prize, Goldsmith or no Goldsmith.

Warming to the idea of some overdue violence, he felt his stomach applauding the idea of his soon to be trip. He had read about the restaurants in England and certainly meant to mix business with pleasure.

Jack, exasperated at the day's events, jumped from his Land Rover and, despite his son's protests, made straight for the barn where the stray had secreted its kittens. He did not like hurting animals but if his uninvited guest was going to interfere with his chickens, quite simply it had to be moved on.

Getting angrier by the minute, he wondered why his son had admitted climbing the oak. Crossing his fingers, he prayed that his old friend did not spread the information any further.

Looking at his watch, he recognised he was way behind schedule with his new boss soon to make a visit. Hastening his footsteps, he made his way to the large barn. Throwing the large door open, he quickly closed his eyes, not wishing to witness the sad scene in front of him. His hands rising involuntarily to shield his nostrils from an over powering smell, he kicked the door of the barn shut. Not wanting JJ to see the horrible spectacle he motioned him back to the farmhouse. Staring momentarily at the dead cat and her dead brood, he grabbed a bin liner and set about the task of piling the dead carcasses, intending to take them over to the bonfire later. Shaking his head sadly it dawned on him, by the disgusting smell, that the felines must have been dead a few days and were not the culprits that had scared his fowls. Wondering how the streetwise feline had come to such an end, he started to feel bile enter his throat. Whilst exercising his unpleasant task he stood back trying to breathe the fresh air from outside. Satisfied that he had inhaled enough air to complete his chore he quickly threw the decaying carcases into a bin liner, until disturbed by the pitiful whining of a small animal. Abruptly stooping down, he was shocked to see one of the kittens move. Amazed that it was still alive, he quickly wrapped it in some old towelling. Looking sadly at a bulging bin liner, he mumbled about protecting the sole survivor and made his way over to the farmhouse.

During the short journey he envisioned April's delight at the new occupant, shaking his head sadly. Sure, they would nurse the mite to health then (he already knew against his wife's objections) it would have to move on. Cats and chickens were not a good mix.

As he strode noisily through his front door he had absolutely no idea what impact the straggly creature would have on the future of November Keys.

April gave JJ one of her forgiving smiles and gestured for him to hand her the small kitten. It was certainly ugly and ate enough for all of its brothers and sisters combined, but there was also a cuteness about it. The small feline, happy after a large feed and three saucers of milk closed it's eyes tiredly and snuggled in to April's waist purring contently. "So now you have eaten enough for an entire family, you want to go to sleep?" April laughed, stroking the cat gently. "We will have to call you Well Fed."

JJ raised his eyes, staring at his mother disapprovingly.

"Ah we need to give our hungry guest a name." JJ laughed loudly, looking at the ugly kitten with disdain. "How about, Wilfred the barn rat cat?"

April, pouting, wrapped a collar around the small animal's neck. "I know we will call you Wilfred." She looked triumphantly at JJ. "Now if you get lost, people will know your name."

Jack Carpet who had entered the room shook his head sadly. If it was not bad enough that his wife had fallen for the ugly stray, she was now trying to settle the odd creature in to his house.

The Echo
Maysoni reveals his brilliant plans for Keys' Football

Club.
The state-of-the-art Caterpillar Express almost certain for Keys' residents.
Talks of a statue to express village's gratitude at Maysoni's generosity.
Committee to investigate rumours of JJ violating the oak.

Chapter Seven
Cheryl's Pub Grub

Maysoni squinted at the fading August sun, trying to close his ears to the thundering noise of a small jet plane screaming along a dusty runway. Glaring at Reuccio, he pressed his fingers down the lapels of his expensive suit, ready to greet his unwanted guest. Continuing to glare at his sidekick who was now trying to advert his gaze by playing with a flower picked from an over-growing hedge, he kicked the dusty road vindictively.

Maysoni was angry, as always he imagined Reuccio was responsible. Maysoni was angry because he did not want Decesso on his back and he was further angry that he was not getting the information he required. Which meant he was not afforded the respect he felt he was due. If the recipe that Decesso never stopped complaining about had anything to do with his operation, he felt he had the right to be told. However, he thought disdainfully, it was unlikely that he would be told. He hated to admit it, even to himself, but truth was he was scared of his overawing boss. But then most were.

The man had fought, murdered and manipulated himself to the top of the ladder. It was rumoured that even the organisation's top boss resigned himself to the fact that Decesso would one day lead the whole pack. Watching the rising dust settle and familiar figures emerging from the jet he cursed softly.

"Alphonso," Maysoni's glare channelled into a feigned smile, "It is nice to see you." As Maysoni lied, he eyed his boss up and down reluctantly acknowledging how resplendent he looked. His suit fitted like it had been tailored to the nearest fraction of an inch. On the cuffs of his thousand-dollar silk shirt sat cuff-links with multiple emeralds proclaiming the initials AD. Drooped around his large neck hung a hand woven scarf whose cost would have paid off half of Britain's overdrafts.

"Alberto," Alphonso Decesso lumbered across the cracking tarmac, "it is good to be here." Decesso grinned broadly, the last of the sun glinting on his gold teeth.

The two men hugged which lessened Maysoni's immediate concerns over Decesso's unexpected visit. When they had argued on the phone Maysoni had the whole of the Atlantic to protect him, now he felt vulnerable, fully aware that he might have written his own death warrant. However, when Decesso hugged his co-conspirator he knew he was still good for some more days on the planet. Anyway, Maysoni thought foolishly, he would not be 'done away' on English soil.

Following the large Italian at a discreet distance were three of his trusted henchmen. Maysoni knew he only travelled with them when something serious was afoot and steered his mind back to what could be going down. Making a mental note to get Reuccio to prise some information, he feigned the best smile he could muster, turning reluctantly towards his unwanted guest.

"This is a surprise Alphonso." Maysoni stood waiting for an answer to a question he felt he did not have to ask. He looked at his guest expectantly.

"Alberto you must not worry." Decesso looked coyly back at his travelling companions. "You have mastered a grand job, this is strictly pleasure." He looked admiringly at the private jet he had vacated. "And Alberto you only add to that pleasure."

With the basic formalities over, the posse climbed in to Maysoni's Rolls Royce, which Reuccio steered into the English countryside. The two leaders sat in silence as the car sped through narrow lanes. Everyone knew that business, regardless how urgent, would be conducted later and privately between the two men.

Gazing out of the window Decesso put his thoughts to pressing issues. He was ravenous and mused hungrily where they would be eating. Before leaving New York he had his administrator locate six of the best Italian restaurants in England. He was sure, if he knew Maysoni as well as he did, one of them would be expecting a visit. The thought of meatballs and pasta stirred his appetite and he looked longingly at the passing trees.

"We eat first." His words punctured the silence, sounding more an order then a request, "I am hungry."

"Yes me too." Voices that had been restrained responded in noisy unison. "I only had a bag of potato chips."

"And they only had salt and vinegar." A voice complained noisily.

Decesso glared at his companions. "We eat soon." He looked affectionately at Maysoni. "I am sure it will be a delight."

The remainder of the journey passed quietly, the passengers deep in their own thoughts. Finally the luxury car entered November Keys, where Maysoni broke the silence. "This is the place where our fortune lies." He pointed to a building site still very active, "Very soon we shall see the beginning of the new stadium." Pointing to a small farmhouse, he crossed his finger across his throat. "And very soon we will have the land to build the Caterpillar Express."

"Alberto, you have done well." Decesso spoke in a strained voice. "And we will discuss this many times over the next few days." He gently rubbed his stomach. "But now before I can pay any attention to your marvellous plans, I must eat."

"Yes me too, it must be hours since food passed my mouth."

The noise in the rear of the vehicle became chaotic with Decesso's henchmen proclaiming their hunger. As Decesso was about to remonstrate, Reuccio stopped the car immediately outside the Black Cat Inn. Maysoni leaned back and gestured at the small hostelry.

"Gentlemen, your accommodation."

Decesso looked at his counterpart questionably.

"Alberto, I do not understand, where is our hotel?"

"Alphonso this is your hotel." Maysoni looked at Reuccio for support. "It was the best I, er Reuccio, could manage at such a short notice." He spoke sarcastically. "You must remember this is the English vacation time. All the bigger hotels are booked." He looked apologetically at the occupants in the car. "I have booked a table to be ready in twenty minutes."

After some grumbling the group made their way through the decaying door of the inn, shuffling into the smoke filled bar. Immediately, as though someone had called for an abolition of noise, the packed bar fell into silence. The silence was maintained for a while until a chubby man in his late fifties stepped forward.

"You must be the party of six." He nodded at his gawking customers. "That's a relief, for a moment I thought you was gangsters."

Maysoni put his hand on Decesso's shoulder, whispering that the balding bartender did not mean any insult. Pushing him forward he warned that there was more strange behaviour to come, as all English were like this. The six outsiders were seated at a table with enough room for four. They sat dejectedly until the balding barman requested their order for drinks. Looking around the packed bar Maysoni quietly asked what the popular beverage everyone seemed to be drinking was. He was quietly enjoying Decesso's discomfort but did not want it to appear obvious.

"Ah that's our famous honey beer." The chubby barman rubbed his grubby hands gleefully. "It's famous around here."

Decesso, who had his enormous bulk squeezed into a small corner of the table, reeled forward nearly knocking Reuccio from his chair. "No, no we will not want to drink that." The horrified look on the Italian's face certified there would be no arguments over the matter causing the group to stare at the crestfallen bartender expectantly.

"Well, you can try our home made cider." The bar man

spoke sadly. "If our honey beer is not good enough."

Maysoni nodded his head, gesturing for six glasses to be brought to the under-sized table. He looked at Decesso curiously. He knew the fat man was disgruntled but at the mention of honey beer what was left of his greasy hair had nearly stood on end. Maysoni recalled recent arguments over a missing recipe, making a mental note to investigate. There was something going down and he was going to make it his business to find out what it was.

"Six pints of our best." The barman's return quelled Maysoni's occupied thoughts and he smiled at his colleagues.

"Here is to Keys, gentlemen." He raised his glass, taking a large gulp from the strange looking mixture. As the cider made contact with his tongue he spluttered, quickly attempting to force it forwards to the front of his mouth. The last time he had tasted anything so vile was when his father had owned a restaurant. It had been plagued with rats and his father had brewed a concoction that he maintained would rid the place of elephants. Maysoni had unwittingly placed some of the mixture into his mouth and been confined to his bed for a week.

He looked over at Decesso whose normally red face had turned bright crimson. He appeared bemused and upset. Maysoni feared that any moment the big man would erupt and cause mayhem.

"Your evening meal gentlemen." A large woman whose physique made the barman look slender beamed at the six men. "My name is Cheryl and I prepared this with my own hands."

Maysoni, grateful for the interruption, looked at the six plates hastily dispatched onto the table. He gulped, watching Decesso alarmingly. In truth he had heard some stories about the infamous cuisine offered by the village inn but, as he took in the mess on the plates, he could not comprehend how anyone could possibly offer anything like this as food.

Each plate contained a soggy white lump that was presumably meant to be mashed potatoes. Accompanying this was a small handful of soggy green peas, while nesting on top were two sausages that appeared to have sat on a barbecue for an hour or more. The completely unpalatable mess was saturated in strange lumpy gravy.

Maysoni immediately felt relieved that he would be able to summon the room service at his hotel later and eat something digestible. Meanwhile his concerns stayed with his guests.

Decesso stared at the burnt offerings as though they had fallen from a dustcart. If Maysoni had thought the man's face could not have turned any redder he was entirely wrong. Decesso looked like he was going to explode.

"It is authentic English cooking." Maysoni felt that he had better make some type of excuse or very likely everyone in the strange bar would end up dead. He looked coyly at his guest. "It takes some getting used to."

"Are you trying to poison us?" Decesso spluttered with rage. "I have seen better, fed to the pigs." Fortunately he spoke quietly and the regulars in the inn were oblivious to his discomfort. Decesso had a passion for good food and had automatically assumed Maysoni was aware of this fact and that they would be dining in one of England's top restaurants. "Who would you expect to eat this muck?"

He felt so incensed that, if Maysoni were not so important to his plans, the man would be wearing a concrete overcoat. Looking around the crowded pub, he gestured at the other guests. "Alphonso I feel that I should offer these people some decent food. They are under our employ now." He shook his head vigorously. "What type of employer could see their workers eat this mess?"

"Are you going to eat that boss?" Decesso's companions spoke together. "It tasted pretty good."

Decesso reeled around, disgusted to see his three henchmen scraping his uneaten meal onto their plates. He made to stand up, happy that this culinary nightmare was ending.

"Ah nice to see men with appetites." Cheryl had appeared with six bowls of an unidentifiable mixture. She stood proudly examining the empty plates. "As you ate your dinner you are in for a special treat." She rubbed her hands down her soiled apron. "Tomorrow I will do one of my special curries."

Decesso, Maysoni and Reuccio sat silently as their companions finished all the food in sight. Maysoni felt it was a good time to take his leave. Decesso was looking very unhappy. As he stood up to leave, he felt he should say some words of apology about the revolting food that his guest had been offered. Before he could offer his words, he noticed Decesso's face screw up in pure hatred, his eyes bulging like a swamp frog. The bulging eyes were glaring directly at a young girl who had made her way, noisily, into the inn.

Recognising her as the youngster who sometimes worked on the chicken farmer's land, Maysoni himself studied her intently. Word had reached him that she had been opposed to his takeover but as she was of no concern he had shrugged his shoulders and laughed.

Why his guest had taken offence, he had no idea. Maysoni noticed that the girl had sensed she was being glared at and in response pouted at the large American. Mystified why two strangers should dislike each other he continued to make his exit. On passing the girl, he noticed she was cradling a pasty in her tiny hand. That is why his boss had glared. He made a note to change Decesso's accommodation. If a girl with a pasty upset the man, he must be starving he mused happily.

Jack Carpet stood silently, staring upwards to a blue sky. He loved the noise of the bees droning and wanted to savour the moment. It crossed his mind how many times, as man and boy, he had collected honey from the busy hives. The pattern had never changed. He would collect the honey, mix it according to the farm's recipe and wait for his chickens to appear from nowhere. He smiled to himself as he recalled the horses kicking up a fuss until they got their share also. The recipe had been handed down through the ages and he wondered if all those years ago the animals went potty over the mixture as his did. One thing for sure, he mused, those chickens laid the biggest eggs this side of the Atlantic.

"I cannot lose this farm, not to a football pitch." Jack pulled his five feet ten frame upright, not happy with this unwelcome thought. "Goodness me I am talking to myself now." Trying to occupy his mind, he ventured over to the hives, carefully taking out one of the honeycombs. Dipping his finger, he tasted the delightful honey and acknowledged the bees circling above him. "Well done my winged caterers." Placing the honeycomb carefully back in place he spun around checking the space behind him. He thought he had heard a giggling noise and stood quietly hoping the unidentified noise might echo itself.

Seeing nothing untoward, he shrugged his shoulders and made his way over to the chicken coops. As he approached the hens clucked in anticipation, their excited chirping only overshadowed by the sound of the horses' snorting, trying to attract Jack's attention. "Alright my farmyard friends, there is enough for everyone." Jack never fully understood why his animals were so fond of honey and stood for a while listening to their protests at the lack of refreshments.

"Hi, I brought you some tea." JJ interrupted his thoughts. Standing, grinning ear-to-ear, he proffered a steaming mug of tea. "Guess you could use it."

Jack took the drink gratefully, eyeing up his son. The bruises that he had suffered were starting to fade helping him to look like his old self. Putting the mug to his lips, he gestured to his son with his thumb. The men had gone through this ritual for many years as a way of thanking each other for little services rendered.

Looking to JJ for his reciprocation, he was amazed to see him rooted to the spot staring madly into the hedges, his face as white as a sheet.

"JJ, what is it?" Jack rushed towards his son thinking he was having some sort of delayed shock.

JJ did not move but stood staring transfixed into the hedge. As his father got nearer, he pointed with a shaking finger. "There's one of those things." He could hardly talk through fear. "What I saw up the tree."

Looking into the hedge Jack spotted the cause of his son's fear and jumped back.

Decesso glared at Maysoni menacingly. They had inspected the site together, meticulously discussing plans. Reluctantly he registered that his counterpart had everything spot on, leaving no reasons for complaint. However, he wanted to complain. He wanted to complain loudly, about the horrendous place that Maysoni expected him to stay. He wanted to complain about an owl hooting all night long. He wanted to complain that when he sent his posse to shoot the offending creature the noise woke up some chicken farmer who had run about screeching at the top of his voice. He also wanted to complain about the slops he had been served up. He thought the previous evening's meal had been bad enough, that was until he had been served up some revolting concoction that strange woman called an English breakfast. If the English truthfully had to eat that stuff every day, he thought dismally, there would soon be a worldwide cry for help.

Although Maysoni had apologised incessantly, that was still not good enough. He insisted that Maysoni find him somewhere else. He did not care, he had ranted, if places were packed to the rafters, shoot a few guests and there would be plenty of room.

Eventually Maysoni had relented, sending Reuccio scouring around the countryside, ordering him not to return until he had successfully completed his mission. When Reuccio had phoned and informed him that he had managed to find them a five star hotel a relieved Maysoni had happily told the big Italian he would be moving that evening.

Nevertheless, Decesso was still angry for the suffering he had endured and scribbled into his notebook that when Maysoni eventually returned to America he would be made to remember every detail. However, there was business to conduct, he wanted that recipe.

After an hour of grilling an amazed Maysoni, he reluctantly acknowledged that he would have to follow a different strategy. Goldsmith had his paperwork and he quietly surmised how he was going to obtain it while the restaurateur was under the protection of the bosses. Making a mental note to visit the chicken farmer he brushed down his suit, happily visualising the farmer screaming in terror as the contents buried deep in his brain were revealed.

"We are ready Mr Decesso."

Reuccio's soft tone interrupted his thoughts and his mind turned once more to his stomach. He was feeling irritable but knew that a good meal followed by a good rest would put him in a better frame of mind. The supposed food that he had been subject to would have been thrown out of all the prisons in The United States. Flashing his gold teeth to the sky he inwardly prayed for a sumptuous meal and climbed into the waiting Rolls Royce.

As the Rolls Royce neared the Black Cat Inn, the occupants of the car sat up in alarm. They had planned to fetch their luggage and make a hasty retreat. There was to be no fuss but on witnessing a big crowd outside the inn, they knew their plans might change.

Reuccio parked the car outside the inn door, each of the occupants had a hand on their gun. Decesso looked into the rear of the car, pleased that his bodyguards were fully alert to any danger. He could not see why any of the villagers should want to cause any fuss but descended from the car cautiously. Stepping out of the car, he was amazed to be greeted with a loud cheering. Looking around, his shocked eyes were met by hundreds of faces grinning like apes. Trying to take in the ridiculous scenario his nostrils were attacked with a disgusting smell coming from the inn. Wondering what could cause such an unpleasant odour he looked around to Maysoni gesturing for the car to move on. He would buy some new luggage he thought nervously. He did not want to be amongst these people any longer than he had to. As he made to get back in the car, his eyes were averted to a crudely written banner hanging precariously from the inn's sign.

THE AMERICANS EMPLOY US BUT THEY EAT
WITH US.
THREE CHEERS FOR THE AMERICANS.
TONIGHT THE AMERICANS ARE GOING TO
ENJOY A HOMEMADE CURRY AND IT WILL BE
HAPPY HOUR ALL NIGHT.

Decesso stood rooted to the spot looking contemptuously at the home-made banner. He was soon joined by his companions.

"Three cheers for the Americans." Cheryl had appeared waving a flag em-blazed with the Stars and Stripes. As although attending a film premier cameras appeared from nowhere, their flashbulbs illuminating the dusky evening. Decesso spluttered, recoiling in horror as hands thrust grubby notebooks into his begging for autographs. Looking helplessly at his posse, he was starting to understand why Maysoni complained so bitterly. His ruddy face exploding a gross scarlet hue he winced as a camera flashed in his face.

When he had the recipe, he thought moodily, he would have all of these mad people obliterated. For a moment, his face creased into a smile. If this was a sample of what his influence could achieve in such a short space of time, he would soon be ruling the world. His greedy mind imagined his new-found wealth until a mad shrieking interrupted him.

"Let's show them some real English hospitality." Cheryl's frenzied voice punctured the air. As though going through a well-rehearsed, routine the small crowd pushed the Americans through the door of the Black Cat Inn. "No charge tonight." Cheryl's excited voice reached an unhealthy pitch. "The delicious food is on the house."

Decesso turning to his henchmen for help looked on disgusted as they were seated at the same table they had frequented the night before, banging their cutlery in hungry anticipation.

Maysoni, his nose taking in the repugnant smell, could only put his hands on his head looking down in despair. As another camera waved in his face, he acknowledged he needed to have these strange peoples' cooperation, he picked up a glass, smiling at the lens.

The head-waiter at The Dorchester Hotel sadly stared at an empty table, shaking his well-groomed head. He had no idea why his guests had not arrived and hoped it had nothing to do with the reputation of his establishment. He knew all about the reputation of the missing party and hoped there would be no repercussions for him personally.

He stood motionless for a while, aimlessly shrugging his shoulders. When the little Italian man had turned up earlier and requested, rather forcibly, accommodation and the best food in town he had made every effort to impress. It had meant shuffling some guests and calling his Italian chef into work on his day off. The irate chef had laboured all afternoon abusing everyone in sight. Nevertheless, he was pleased with the outcome. The best Italian food this side of the Mediterranean. He had even managed to procure some of the finest Italian wines.

He had hoped that the grateful Italians would remember and use the hotel when the new stadium was built. For a brief while he thought he had taken another step up the promotion ladder. Now here he was with six extra staff and no customers to serve. Realising the repercussions that might follow when the hotel's owners got wind of his extravagance he took off his frock coat and drooped it over an empty chair. Hastening his footsteps, he figured he would not have much use for it in the future.

JJ ate his toast whilst idly reading The Echo. He was feeling a bit down but laughed when he read the article about the Americans loving The Black Cat's food. Cheryl the proprietor had exclaimed that because of her undisputed culinary skills the pub would be holding theme nights. If the Americans loved her cooking then so would everyone else. He wondered what she had given them to eat because not many people went back twice. Flicking the pages, he laughed at the photographs of Maysoni and his overweight guest. The fat American looked like he was going to explode whilst Maysoni, with his sickly grin, raised his glass to the camera.

JJ stopped laughing, his eyes resting on a photograph of his parents, which had been taken at John Goldsmith's restaurant. He squirmed a little, feeling a bit guilty. He could see, studying the picture, that they were happy and having a good time. He had been stupid climbing the oak and felt he had let them down. It had ruined their evening. They had enough on their plates without him acting up. What with trying to keep the orders going for Goldsmith and worrying about the plans for the new stadium his father had much to keep him occupied.

Goldsmith, who had already picked up an award for the honey ale, had now requisitioned the farm to supply his restaurants with free-range eggs. It was going to necessitate more chickens and a lot more work.

For a short while he pondered why a man like Goldsmith should need a small farm's eggs and honey. Whatever it was, was not for him to say. His father had done a deal and needed all hands on deck. He certainly did not need his second-in-command losing control and certainly did not have time to hear stories about leaves with legs.

He sat silently for a moment, wondering what he had seen firstly up the oak and then in the gardens. When his father had responded to his shouts, a grass snake that had vanished quicker than a puff of smoke had lay there staring at them. His father, not liking snakes, had jumped back and then fell into a fit of laughter. JJ protested saying he was certain he had seen something different. His father had been good about it but he could tell by the strange looks he was getting that his parents thought he had cracked up.

He shuddered, remembering hearing their hushed conversation that the fall from the tree had done something to his head. One-minute owls were scaring him out of trees, now harmless grass snakes were spooking him. Shrugging his shoulders, he placed his paper down and wandered out to the farm. If he were to work twice as hard, he thought benevolently, it might make up for the previous day's adventure.

John Goldsmith quietly watched his diners tuck into their meals, silently crossing his fingers. In his restaurant sat, as always, the top leaders of the mob. To an unsuspecting eye, each of them looked like slightly overweight men enjoying a night out. Goldsmith knew different. Every one of them was outrageously violent. Each one had killed so many people the bodies were still being counted.

Watching them roll up the sleeves of their ten thousands dollar suits, he blew air upwards to his nose. Why they were so protective of their clothing he had no idea. The suits would be discarded for new ones the next day. No one in the hierarchy wore the same suit twice. Their decadence knew no boundaries and no one stood in their way.

Allowing his mind to wander he sadly thought of the young witness. A very brave man indeed. He knew the man, despite countless witness protection programmes, would inevitably end up dead. That was after he had been severely tortured. Goldsmith would not wish that on any man but if the witness could take Decesso out of the picture, then it had to be done.

He listened carefully, through the monitors he had

secreted, as the bosses instructed their aides to recall Decesso back to America. There was a lot of muck hitting the walls and they did not want any involvement. Of course, they would hunt the witness down before he could make any damaging testimony but in the meanwhile, Decesso would have to face the music on his own. Hopefully he would be incarcerated.

Goldsmith grimaced as he recalled how he had bribed the witness to give his testimony. He knew he had saved his own life whilst putting the unfortunate man's life in jeopardy. However, no way could he let the recipe fall into Decesso's hands. Whilst the bosses frequented his establishments Decesso would not dare make his move. He knew Goldsmith had their protection, but for how long? Too much salt or not enough seasoning could send anyone of them into a blind fury. He felt a bead of sweat run down his chubby neck and thanked the heavens, that Decesso had kept his greedy secret to himself. If any of those in the room had any idea about the recipe then he might as well settle his funeral arrangements.

After a short while he tired of watching the mountains of food disappear, switching his mind to the Carpets. Very soon, if Decesso remained at liberty, Jack Carpet would be a very dead man. Shuddering with this unwanted thought, he patted his gold suit and wandered into the eating area to mix with his guests.

The Echo
Maestro Maysoni unveils his plans for the future.
The outlook for November Keys looks spectacular.
The Americans enjoy a night at The Black Cat Inn.
The Black Cat announces due to unqualified success, the inn, in future, would be serving meals based on different theme nights.
Jack Carpet's farm grows after being rewarded with huge order for his famous eggs.

Chapter Eight
Angry Bees Do Not Make Honey

Maysoni stood silently, glancing up to the October sky. The autumn breeze made him feel unusually good, enthusing him to inhale large gulps of country air. Quickly scanning his building site, his brown eyes beamed with delight. He felt happy. Especially with the stadium's progress. In fact, he thought contently, everything was going perfectly to plan. Keys, as expected, were top of their new league and even at the early stages of a long season experts were predicting another promotion.

Watching some browning leaves detach themselves from the old oak, he briefly allowed himself a vote of confidence. The odds of his plans succeeding, he thought happily, were as certain as those leaves reappearing in springtime. The building work was ahead of schedule, whilst the team was exceeding all expectations.

His face contorted into a sneer as he deliberated on the inhabitants of November Keys. Strange, every one of them, he thought gruffly. He had heard many rumours about the English but had generously assumed that they were far-fetched. Now he was entirely sure the bizarre stories were as accurate as told. However, what other nation could be so gullible he thought happily? Did they seriously think that he had spent millions just to give these country hicks some low-life entertainment?

He laughed aloud, recalling the strange man who had requested an exhibition in the stadium. He wanted to show pictures of leaves and witches. Normally he would have sent the mad man scuttling away with something painful to take as a present. Ironically, however, a dimly lit area with secret niches suited his plans very well. Lionel Bains, the strange editor of The Echo, was forever singing his praises, making his job a whole lot easier. He shook his head in bewilderment, pulling on his cigar.

"What a clever man I am." He chuckled loudly to himself, slowly making his way to his make-shift office. "A couple of outstanding issues and I am right back on track."

On entering the office his nostrils were attacked with a familiar smell making him cough involuntarily. "What on earth are you doing?" He glared at the four men sprawling across the room. Each of them eating hungrily from brown paper bags.

"Cheryl had some curry left from last night." Reuccio spoke cheerfully, sticking his fingers into a messy bag.

Maysoni shuddered, glaring again, the sickening smell making him retch. "All you want to do is eat." He stood staring contemptuously at his companions, suddenly thinking wistfully of the evening they had all sat in the strange pub eating the same foul concoction. Decesso had gone outright crazy. Maysoni had thought he was going to shoot everyone in sight. Out of respect he stifled an unwanted smile, remembering the fat man taking a gulp of the putrid mixture. His features had taken on the expression of a man being garrotted. Maysoni, at first, thought he was going to die. Until he had spat out the offending food, spluttering at everyone in the bar, promising all sorts of nasty and unimaginable retribution. Maysoni shuddered, remembering the fat man's threats that he, Maysoni, would be hung up and left to die. By the time he had finished, Decesso had promised, Maysoni would smell worse than the vile food he had procured for them to eat.

Fortunately for Maysoni the Italian had been called back to the States the next day. Some very foolish person had decided to go canary, incriminating the boss in various crimes including Decesso's party trick of chopping off an enemy's fingers one by one, to the tune of jail-house rock. Decesso's attorneys had stipulated he return and defend his name. Stepping back on to American soil, he was promptly arrested and his posse of legal representatives had spent every moment since trying to get him released. If found guilty he faced a back to back sentence of ninety-nine years, so Maysoni reasoned he would not be bothered by the fat man for some time to come.

The noise of drilling and busy machinery brought him back to earth, he stood glaring at the men in front of him. In a short while they were going to earn some of their enormous wages. That chicken farmer was going to need a hand to move on and if his plans were going to go as planned that would have to be very quick. Decesso, although incarcerated, was still ranting about some recipe. Maysoni reasoned that if he got the recipe, for whatever reason, it might ease his boss's memory if he was not put away.

Tom Doulby pulled his ageing deckchair under the oak, sitting down thankfully. "What on earth am I doing this for, at my age?" He spoke to the evening shadows gruffly, whilst attempting to roll himself a cigarette. "Sitting in the middle of a building site breathing in dust and whatever." He took a long satisfying pull on his handmade fag. "It could damage me for life." For a moment he sat silently listening to the hooting of an owl. "As if I don't have better things to do." Pulling hard on his cigarette he took a hip flask from his pocket, opening it casually. Looking hard from right to left, he took a large gulp from the container, coughing loudly. "Ah that's better, nothing like being with nature."

Taking another gulp he recalled smugly how Vera had nagged him about his drinking. Well sitting here, he thought coyly, he could do as he darn well chose to. Looking up he spotted a shooting star lighten the dark sky. "Well I'll be." He helped himself to another drink. "Time to make a wish." He chuckled loudly, gulping greedily from his hip flask. "Good bye Vera."

As the potent mixture worked its wonders on him, he closed his eyes, soon falling into a drunken sleep. His dreams of a single life with an abundance of whisky were soon brought to an abrupt halt. Something hard hit him on the crown of his head causing him to wake, cursing angrily. "Ow, that hurt." Glaring at the sky, he shook his flask, happy to hear the sound of liquid before greedily consuming what was left. As he sat contemplating how long he had to go to finish his shift, he was rudely brought to his senses by another falling object, this time skimming his right ear. "What on earth!" He pulled his large bulk out of his chair, staring up at the huge oak. "Is anyone up there?" He spoke gruffly, his harsh tone betrayed by nervousness.

Twang, twang, two more objects hit him full on the head. Despite his age and intoxication Tom acted fast, quickly producing a large torch from his inside pocket. Pointing the beam towards the top of the tree he was taken aback to hear giggling noises. Again, his thoughts were interrupted when another two missiles came hurtling down on him. Shining the torch on the floor, he strained his eyes to recognise acorns lying by his feet. "Who's up there?" He spoke angrily picking up the acorns and tossing them into the air. "You shouldn't be trespassing anyway." Shining his torch, he tried to identify his attackers. "If you don't come down I will call the police." He knew that he would not but he hoped his threat would frighten his assailants. "And if you do we won't say any more about it." Getting no reply, he shone his torch up into the tree again, quickly stepping back in terror. He wanted to verify what he thought he had seen but stood trembling not quite sure what to do. Kicking his flask that was lying by his chair, he plucked up enough courage to have another look. Aiming his torch carefully, the beam caught his assailant full in the face, causing it to stand mortified. "Well I'll be," Tom shook his head stupidly, "a flipping squirrel." He looked at his feet, cursing the spent liquid in his flask. "Making me see things what isn't there."

As he spoke, a leaf fluttered from the tree, hovering lightly in front of his face. Grabbing it roughly, he thrust it into his top pocket. "Another wish," he spoke happily, "good bye Vera."

Jack Carpet ate his breakfast, lazily scanning the pages of his newly acquired Farmer's Advertiser. It had been several weeks since the American had tried to buy his farm and he was now feeling quite confident that he was going to be left alone. Pushing some toast into his mouth, he sat up abruptly as an article caught his eye.

"Just what I need." He ate quickly. "Two beehives with queens for the price of one." Circling the advertisement with a red felt pen, he sat back contently. Things were going well and he felt he could relax a little. The American had agreed with the village committee to reroute his so-called train line and Carpet was going to be left in peace. Further to that, Goldsmith was buying everything the farm could grow. At last, he thought happily, he could purchase some much-needed equipment, which would enable him to expand a little.

Daydreaming for a moment, he realised how lucky he was. April, JJ and now the farm were prospering. Gold Foods was demanding more and more and the farm was at last making ends meet.

"All I need is a couple more good layers and Monsieur Goldsmith can have as many eggs as he requires." He smiled to himself hardly believing his luck when on flicking the pages of his magazine he spotted an advert for two extremely good layers for sale at a decent price. Again marking the advertisement, he made to get up intending to start on some much-needed work. Before he could decide where to begin, a frantic hammering on his front door stopped him in his tracks. Rose was barking furiously which meant there was a stranger at his door. Muttering angrily to himself, he pulled the door open and was amazed to see Maysoni standing grinning like a Cheshire cat.

"Good morning Mr Carpet." The American walked into the cottage without invitation. His eyes roving around the small room he sat down, again uninvited, staring menacingly at his reluctant host. "Time is money and neither of us have much to spare." He stared moodily, pointing at the bemused farmer. "I have a problem, not unsolvable, but nevertheless a problem." Without waiting for a reply, he gestured towards the land outside the humble dwelling. "Your property is stopping my developments."

Jack who could feel anger rising inside him wanted to get the American by the scruff of the neck and push him through the front door. However, he knew the wealth the American was bringing to the village and desperately tried to stay calm. "Would you like some tea Mr Maysoni?" Jack thought that a little politeness might go a long way.

"Yeah sure, why not?" Maysoni slouched back in his chair. "You get the tea because we need to talk."

As Jack left the room, Maysoni allowed his eyes to roam around the small room, finally resting on Jack's magazine. Picking it up he sneered and flicked through the pages. "You won't be needing this, mister chicken farmer." Resting the magazine down his eyes focused on a red highlighted advertisement causing him to chuckle. Quickly copying the advertisement, he sat back contented in his chair. Things were getting easier and easier all the time, he thought smugly.

"Do you have sugar?" Jack having returned with the tea hoped his voice, unlike himself, sounded relaxed.

Maysoni accepted the tea without thanks, staring at Jack intently. "Do you know Mr Carpet the wealth I am bringing to your village?" He slurped his tea, not waiting for a reply. "In just a few years Keys will have grown into a town." He gestured with his hand for Jack to remain silent. "The people here will be wealthier than their dreams would allow." Placing his cup onto a small table, he fixed Jack with an ugly glare. "Now are you going to stand in the way of all this?" Maysoni stood up abruptly, walking slowly to the farmhouse's small bay window. "Or are you going to be pushed down and walked over?" Maysoni burst out laughing. "Walked over, carpet, funny eh?"

"What is it you want?" Jack was pleased that his voice still resembled some type of politeness. "I thought the committee had resolved all of the problems."

"Ah, a man who likes to get to the point. I like that." Maysoni feigned a smile. "Mr Carpet am I going to get this farm the hard way or the easy way?" He sneered at Jack. "Committee or no committee." He glared at the farmer intently. "I hope for your sake it will be the easy way. Now here is my offer." Sitting down heavily, he put his hand out to stroke Rose who rewarded his boldness by snapping at him whilst omitting a series of hysterical yelps. Violently pulling his hand back, he glared at the dog and then its owner. "Mr Carpet for your land deeds I will pay you double what your property is worth. I will also find you another farm at my own expense." Maysoni sat back grinning. "The only problem you will encounter is the move, again funded by me."

Before Jack could utter any reply, the American remembered Decesso's darned recipe. "And oh yes, for your honey recipe you will have a fully run shop in the stadium with seventy five percent of profits." Sitting back snugly, he studied Jack's face with the air of a lawyer who had just unleashed some spectacular evidence on an unsuspecting jury. "I will get my attorney to draw up the papers." Rising to his feet he nodded at Jack and made towards the door.

"I am not selling Mr Maysoni." Jack spluttered with an unwanted rage. "Either my business or any recipe." Looking at Rose, he pointed at his door. "Now I suggest you leave before my faithful friend decides you have outstayed your welcome." Rose duly snarled at the American causing him to jump back.

"Mr Carpet, you obviously prefer things the hard way." Maysoni regained his posture, glaring at the dog and its owner in turn. "We will speak again soon." He shook his head angrily. "Good day to you."

Maysoni stormed from Jack Carpet's house, angrily barking at Reuccio to drive him back. As Reuccio pointed the car at the site, just a few hundred yards away, he shook his head in disbelief. His boss was very angry, ranting on about bees and chickens and saying he had important phone calls to make. Decesso's three henchmen smiled simultaneously. They could see some action coming their way at last.

Jack Carpet sprung out of bed to face another busy day. He tried to put the unpleasant meeting with the American to the back of his mind and concentrate on the day's chores. Friday was always a busy day on the farm and this Friday was not going to be an exception. Having quickly placed some bread in a well-used toaster and boiled water for tea, he summoned JJ for the daily activities. As the pair quickly ate, a tapping on the door interrupted them. As usual, Rose went into one of her 'get off my property' barking fits, running around in circles until JJ opened the door.

"Bees' hives and two chickens." The visitor smiled and spoke quickly. "Sign here please."

"Well I'll be," Jack Carpet beamed, "and I only ordered these yesterday." He quietly inspected his new goods that stood outside his front door. "I will definitely use this company again." He nodded towards his magazine, shrugging his muscular shoulders. "Anyway," he grinned at his son, "as if we did not have enough to do, we have to get these housed."

JJ appreciating there was much to do put his elbow to the grease while Jack prepared the bees and their hives.

"Welcome my little honey makers." Jack spoke loudly trying to make himself heard over the din from the neighbouring building site. "I hope you are as productive as our residents are." Having left the bees to their own devices he attempted to make accommodation for his two new hens. He laughed loudly when they clucked with delight on receiving a sample of the farm honey. He intended to keep them isolated for a few days while they got used to their new surroundings and then they could meet Ben the cockerel and his countless mistresses.

"Dad, come and have a look at these monsters." JJ spoke excitedly. "They are the size of rugby balls."

Jack rubbed his eyes, stepping out into a new Sunday morning. He had not expected to rise so early but on hearing his son's calls, made his way to the shed that housed his two new chickens.

"Look at these." JJ stood proudly holding a basket containing numerous eggs.

Jack shook his head in delight trying to shake off his drowsiness. He marvelled how two grown men could become so excited over some eggs whilst promising himself that he would never sell up, at whatever cost.

Maysoni glared at Reuccio, roughly handing him a bottle of colourless liquid.

"Make sure you get near to our man and sprinkle this over him." He glared again, quickly checking his busy building site. Hearing the harsh grating of cement mixers caused a cruel smile to creep across his face. Very soon, he thought smugly, he would have his next piece of revenge whilst killing two birds with one stone.

Keys were playing at home, a Tuesday fixture and despite the extensive building work, five hundred or more lucky fans were expected to show. Seats were limited due to the extensive work causing much discontentment for those who could not get tickets. However, they were urged by Bains from the Echo to be patient. The new ground that could accommodate a hundred thousand bodies would soon be built, he maintained in large print. Then everyone would get a piece of the action.

The press, out in their droves along with Moon TV, were giving the coming game some high profile attention. Anyone with any knowledge of football knew that it was only a matter of time before Keys were in the big time. Maysoni was big news and everyone wanted a piece of him. In his pre-match interview, even the over-confident American had surpassed himself. He had spoken happily, advising those without tickets to find a television. The people would have something special to see tonight he had maintained coyly, a little bit more than their licence's worth.

John Purdy from the Daily Games was attending and Maysoni was making sure he was going to get some special attention. Mr Purdy had upset the American tremendously. Using his weekly column in the Games, he had continuously attacked Maysoni, angrily questioning his involvement in British sport. On one occasion he had openly referred to him as a gangster, asking the Keys' fans if this was the type of role model they wanted as their figurehead. At first Maysoni had laughed the insults off, writing the reporter off as another English hick. However, after continuous insults from the angry pressman, Maysoni decided, in good gangster ethics, to take matters into his own hands.

Clearly irritated by Purdy's presence Maysoni purred smoothly into his microphone apologising for the noise from the neighbouring building site he explained how he had given the construction workers Monday off. "Time to be with their families." He cooed. Unfortunately, he continued, work had got a little behind necessitating a few of the workers, on big bonus of course, to work through the game. He apologised again for any inconvenience.

Everyone took his or her seat, waiting excitedly for the referee to blow his whistle. The Keys' players were becoming big news and each Keys' resident felt they had their own small part in the story.

John Purdy acknowledged privately that Maysoni had done a good job for Keys' football club but he disliked the man vigorously. He had constantly heard of his bullying tactics and used every inch of space in his paper to run the egomaniac gangster down. After some extensive research, he had uncovered some of the unsavoury American's past. He had shuddered reading the reports. This man, taking over the reins of an English club, would make the devil himself look respectful.

Why he had been invited to the game, he had no idea. If Maysoni thought he could be bribed then he would have to think again. Nevertheless, he had made an appearance, mostly due to his uncompromising editor and was sitting uncomfortably in his supposed VIP seat.

Earlier some idiot had splashed some foul smelling liquid over him causing him the discomfort of wet clothing. He waited impatiently for the start of the game. He wanted to get home, back into the warm.

Jack Carpet watched his new bees apprehensively, monitoring their movements carefully. Their behaviour having become erratic concerned him immensely. Normally, happy bees would go about their work humming softly. However, the aggressive moans from his new additions were far from happy. He watched carefully as they hovered angrily together, assembling into one black cloud, which then nosily propelled its self towards the busy building site. The cloud ignored the dancing flowers, concentrating its attention on a churning cement mixer. Jack watched in amazement as the bees hovered around the machinery, chanting viciously. The mixer's operator, blissfully ignorant of the distress his machine was causing, watched in amusement as the bees circled it repeatedly. Jack, shaking his head, called to his son, constantly reminding himself, that in all his time of honey farming he had never witnessed anything like it before.

The bees now tired of taking their anger out on the huge beast that was taunting them rose into the sky, furiously making their way towards Keys' temporary football ground. The leader having picked up an unfriendly scent beckoned his flock to follow. Spectators jumped up concerned when the angry bees made their entrance. They did not have to worry however, the bees had only one purpose, to track the aroma that was whipping them into frenzy. The very fragrance that had been splashed over the unfortunate John Purdy. Purdy reacted quickly and tried to use whatever came to hand, to beat off his attackers. Outnumbered greatly he soon succumbed to their violent stings. Much of the nation watched in horror as he screamed his last words in pain and terror.

John Goldsmith sat back contently, humming inharmoniously to the music of the brass band he had hurriedly hired. The setting was perfect, he thought smugly, to launch his new creation and tapped his feet happily, craftily scanning the busy dining room. He had a full house and none other than Jose Mahodo and his various hangers-on were seated, waiting expectantly. He had instructed his waiters to keep gallons of complimentary wine and champagne flowing and grinned widely, recognising the familiar stages of intoxication amongst his guests.

Jose in particular was quite loud which meant he was enjoying himself. If Jose enjoyed himself, it was customary for everyone else to enjoy themselves.

The chubby restaurateur sat quietly, a busy imaginary cash register in his head totalling the evening's takings. He charged a lot but got few complaints. Indeed, for the privileged few, his eating-houses were a social must. It was said that the rich and powerful often trembled in case a table could not be booked. However, tonight was not about money. Goldsmith's mood changed swiftly. If his new dish were acclaimed, as he expected it to be, the heat would be off Jack Carpet for a little while. After a time he reluctantly rose, tidied his gold suit and made his awaited entrance into the busy dining area.

"Ladies and Gentlemen." Goldsmith's squeaky voice rose above the now irritating band. "Tonight you will dine on golden omelettes from hens that are reared in luxury." He bowed humbly to loud cheers, nodding to his head-waiter. "Cooked in a very special way by my very special chef. Accompanied by vegetables that have been touched. only by the sun." His words sent the diners into a frenzy of cheering "Do not forget every day is a gold day, enjoy your meals."

Goldsmith ordered the lights to be dimmed, watching happily as his busy waiters served up the appetising meal. It was just has he had planned, a very special meal. As the waiters, much to the diner's approval, hovered from table to table, each plate glowed in the dim light. This time he had even surpassed his own expectations, an omelette cooked in a luminous gold sauce. As the diners gasped in delight, jugs of honey ale were placed onto their tables. The eating area descended into a contented silence.

For a while he watched the criminal boss tuck into his meal, crossing his fingers tightly. If the mobster enjoyed this new creation, he would demand Goldsmith's audience, determined to enquire where the brain-wave had come from. On cue, Goldsmith would explain about the eggs and honey ale coming from Jack Carpet's farm. He would drop subtle hints that the farm was in danger because of the new stadium. In turn, Jose Mahodo would rage and splutter, threatening anyone that dared interfere with his gastronomic delights. No one on the planet, certainly not Maysoni, would dare go anywhere near the farm again. Which meant Jack Carpet would be left in peace.

A chorus of angry chants brought Goldsmith back to reality. Hurrying out to the busy eating area, his face dropped a hundred miles, his ears trying to comprehend what they were being forced to hear. Instead of the usual complementary cheering, he was being booed.

Jack Carpet sat mesmerized by his television's flashing lights. He miserably listened for the umpteenth time how John Purdy had been stung to death. Stung by bees that had come from Jack Carpet's farm.

Everyone had told him it was not his fault. The young constable had tried to explain that the bees were from a killing breed. The noise from the cement mixer had tipped them over the edge. John Purdy was just unlucky to be in the way of their flight. The police officer had stopped for tea, taking the details of where Jack had purchased the unlikely killers. He had told Jack not to worry.

Jack shook his head, trying to concentrate on the day ahead. Rising to switch off his intrusive television he jumped back in alarm. Another news bulletin flashed across his screen causing an involuntary shudder across the whole of his body. A sombre voice explained how John Goldsmith's restaurant in New York had been closed pending complaints of food poisoning. Goldsmith had fervently denied the claims stating his legal team was calling in hygiene specialists. Reading from a script prepared by his lawyers, he added that he had been sold a consignment of bad eggs. He stressed that his standards were very high which would result in the offending supplier being struck off his catering suppliers list permanently.

Jack sat, head in hands. He knew he was the only one who supplied the restaurant and reasoned it was his eggs, which had caused the eccentric millionaire his problems. Trying to take in the disastrous events, he was disturbed by the shrilling of his telephone. Dejectedly picking up the receiver his face turned white as he listened to his caller calmly informing him that Maysoni intended to sue his farm and he should consult his lawyers in the first instance.

Maysoni sat in the lounge of the Black Cat Inn beaming with content. Things had gone exactly to plan. That irritating journalist was out of the way and the chicken farmer was all but ruined. John Goldsmith was out on a limb with much of his clientele shunning his establishments. Rich people do not like getting bellyache and they were staying away in droves. Indeed, the bosses in New York had already let it be known that Goldsmith was history. In truth, Maysoni did not know the man but knew that Decesso hated him vigorously. Another few points for his good deeds, he mused happily.

Looking slyly around the crowded bar he shouted for drinks all round. The people of Keys had become used to his generosity and nodded happily. It seemed the giant American was keen to look after every one of their needs. Although not eating there, he frequented the pub a lot, installing at his own expense a wide-screen television complete with Moon Sports. In addition he had insisted on purchasing video games for his exhausted work force.

People now loved him listening intently as he explained how he had tried to help the chicken farmer expand his business. What did he get in return, he lamented? A load of bees killing his special guest.

The villagers, supping their free drinks, nodded their heads in sympathy. After many years living harmoniously alongside Jack Carpet and his family, Keys' people were now finding the troubled farmer a little irksome.

Jack sat at his kitchen table studying his untouched meal. He could not believe that just a few days ago things had been going so well, yet now they were suddenly turning to the point of ruin. The American was taking him to court and according to his solicitor had a fair chance of winning his case. The amount of damages he would have to find would be devastating and, even worse, his friends for years were turning their backs on him. The American, charitable as ever, publicly announced he was willing to drop his lawsuit on completion of the sale of the farm.

Jack's friends could not praise their new benefactor's generosity and understanding enough. The American, they constantly reminded him, had brought an abundance of wealth to the village whilst he Jack Carpet had nearly sabotaged their future. Some even accused him of meanness, openly stating that he was trying to cut costs by buying dangerous bees. A man had died they reminded him and if that were not his fault how could he explain his rotten eggs bringing a shameful name to Keys? Despite all the bad publicity the American had to endure, he was still willing to try to help the hapless farmer. Their message was loud and clear, it was a good time for Jack Carpet not to be around.

As he sat mournfully contemplating his future, his phone rang in its familiar shrill. He listened intently as Goldsmith explained the grave situation Jack was in. They spoke for fifteen minutes until Jack sullenly rested the receiver back. Jack felt a tear form in his eye. He loved this farm, so had his father and his father before him. However, now was the time to be prudent. It seemed he did not have a friend in the village. If he went now he might be able to start again somewhere else. He owed it to April and JJ, he reasoned, to do something. Muttering sadly to himself, he made up his mind. He sat for a moment fiddling nervously with the torn paper that Maysoni had scribbled his phone number on. Sighing deeply, he picked up his phone.

Bridget Bluestone hastened her steps, impatiently trying to reach Jack and April's farm. She had acquired her first passport and wanted the Carpets to be the first to know. She was extremely fond of them both and knew that they would be as proud as punch. In a few days she was leaving for a new life, first backpacking and then on to university. And it was their kindness that had helped her achieve her dreams. Clutching a red envelope she smiled, promising herself she would confront JJ about the card's contents. He did not give her much credit, she thought defiantly, if he thought she could not decipher his awful writing, even if he had tried to disguise it. Typical, she thought loftily, an overdue Valentines card with disguised handwriting.

As she approached the small farm building she stopped for a while trying to work out what was different to her other visits. Suddenly it dawned on her the noises that she had grown accustomed too were missing. The whole farm sat in an eerie silence. Not quite understanding why, she could feel her feet quicken, arriving at the oak door of the farmhouse breathless. Gulping a lungful of air her eyes were summoned to a small notice pinned on the far corner of the door. After reading it repeatedly, she stood motionless praying that her eyes were deceiving her.

The notice, in short and sharp terms, conveyed that the farm was now the property of Alberto Maysoni. It went on to state that trespassers would be prosecuted. Putting a hand to her face, she felt wetness as tears at first trickled and then ran freely from her eyes. She could not imagine November Keys without the Carpets and she desperately hoped they might find somewhere close by to continue their farming. As though someone was reading her mind her thoughts were interrupted by a voice, much slurred, due to the effects of alcohol.

"They have all gone and won't be coming back." Tom Doulby looked triumphantly at the bewildered girl. "I overheard that nice American, telling them to clear off and don't come back." Taking a shining hip flask from his pocket, he unscrewed the top hurriedly and greedily gulped the liquid inside. "That nice American gave me a permanent job." He pointed at the building site. "Over there." Shaking his flask happily, he jigged from one foot to the other. "And he filled me flask up. That nice American knows how to treat people properly." Screwing his bloated face into what he assumed was a smile he leered at Bridget whilst taking another long gulp from his flask. "Not like that Carpet and his lot." Trying to steady himself, he knocked impatiently on the farmhouse door. "Killing people with his bees and then poisoning decent people with his rotten eggs."

Realising he was in the presence of a lady he remembered one of the manners he had been taught as a child and reluctantly offered his quickly diminishing flask to Bridget Bluestone. "Let's drink to the kind American and good riddance to Jack Carpet."

Bridget who had stood open mouthed dried her tears, looking at the drunken man standing before her, scornfully. She realised he was intoxicated but she was not going to stand and hear her adopted uncle and aunt being humiliated. Stamping her tiny foot, she stared Tom Doulby in the eye, defiantly refusing his offer of a drink.

"Mr Doulby, Jack and April Carpet," she emphasised her

words for effect, "are two of the nicest people in the world." She eyed the drunk menacingly. "Certainly a lot nicer than a drunken man who has no loyalty to his fellow villagers." Bridget apprehending that the man standing in front of her was probably airing the views of the majority of the village, reluctantly felt another tear trickle down her cheek. "And I hope Mr Doulby that you fall from a tree and puncture your rotten hip flask."

Tom Doulby stood for a while clutching his prized flask, not sure what to do or say next. Although he had consumed a great amount of alcohol, he could still comprehend what was being said and that the naughty girl standing in front of him hoped he fell down a tree. Well, he thought defiantly, he was not going up any tree in the first place. Therefore, that would be the end of that. However, his hazy mind reminded him of the extreme insult he had been subjected to and retaliation was the only possible remedy. Pointing a shaking finger at his tormentor. "I hope you fall down a tree miss, and I hope you fail your tests when you go to school." Satisfied he had passed on his insults in his best manner, he clumsily turned, staggering back to the building site. His cherished flask was becoming empty and he hoped the nice American might fill it up again, especially as he was on the pay roll.

Bridget Bluestone rolled her eyes at Tom Doulby with disdain. She had known the awful man for years. Every time she saw him, he was intoxicated but as far as she was concerned, that was a matter for him and his family. However, he was now insulting her and her adopted family. Wiping a tear from her swollen eye, she jumped forward, snatching the drunk's prized possession from his hand. He had had the audacity to raise his flask to toast the vile American. Well she thought angrily he was going to pay the price. Tossing the flask in to the air, she glared at the crestfallen man in front of her, cursing silently.

"Your flask is in the hedge Mr Doulby." She eyed the man with satisfaction. "Just where you belong with your horrible manners."

Tom stood rooted to the spot staring at the sky for support. The young girl standing in front of him had insulted him for no good reason and then took his most cherished possession and thrown it into a hedge. He was not a violent man but he felt the need for retribution and heaved his large bulk towards Bridget who was now smiling with satisfaction.

As he lunged forwards, his drunken eyes registered an object around Bridget's neck that glittered in the weak sunlight. She had thrown his shiny flask away, he thought hazily, so he would throw her shiny necklace away. Then they would be even. Pushing a shaky hand towards the unsuspecting girl's throat, he grabbed the necklace, yanking it roughly from her neck. Eyeing her triumphantly, he gestured that he intended to propel it to the same place where his flask rested.

"See you should not mess around with a gentlemen like me." He eyed Bridget defiantly. "I am of a good mind to report you to the nice American. He doesn't like trouble makers."

Before he could utter any more threats, he was interrupted by a familiar noise. His groggy mind trying to distinguish the eerie sound caused him to spin around, to be confronted by hundreds of leaves circling around his head. Suddenly he quickly sobered up as a hideous giggling noise penetrated his ears. Certain that monsters from Hell were attacking him he handed the necklace back to Bridget and ran as fast as his legs could carry him.

Maysoni sat in his favourite chair trying to speak over the din in the noisy pub. "Now listen up everybody." He pulled heavily on his cigar. "Your friend with the murdering bees and poisonous chickens has decided to sell up and leave." He looked warily around the bar for any sympathisers. "It was his choice, he thought it would be for the better." Looking over at Reuccio and the three henchmen's knowing smiles before he hurriedly continued. "He got a fair price and will do well." Relived that no one had uttered a word about Jack's eviction he smiled and raised his glass. "Drinks all round and I will toast to the future of your football club, Keys."

A few of the drinkers refused, on that occasion, for their glasses to be refreshed. Indeed some even hung their heads in shame. Their long-time friend had disappeared overnight lock, stock and barrel. In just a few days his once proud farm would become a building site.

The young driver cursed again and slammed the door of his yellowing van noisily. It had taken him ages to find his destination only to find a deserted house with no customers. He fleetingly wondered what Mr Sand was going to say when he returned with the bees and chickens. Mr Sand did not tolerate lightly, people who ordered goods and did not complete their transactions. Shrugging his slim shoulders, he mused why someone who read such an illustrious magazine like Farmer's Advertiser would order bees and chickens, then disappear. Well it was nothing to do with him, he thought happily. Turning the ignition key impatiently, causing his over-worked van to stutter into life, he rendered a tuneless song to the deserted fields.

The Echo
Killer Bees kill reporter in horrific attack...
The bees were reported to reside on Jack Carpet's farm, who has consequently decided to sell up and move.
Reports of foul eggs from Jack Carpet's farm, upset diners in America.
Keys win again paving the way for another promotion.

Chapter Nine
A Gangster's Memories

Maysoni sat back contently, inhaling deeply on his expensive cigar. Leaning over to pour himself another glass of his favourite Scotch whisky, he pondered how good life was and promising to get better. Brushing imaginary dust from his silk dressing gown he sat back, happily wallowing in his numerous achievements. Arching his head he caught his reflection in a greying mirror and congratulated himself on being one of the most successful human beings on planet earth. Not even his arch-enemies could argue with that, he thought ruefully.

If anyone read any selection of newspapers, they too would agree, he must be the most successful chairman of any football club in modern times. Furthermore, feedback insinuated that the bosses were pleased with his activities. That could mean only one thing, wealth and fame. If Keys continued to progress as they had, in about six to eight years he would be the owner of the biggest football club in Europe, if not the world. That was no mean feat, he thought proudly, for someone who had no education and had spent most of their years ducking bullets.

He grinned broadly, remembering his teachers and a long list of probation officers constantly telling him how he was throwing his life away. If they had a fraction of his vast wealth, he thought contently, they could get a proper life and give up on lecturing people.

His lips curled into a smile as he recalled Decesso discussing plans for the new club. The big man had become very animated, waving his podgy hands into the air. He could not stop repeating himself, stressing manically how the bosses had given the project their full blessing. Decesso had continuously reminded him that, if he pulled this particular caper off with no hitches, his name would be repeated in all the right circles. They had sat in the front row, ten thousand dollar seats, watching the bosses' prize fighter winning his bout on a dubious points win. Decesso, running a podgy finger down the silk lapel of his dinner suit, had proffered one of his best smiles. Gold teeth glinting against the bright lights in the packed arena.

Maysoni shuddered recalling that meeting, gulped hungrily at the liquid in his glass. He knew he had acted stupidly. Despite the honour of being picked for such a project, he had been reluctant to get involved. He had asked Decesso to find someone else. Explained he did not want to be uprooted. Had far too much to worry about at home. Decesso had hunched his enormous shoulders, staring at him worriedly. After an unpleasant silence the big man had shook his head, commanding him to get packed. Asking him if he would prefer a concrete overcoat.

Maysoni had learnt that day facts he should have known much earlier. You do not refuse the bosses' bidding. He had not really known, or been told, why they had chosen him over many of the other hopeful up and coming crew, but he was now glad they had. At last, the bosses had recognised his cunning and aptitude. In just a few years, he mused smugly, he would be just where he belonged, at the top of the tree.

His mind travelled hazily, back many years, recalling his school days. Even then he had been a leader of men, he thought proudly. He had supplemented his insufficient allowance by taking protection money from local paper-boys and charging harassed tutors a fee for establishing order in the classrooms. He became known as a no-rules fighter and consistent troublemaker. Eventually he had the honour bestowed on him by the authorities of being expelled from school.

He prospered at his chosen vocation, graduating onto petty crimes and larceny. Of course, he ran the risk of incarceration, but each time he was arrested he felt he was moving on. Each arrest seemed like a badge of honour for services rendered. Consequently, he had spent much of his youth in correctional houses and eventually went to Crime University aka prison, where he learnt a lot and made important contacts. It was whilst in prison he had first heard about the bosses and their considerable power.

Any inmate that was incarcerated due to working for the bosses, was treated like a lord. Food parcels were frequently sent, as were copious amounts of tobacco and alcohol. Everyday Maysoni enviously eyed the young men swaggering around the exercise yard, promising himself that very soon he would be joining them on the same pay roll.

Maysoni paused for a moment, standing to pour himself another whisky. He liked Scotch whisky and reasoned that he would be drinking a vast amount of it over the next few years. Now he was settled he had a grudging liking for the English and some of their strange ways. Furthermore, he loved the fact they were all, without exception, gullible and stupid. He pondered over the fortress he had the English labourers building, laughing aloud, his alcohol releasing his inhibitions.

Indeed, through the eyes of an average onlooker, the building would function as a successful football club. The people of the United Kingdom were falling in love with him. The Echo had even questioned the prime minister's failure to ask the Queen for a knighthood. However, he had vastly different plans.

When the stadium was completed he would have a building that could conceal five hundred top soldiers along with an armoury to keep them in battle for months. November Keys' location had not been chosen without a lot of thought. Decesso maintained the geography of the club meant that every country in Europe would be in striking distance. After he had overrun all the English mobs, he would go continental, with an army at his disposal they would systematically takeover each crime family. The families would be allowed to continue their dubious practices but only under Maysoni's directions and with heavy taxes.

Pouring himself another drink, he allowed himself the luxury of relaxation whilst the pungent alcohol rolled around his gums. He smiled broadly as he recalled the time when the bosses had at last noticed him and he was taken on the team. Just as in any fine movie, a black limousine had pulled up alongside him and a gruff voice ordered him to get in. Subsequently he was delivered to the man who would become his boss and mentor and who reminded him of the honour and pitfalls of working for such illustrious bosses. The man needlessly had questioned him about messing up. Warned him he might become dinner for the fat fish that inhabited the Atlantic. He had smiled, visualising himself rising virtuously through the ranks. Cockily telling his new boss not to worry, that everything he, Maysoni, touched turned to gold.

Predictably, he had revelled in his first job. A visit to a puny hot dog vendor who did not have the courtesy to pay his insurance premiums. The bosses had kindly protected the man against all types of low life, however the disrespectful wretch had forgotten to pay his dues.

Maysoni writhed with satisfaction, recalling his enterprise, dealing with the situation perfectly. He had smashed the operator's hand with a baseball bat until the poor man had screamed in agony. Through his screams the vendor had protested that he could not afford the twenty-percent levy imposed on him. Whined that he had a wife and children to feed. Maysoni had smiled sympathetically, increasing the sum to thirty percent. Following the same practice, he soon had a string of hot dog stalls in prominent parts of New York. Their previous owners being somewhat indisposed.

Quickly realising that violence was the be all and end all, he continued handing out his punishments to those who he felt were justly deserving of them. Eventually he devised a horrific torture that necessitated rats for its application. This spontaneous punishment began to be widely feared, known as Mr Maysoni's nature lesson. One thing was for sure, those who had the unfortunate pleasure of its acquaintance never volunteered for homework.

Maysoni laughed aloud, remembering his yesterdays, looking forward to his tomorrows. When the bosses had control of all the European crime families they would control all narcotics and arms running in Europe. Picking up politicians and police officials they would not only control crime, they would dictate its terms and conditions. There would be no winners other than the bosses. Any family offering resistance would be crushed.

The football club that Maysoni intended to champion would be playing for the highest honours all over the world, which in turn would make transportation seamless. Nothing would seem out of place as thousands of fans travelled to England. Amongst them an assortment of the best hit men and killers in the world. Others would be selected to smuggle guns and vast amounts of drugs.

Maysoni purred with satisfaction. His whisky taking its effect on his sharp mind, it led him back down memory lane.

Very quickly his reputation had commanded more work until he was working actively for the bosses. Albeit, he was working on the lowest rungs of the ladder, but that did not bother him. He happily handled any request, from simple hoists to arranging some unfortunate's last ride. His name was echoed in the right circles all around the big apple.

As his reputation grew so did his wealth. A vast apartment with views of the Statue of Liberty replaced his once humble tenement two-roomed apartment that he always struggled to pay the rent for. Visitors to his grand abode would comment on his personal collection of classic paintings with Van Gough and Picasso amongst the contributors. He relished his up and coming reputation and thought nothing of spending thousands of dollars on extravagances like an ivory chess set and his favourite possession, a World Cup winner's medal won by The Uruguay football team in nineteen thirty.

He sat back contently, savouring his achievements. When Keys became a prominent force in football the bosses' money-men estimated that around two million dollars could be laundered weekly. That would eliminate the massive headaches that high profile crime produced. The money-men also maintained that the bosses could then dictate the street price and locations for every drug consumed in Europe.

The new look Keys would attract an important band of followers and hangers on. Consequently, prominent politicians and anyone of importance would be sucked into the bosses' web of vice. Their easy life would be short-lived however. The bosses new groupies would be expected, under controlled blackmail, to influence important Parliamentary decisions. Within a short time the bosses' illicit gaming houses would become legal. Playboys would lose their millions along with their reputations. The bosses would grow rich beyond measure and he, Maysoni thought happily, would be one of those bosses.

As the whisky took hold, his mind wandered to the three henchmen that Decesso had left in his custody. That on its own was a good sign. Only the upper hierarchy were allowed the luxury of three bodyguards, indicating his climb up the slippery crime ladder. He had to admit, Decesso had chosen well. Each man reminded him of himself in former years. They were hardened to any crime, happy to be called to perform any dubious request at the drop of a hat. Being fearless, he was never frightened of doing things alone. However, having the company of three hardened assassins sure made him feel comfortable. Each man was as fearless as he was, with a pedigree in crime that had his victims quaking with fear.

Stingray was an amazing example. The man had walked into a restaurant full of rival gang members. Wielding a samurai sword shouting insults, rudely demanding his reluctant hosts immediately vacate the premises. The gang had first laughed at his audacity that was until parts of their limbs were flying everywhere. They shrieked in terror. Satisfied with his exploits, Stingray had calmly wiped the blood from his blade, casually helping himself to a bowl of spaghetti, which had been especially prepared for his bloodied rivals.

Records had lost count of the men who had met their demise at the hands of Beesting's ingenuity. The only weapon he used was a poisonous needle, with which he lovingly pierced his victim, proudly referring to its fatality as his sting. Beesting was much in demand, able to perform his unexpected attacks in crowded areas. Indeed, many would-be witnesses that had turned up in court, ready to indict one of the bosses, arrived with a healthy glow and left with a grey pallor. Rumours maintained that the hit-man had once stung a whole jury who were ready to bring a guilty verdict. Beesting was a true artist.

Snakebite, a giant of a man, usually only used his hands. Nevertheless, what hands they were. It was said he could crush a man in thirty seconds. Grabbing his victim in a vice lock, strangling the life out of them as he recited poetry. His victim, held in a vice type grip, prayed the poems were not going to be long. It was once said that some unfortunate who had crossed Snakebite's path rather foolishly taunted him from afar. When word got round that Snakebite had purchased several volumes of poetry books, the tormentor shot himself before the big man could get to him.

Maysoni poured himself another whisky, gulping it greedily. Picking up his phone for room service, he wondered what the bosses would think of the strange place they had sent him to. There had been talk of them flying over but Decesso, even from the depths of his cell, had been less than complimentary about English hospitality, causing them to delay their trip.

Shrugging his broad shoulders, he shook his phone impatiently. He fleetingly wondered how Decesso was fairing holed up in a stinking cell. He knew he would not be happy. Decesso was demanding the bosses use their strong influence and have him bailed. However, this was not your local police whose heads could sometimes be turned with a brown package. This was the FBI, who had a strong case against him and were holding him in maximum security. They were not taking any chances. Decesso was deemed one of the top bosses and his subsequent indictment would wipe an abundance of controlled crime from the streets of New York.

Maysoni had never really liked the man but knew everyone else would be safe. Decesso followed the bosses' unwritten rules to the letter and would not breathe a word. There would be no dealing to gain his release. Indeed, the big man was held in esteem right through the ranks of the bosses' empire. It had been Decesso who had first thought up the elaborate scheme to invade England via a football club.

Europe was the one place that the bosses felt was missing their expertise and they sucked up Decesso's scheme as a baby sucks up milk.

Maysoni inhaled the smoky air hovering in his small room, coughing loudly. He could hardly believe how he had let his temper get the better of him, resulting in a stupid argument with Decesso. The man was ultra-dangerous and it had been a very rash thing to do. Doubtlessly he had broadcast Maysoni's reluctance to the bosses.

Gripping his cigar tightly, he silently prayed that his achievements would outweigh his misdemeanours. He knew the bosses had long memories however willing they might be to overlook shortcomings if their plans were successful. He planned to unscrupulously make them successful.

Already controlling illicit activities in parts of Florida Keys, including Key Largo, The Lower Key and Key West, November Keys was going to be another key on his vast ring.

Disturbed by the knocking of an impatient waiter, he weaved across the room, happily receiving a fresh bottle. He laughed, watching his waiter look firstly in amazement before quickly turning to unconcealed delight at the fifty-pound note Maysoni placed into his hand. Maysoni always tipped generously, thinking nothing of handing out large notes to those who pleased him.

Ironically, he thought, he had given less for the whole of the chicken farmer's property. He had not intended to act so savagely but as far as he was concerned, the chicken farmer had got his just desserts. From day one, he had disliked him. He glared at his heavy tumbler, recalling the man's arrogant back-chat. Refusing to sell his run-down farm at a decent price. He could not believe the man's bravado. Carpet had deemed himself unapproachable. That was until he had met the three henchmen, deciding appropriately that Keys was not a good place for him and his family to live any-more. It had not taken him long to disappear. Shaking his head, he wondered why Decesso had been so excited about the man's recipe for some undrinkable beer.

Closing his eyes, he let the warm glow of whisky relax him again, cherishing his new role and contemplating his prosperous future.

The New York Echo
Hospitals concerned about the large amount of hot dog vendors being admitted with broken bones.
Decesso attempts his thirty-first escape attempt from maximum security jail.
November Keys in Europe, proving to be popular destination for American tourists.

Chapter Ten
A November Fairytale

Leonard Small peered through bleary eyes at his fading curtains, amazed that the morning sun had started to shine through their thin material. Wearily rising to make more coffee, his eyes focused on a dusty clock nesting precariously on a flimsy shelf. The clock's fading hands reminded him he had been working through another night. Catching a glimpse of himself in a tainted mirror, he ran his fingers down a frayed corduroy jacket, half-heartedly watching the sunlight dancing on a dusty window. He reprimanded himself in a hoarse voice, promising to get more sleep.

He felt that improbable however, ever since the American had conceded that he could have an exhibition within the stadium, he realised that he had become like a man possessed. Delighted that he was going to get the chance to display his painstaking research he had worked flat out to get his life-absorbing project completed. He was fully aware that the exhibition had become an obsession, but felt he was being given a once-in-a-blue moon opportunity and was not prepared to waste it.

For a brief while he contemplated happily that the rich American was apparently as absorbed with history as he was. He fleetingly hoped that some of the visitors to the complex would be as interested in the folklore of the village and would enjoy his exhibition, leaving enriched.

He knew that some, if not most of the villagers, thought he was a bit cranky. Often they would call after him in the street, he had lost count of the times he had berated them, after all this was the history not just of their proud village but of their ancestors too.

Fleetingly he wondered why he had turned out different from the others. He certainly had not intended for that to happen. Up until his teenage years he had been just like the other boys in the village. Indeed, he and Jack had hunted, stolen apples, and generally got up to all types of mischief. Suddenly though, as if a light had switched on in his head, he had the learning bug. Things would never be the same for him again. Whilst Jack and his friends helped their fathers on their farms, he would prefer to have a book stuffed under his nose. Very quickly, especially to those who were forced to squeeze past him in the most unlikely places, he became known as the professor.

His parents, somewhat bewildered but nevertheless pleased at his new behaviour, dedicated themselves to sending him to university. He repaid them, proudly graduating with an honours in history. Whether it was the burden to find extra finances or just a quirk in their health it was never quite known. Nevertheless, only a short time later both Mr and Mrs Small journeyed to the life after, leaving the young historian to fend for himself.

Naturally deeply saddened at his sudden loss, he devoted his waking hours to researching Keys' history, determined to keep his mind active and forcing his thoughts away from his sudden void. Pawing over dusty books, uncovering facts of old, he was himself amazed how the village had grown. He was also amazed at the intolerance and superstition prolific in the village, especially against those who did not fit into the mainstream.

During his studies he was surprised to learn how authentic the recipe owned by the Carpets turned out to be. It was indeed as old as Jack had always claimed. Rumours abounded that the recipe was an idea thought up by the enterprising Carpets to increase sales of their honey and ales. However, his investigations confirmed that just as the Carpets claimed the recipe dated back hundreds of years.

Pouring himself more coffee, he sat back admiring his completed paperwork. He had worked relentlessly to finish his project, stubbornly insisting his forthcoming exhibition was necessary not just for the villagers but also for everyone who might be interested in folklore and history. Closing his eyes, he visualised himself standing in front of a wide audience, young and old, startling them with facts and fiction from the past.

"Ladies, gentlemen and children settle back and hear the real history of November Keys and its legendary myth. Firstly, why the name, November Keys? Well this village, soon to be home to the best football club in the world was built in the dusky month of November. As the new residents hauled rocks and cut down reeds they sang. There was no radio in those days."

Leonard paused, allowing his imaginary audience to have a little laugh. "Now some of those who sang were out of tune, causing their neighbours to scorn them, berating them to sing in key. Those who could hit the right notes boasted that they could sing in key. Hence November Keys. Now you must imagine what it was like about this time, the year would be around 1562. Yes that's right 1562."

Leonard imagined his audience sitting back in surprise. "Most of the accommodation would be simple huts made from straw, their inhabitants depending on water from a nearby river. They would generally be happy people, contented, living from the land, possibly catching one of the chickens that roamed freely."

He paused again, brushing a tear from his eye. The thought of chickens brought back memories of his friend Jack and although he was eager to promote his exhibition he felt sad at his old pal's demise. Briefly he felt ashamed for voting against him. Back then he had no idea Jack would be forced off his land. Shrugging his shoulders, reprimanding his unwanted thoughts, he pointed a bony finger at an imaginary visitor drinking water from a plastic bottle.

"Yes the water from that river would probably have been good enough to put in that bottle. As I have said, they were a contented bunch, dependant on their harvests and livestock. Certainly, they were grateful for the milk from the goats that noisily occupied their straw huts. As like all people during that era, our villagers would have been very superstitious and, without fail, God-fearing. Hence the huge popularity of their village church. On a Sunday, these pious villagers would assemble, taking age-old vows whilst listening solemnly to their monk's sermon. The church was also, conveniently, a popular place to gossip and barter unwanted possessions. Now this is where our story begins."

Leonard rubbed his hands in excitement. His hard work was paying off, he mused smugly. "Now the monk in charge, whilst awaiting the arrival of a new clergyman, of our little chapel was a chap called Alfred. Rumour had it that he was the kindest man that God had deigned to reside in our charming domain. Not only did he diligently look after his parishioners, his kindness extended to all of God's creatures, large and small. It was quite common for his flock to witness him pulling unfortunate flies from hungry spider webs. Perhaps, more subtly, he was seen placing cheese for numerous mice vehemently despised by the villagers. Now, if Alfred had a weakness, which we all do, it was for a drop of what makes you happy."

The historian decided to pause at this stage. He contemplated girlfriends and wives, staring knowingly at their embarrassed partners. "Yes, it was not uncommon to see our man of the cloth staggering around after one too many. However, if the villagers noticed this they kept it to themselves. Indeed, when they sang together on a Sunday, Alfred's voice reaching a frenzied drunken crescendo, no one turned a hair. Of course there were no bars and clubs then."

Leonard expected a gasp from the younger members of his audience. "Alfred's brew would be made from honey that he collected from his abundant hives, diluted with water from the river. These ingredients mixed with a little something mysterious would keep our man happy for hours."

At this part of his narrative, Leonard thought it would be a good idea to plug the local honey ale before continuing to the darker side of his story. Explaining that the ale was now manufactured by a very famous John Goldsmith.

"Now, Alfred extended his kindness to what some might call a strange lady. Isobel her name was and although many thought her weird, she was probably just a little eccentric. She did not help her image however. Dressed in black with matching hat and of course always accompanied by a mandatory black cat, her appearance corresponded to most people's idea of a witch." Leonard imagined his younger audience suddenly taking notice, causing him to chuckle contentedly. Pouring more coffee, he mused why young children were so fascinated by witches.

"Isobel's eccentricities extended to her walking around the forest late at night whispering, intently to various trees. Not surprising then, that many of the villagers compared her erratic behaviour to that of a witch, whilst others simply deemed her mad. Whatever the case, her strange habits did not make her a welcome neighbour."

The story teller grinned at his imaginary audience, sucking air noisily through his teeth. "Her choice of abode did her no favours either. An uninviting stone built cottage isolated in the darkest part of the forest. Now what you must consider."

Leonard forced a cough. "In those times there were no doctor's surgeries and hospitals. If you were sick you somehow made yourself better." The historian could visualise all the young mums gasping in amazement.

"So it was not uncommon for people to produce remedies for the odd cold or sore throat." He nodded sadly. "Our Isobel had many of these remedies scattered around her cottage. Unfortunately the village people regarded her simple, yet nowadays illegal, painkillers as something a lot more sinister." Leonard deliberately paused to allow the penny to drop. "Our villagers thought our Isobel was concocting spells. You see, many of the cures then were made from what are now considered illegal substances. It was not uncommon for people to absorb large amounts of substances like hemlock and cannabis."

The would be narrator, rubbing his hands, beamed into his battered mirror, delighted at his progress. He imagined any teenagers in his audience nudging each other, winking slyly. "This in turn led to many unsuspecting partakers hallucinating, imagining things that were not there." Again he visualised his teenage audience recalling their own experiences.

"Now, many of these supposed manifestations were widely reported to be leaves. Not just any leaves, mind you, but leaves that could talk and fly at will." He decided at this stage he would put his hands up in mock surprise. "Many of the villagers swore on oath to witnessing these strange beings and who do you think they blamed?"

Leonard could imagine the youngsters shouting sadly back to him. At this point, he reasoned, he would inform his now captivated audience about the witch-hunts that included old unmarried women being hanged just because they happened to own a cat. He checked his watch carefully, timing his speech. He was certain that his audience would be so engrossed with his tale they would be in danger of missing their football.

"So, what we had was the usual scenario in those days, people out of their head on drugs, imagining all sorts of weird and wonderful creatures. Blaming these imaginary visions on anyone who was unfortunate enough to be associated with witchcraft. Also, their beleaguered suspects would automatically bear the blame for famines, plagues and whatever ills fell on the village." At this point of his lecture Leonard decided he would utilise some carefully selected slides and photographs found in the archives. His audience's ears could have a little break whilst he got ready for the best bits.

"Now the residents of Keys were becoming more and more antagonised, rumours abounded about mysterious creatures possibly called up from Hell itself. Unfortunately for Isobel, the village also experienced a very bad harvest. Without further ado the villagers proclaimed, and proclaimed loudly, that the cause of their troubles should be expelled immediately from the village. This unpalatable task fell on Alfred whose own reputation was now being questioned. Willing to overlook his excessive drinking, even the easier-going were uncomfortable with his strange friendship let alone his strange habits. Many times he was reported to have chased innocent felines, mumbling incoherently at them to leave his poor mice in peace."

Leonard paused, delighted at his ability and expertise to captivate an audience. Come the day, he thought happily, they would be eating out of his hand. Motivated to his task, he lectured his imaginary audience with gusto.

"Now, as we discussed earlier Alfred was a kind man. His defence for whacking cats, he emphasised, was to save unfortunate mice who, as any church-going people would know, were also God's creatures. Stubbornly he refused to listen to complaints about Isobel. In fact he took to regularly visiting his strange friend, much to the villagers' consternation, laden with jars of his favourite ale. Whilst on one of his benevolent visits he himself became a little suspicious of his eccentric host. Making his way back to the church, seemingly full of honey ale, Alfred supposed he was feeling a little tired so sat down to rest a while."

The historian now intended to show a slide of the monk's handwriting testifying to the horrors he had encountered that afternoon.

As I lay, I thought wearily of the unrest in the village.
As my mind became near a decision of my actions
I was crudely disturbed by a hideous giggling noise.
I swear on oath that my eyes witnessed leafs,
from the trees walking over my torso.

Aware that my reputation of partaking of ale might prejudice my reader's ability to believe what l write. I must, nevertheless, describe which l observed.

The creatures walking freely across my torso did indeed resemble leafs from the trees. However, I would utter on oath, that each creature had eyes protruding from the top of

144

their triangular shaped bodies. Further, they were each able to walk with the assistance of twig like legs and feet, which they did quickly and intently, waving their tiny matching arms and hands whilst chanting in a hideous manner. My mind directed me to suppose that these creatures had been summoned from Hell.

Leonard beaming with delight, poured more coffee, clearing his throat noisily.

"Now although, as discussed, Alfred was a kindly man, he knew he had the responsibility for the villagers' safety. He was also the guardian of their souls and however much he felt sorry for her he could not have Isobel cooking up spells and frighten everyone with talking leaves. For now he was certain she, not his surplus of honey ale, was responsible for their being."

Leonard would smile at the younger visitors, testing their reactions. He wanted to surprise them but not frighten them in any way.

"So amongst his other duties he regularly began to visit the crone hoping to conjure evidence of her meddling in witchcraft. It was whilst returning from such a visit that Alfred was dramatically about to change his mind."

As I returned from my visit l felt the need to refresh my thirst
from the stream. Whatever was causing my mind to wander l
hasten to say, l cannot recall. However, my mind did wander.
Moreover, l foolishly fell causing my head to strike a rounded rock.
My next recollections were of a group of leaves making a hideous noise and
hoisting me from the river to the safety of the river bank.
As l regained my senses, l realised these creatures were of a friendly disposition.

145

"Now Alfred had something of a dilemma to contend with. On one side he had angry villagers demanding he take action against Isobel. On the other, the strange lady's manifestations had saved his life." Leonard decided to lower his voice to a whisper to create more suspense. "Now if Isobel was in trouble it really did not deter her from pursuing more problems. The villagers watched her every move waiting for a chance to have her arrested and hung as a witch. Do not get the wrong idea. These were not nasty people but their harvests were failing without reason and there was much unexplained sickness in the village. So what do you think she did?"

Leonard chuckled thinking that he would once again engage the junior members of his audience. "She went and boiled up a concoction of who knows what and to put it bluntly ended up smashed out of her mind. Her concoction must have been very potent, she decided to defy nature and fly out of a tree. To make matters worse for her tarnished image, she decided to do her flying on a broomstick. Needless to say, Isobel's exploits soon summoned a large and less then friendly crowd to assemble under the said tree."

The happy historian was not sure whether to show some cartoons at this point, undecided whether they would be useful at a later stage. "Can you imagine the pandemonium? There was Isobel up a tree cackling away like a certified Bedlam inmate whilst the vast crowd angrily commanded her to come down. Just to add special effects to her unexpected antics, the moonlight, now at its fullest, caused Isobel's silhouette to appear more sinister than ever. Anyway, come down she did. However, not the way she went up. No, majestically sitting on her broom she hurtled from the tree, emitting dreadful cackling noises. As there are no people residing on our planet that can defy gravity she quickly plummeted towards the hard ground."

Again, the excited narrator paused to allow his invisible audience to gasp.

"As the crone plummeted, nature intervened, a mass of leaves became unattached from their twigs somehow, forming a cushion which cradled the intoxicated woman's fall. To the naked eye this spectacle gave the illusion that our Isobel was actually flying. The villagers not requiring any more evidence vocally expressed their horror at having a witch in their midst."

Leonard decided to include a joke about visiting football supporters.

"The frightened crowd's behaviour became worse than a pack of Starlings' fans. Despite Alfred's intervention, Isobel was badly beaten, the baying mob burning her house to the ground. Alfred, himself injured during the violent scuffle, was powerless to help. Although many wanted to execute her immediately common sense prevailed. Isobel was forcibly incarcerated until a visiting judge could be summoned to pass the ultimate sentence. Alfred desperately tried to plead for her safe release. However, his lamentations were short-lived when a cluster of leaves appeared, seemingly giggling hideously at Isobel's captors. The terrified mob, now convinced Isobel had summoned the very devils from Hell, screeched unanimously for the witch to be locked away. After her trial and execution they steadfastly maintained that her spells would perish with her and the village would fall back in to normality."

The beaming historian, checked his watch again. He did not want anyone leaving as he came to the conclusion of his tale. "Now, it is at this point we introduce the villain in our tale, a certain Mr Decesso. Well Mario Alp Decesso to be precise." Holding up a picture of the ugly man in question, he beckoned his imaginary audience to boo. "Now our Mario was quite an unsavoury character. Although of Italian descent, it was stated that he had been promoted to chief witch hunter, for services rendered, by none other than Queen Elizabeth herself."

Leonard decided to point at one of his audience, gently asking questions. "Do you know what a witch hunter could earn?" Expecting a negative shake of the head, he continued. "Do you know where such a person would expect to live?"

Again, expecting a negative response, he grinned and continued. "Well, we do not know exactly what our Mario did earn, but we do know his allowance allowed him to have Decesso Castle built and to travel around what was known of the world."

Leonard stressed his next words. "However, witch hunters were expected to catch witches. Which contrary to thinking at that time was not always easy. Not that this hindered Mario. His corrupt form of justice often condemned some innocent half-wit to be executed after falsely being convicted of being a witch. Therefore, when our Mario was summoned to judge poor Isobel, his reputation superseded him and caused much rejoicing in the village. Whether Isobel was guilty as charged would never enter his head. Passing the death sentence, he could command another fat purse from the superstitious royal house whilst enlarging his dubious reputation."

Leonard Small decided that he would call for some more booing.

"In addition to his fat purse Mario would often fine the village for hoarding the witch in the first place. Obviously, the funds would go straight into his already bulging coffers. However, Mario had no wish to fine the village on this occasion. Indeed, he distributed gifts which he had collected on his travels. Congratulating the villagers for their dedication to ridding the countryside of sorcerers. There was something else he wanted from the village. Something that was going to make him very rich and powerful."

Shrugging his slim shoulders, Leonard anticipated his audience staring back at him, wide-eyed. "Anyway, back to poor old Isobel. Can you imagine what it was like for this hapless old woman? Her only crime was stewing up an excessive amount of unknown drugs, causing her to behave a little recklessly. Now here she was waiting to die a severe death, her house burned to the ground with her beloved companion, her black cat, on the missing list. Indeed Alfred was so taken aback over her treatment he felt he just had to record his feelings."

Isobel, the dweller from the stone house, has been judged unfairly. She is indeed peculiar to the eye and persists in behaving in an eccentric manner. However, it must be said
she did not manifest the leaves. Their behaviour is unexplainable but they are not from Hell. It is only right that this poor woman be freed.

"Despite Alfred's attempts to help, Isobel was kept under lock and key and treated very badly. The villagers assuming she was grade one in evil practices took no chances, waiting impatiently for her trial on November thirteenth. Mario now arrived on the scene, lavishly distributing exotic gifts to anyone willing to listen to his foolish stories of cunning and valour. Much to the villagers' delight he promised that a hanging would soon take place. During her incarceration, although they disapproved, Isobel's captors did allow daily visits by Alfred. Kindness had not deserted him. He would diligently take slices of bread, praying whilst she ate gratefully. Gradually his pity for the old crone turned into genuine friendship. Friendship into fondness, with Isobel sharing the same feelings."

Leonard decided he would now stare at his teenage audience and await the oohs and aahs. "Alfred and Isobel had fallen in love. Finally, on the eve of the thirteenth, Alfred sat in her makeshift cell where they both cried together. Certain that she would soon be dead he ceremoniously handed her an acorn, instructing her to throw it into the ground before her final demise. He explained that the oak, which would subsequently grow, would remind others of their short-lived love and its hasty demise by her brutal, undeserved death. He also gifted her half of an opalescent gem retaining the other half on his person. Explaining that he had found it in the remains of her cottage he had split it in two and clumsily engraved his undying love. The pair spent what they believed to be the remainder of Isobel's life holding hands and talking."

The historian was sure his audience would be rendered speechless, perhaps some reaching for their hankies. Indeed, he had concocted a love story mingled with superstition and fear. "When the time came for Isobel's would-be trial and subsequent execution, the village square was full to capacity. Neighbours stood shoulder to shoulder, intent on the evil witch's demise. Noisily reasoning that all their curses would be lifted on her death, a posse, waving a parchment commanding her execution, was dispatched to hasten the coming proceedings. Their joviality was short-lived however. Soon the despondent posse returned with news that the old crone had disappeared. On opening the secure door to her prison, it was quickly determined that the cell was empty. Isobel had vanished into thin air. Mario was furious, his heavy purse diminishing before his eyes. Making it clear, if Isobel was not found, the village would have to replace her with a substitution. He warned the crowd, now nervously congregated in the village square, that if their daughters had so much as a wart, the hangman's noose would complete its task. Almost immediately the frenzied crowd went on the rampage. Not leaving a stone unturned they determined to find their lost fugitive, the young women with warts being the most enthusiastic. Very soon, as day turned to night, they attacked every living plant with their blazing torches. As though brainwashed, they were determined to exterminate everything that their once prized prisoner had contaminated. Only then could they rid the village from its evil spells. This mayhem went on for hours until Alfred ceased their rampage. Well to be precise, it was his robes. These were found floating in the river. Nearby, a note lay, exclaiming his undying love for Isobel and detailing the misery he would endure if he lived without

150

her. Well this whipped the mob in to a further state of frenzy. Believing the missing witch was responsible for the death of a member of the cloth they set about cleansing the village and trees of her atrocities."

The historian grinned at his imaginary audience. "Mario could not believe his luck. Alfred owned the one thing he required most in the rapidly growing world. Now he was dead. Further, as he had fraternised with a witch his worldly possessions belonged to Mr Decesso. Mario had inherited, without any real effort, his prized recipe. However, his delight was soon turned into dismay. A few days before his demise Alfred had bestowed his recipe onto a farming family called Carpet. Apparently the Carpets had been benevolent to the tragic Isobel and Alfred wanted them to receive some type of reward. Hearing this, Mario lost his cool. He called on the Carpets, muttering all sorts of threats whilst demanding his rightful property. It is stated that he threatened to hang the Carpet's daughter as a witch unless his recipe was returned immediately."

"Fortunately for Joshua Carpet and his wart-less clan, Mario was summoned to The Tower of London before he could carry out his threats. Apparently, one of the innocent girls he had hung as a witch was a cousin to one of Queen Elizabeth's favourite maids. His execution was carried out two days later. His final words were chosen carefully, damming the Carpet clan, promising he would return and run them off their farm."

Leonard shuddered involuntarily, remembering the fate of his old friend. "It was also chronicled that when Mario's head became detached from his body, his eyes rolled for several seconds, blasphemies were heard coming from his mouth up to several minutes after his death. In many circles, many whispered that he was the Devil himself. Whatever the case, many a young girl slept sounder after his dispersal to another world."

The tired narrator brushed his battered jacket, making himself more coffee. Delighted with his narrative he happily imagined countless, spellbound future audiences. Slurping his lukewarm drink, he turned to his imaginary audience to conclude his lecture.

"Now another promise Mario had made before his head rolled, was that some hideous beings would haunt November Keys. This would happen as soon as he was settled in Hell. He also accused the village of hiding Isobel, threatening them her spells would curse them for eternity. When his ravings reached the ears of the villagers, November winds were causing the leaves to dance in a macabre fashion before falling to the ground. Convinced the leaves were evil manifestations' from Hell the villagers quaked in terror. Most certainly, they thought, the missing Isobel was cursing them from afar. Armed with flaming torches the mob bayed through forest and scrubland, torching any visible falling leaf. Those that had already descended to the floor were scooped up carefully, examined for evidence of protruding eyes and legs and then meticulously thrown onto bonfires. After the leaves had been destroyed, beacons of fire were placed around the corners of the village in the hope that the bright flames would keep any further hideous beings at bay. Ironically, after these strange rituals, life in the village improved. Unknowingly, the fires eradicated the feared plagues whilst the continuous burning beacons frightened away animals that would have ravaged the crops. At last the villagers had something to celebrate. Their village was safe, their crops growing abundantly."

At this stage Leonard considered showing one of the ageing documents testifying how life in the village had improved.

The purge on the foliage from the trees has much improved life.
The beings from Hell have been banished along with the plagues.
No one has indication of the witch Isobel's whereabouts

*and until she is located her legacy from Hell will be strewn
on to bonfires regularly with November thirteenth being
named Harvesting Leaf Day.
No one person residing in the village will be spared
these life-saving duties.*

"To prolong the good wealth of the village, a plaque was bizarrely placed on the outside of the forest to commemorate Isobel's departure .Although she had escaped justice, since her allotted day of trial the village had prospered in leaps and bounds. From now on November thirteenth would be called Harvesting Leaf Day, everyone, without exception, collecting dead and falling leaves and placing them onto the roaring bonfires. Their work not being complete until the very last leaf had been disposed of. Their superstitious task over they would then assemble on the village green partaking in an enormous feast, followed by singing and dancing."

Leonard took a deep breath. "To this day November Keys still celebrates and honours the rituals of Harvesting Leaf Day." He stood back milking his imaginary applause, bowing graciously.

"Oh, and if you were wondering about the acorn."
He took a deep breath. Pointing in the direction of the large oak, he assembled his papers and bowed his head.
"You must draw your own conclusions. Oh and one last thing. Whilst Isobel was imprisoned her beloved feline, pining for its mistress, would roam night and day desperate to make contact with her, it's pitiful screaming heard for miles around. Attempting to pacify the tormented animal sympathisers would leave food and honey ale under one of the trees within the village. As time unfolded, that site was destined to be the home of a new inn. Hence our wonderful watering hole, The Black Cat Inn."

*Ye Olde Echo news Scroll.
Queen Elizabeth orders that all witches are to be*

destroyed.
Noisy black cat disturbs the residents of November Keys
Bountiful harvests and prolonged health after the departure of resident witch.

.

Chapter Eleven
The Myth Takes A Ride

Leonard Small glanced up to the dark November sky, trying to ignore the cold winds billowing through his battered jacket. Determined to focus his tired mind on the day's forthcoming events he ignored the cold, pursing his lips and pitifully attempting to whistle away his discomfort. Although the inclement weather bit through his coat, adrenalin pumping through his veins helped comfort him. He could not remember the last time he had been so excited. It was not everyday people realised their dreams, he thought happily.

When Mr Maysoni had left a message on his mobile inviting him to a conference, he had replayed the message twenty times. To his delight the message confirmed that the big American had been impressed with his articulate paperwork, wishing to discuss things further. It was made quite clear his exhibition was to proceed. Leonard sighed contently. At last the people of Keys could savour their history. Hastening across the muddy building site, although nervous, he felt extremely satisfied. All his efforts, he thought happily, were to be rewarded.

Pausing for a moment, he listened to his message one more time. The familiar drawl of the American, made his blood tingle. Not only had he accepted the idea of an exhibition, he also intended to throw his whole weight and money at the project. Furthermore, he had had his back room staff toiling around the clock to improve every little detail.

Hurrying on his way, Leonard suddenly recalled the date. Coincidently, it was November thirteenth. He was going to discuss a project about the myth on Harvesting Leaf Day. Stopping again, he stood silently, taking in the wonderful artistry of the dome-shaped walls that were to protect the new stadium. Although the building work was still in its infancy, anyone with an eye for architecture could easily imagine the finished project. There was no question, he thought wistfully, that when completed the stadium was going to be very special. He let his emotions overtake him, reminding himself tearfully that his cherished exhibition was going to lie proudly within the crafted walls.

Rebuking himself for his idleness, he cantered across the mud. Mr Maysoni was a busy man, it was not a good idea to insult him by being late.

As his legs dragged him nearer to his dream, he felt guilty, suddenly thinking about his old friend Jack. He had never really understood the friction between Jack and Maysoni. Aware that the farmer could be cantankerous, he put it down to a clash of personalities. It certainly had given him no pleasure to vote against his old friend. Especially as he had now lost his farm. However, children and adults alike needed educating on their village and its folklore.

Now with the wealthy American willing to put his weight behind the project, a dream was quickly turning into reality. Keys' history would live forever. In time he had plans to contact schools across the country, their pupils enriching their minds with the wondrous myth. Perhaps, at some stage, one of the television companies might become interested he pondered excitedly. Although Jack had disagreed whole-heartedly, Leonard considered Mr Maysoni, behind his bluster, to be a kind and generous man.

Reaching the office, breathing heavily, he smoothed his ageing jacket and tapped nervously on the cabin's greying door. Maysoni, glaring at Reuccio and his henchmen, stood up noisily and roughly pulled at the door of his office.

"Ah, Mr Small, come in I have been waiting for you." Maysoni pulled on his cigar, beaming at his guest. "All the plans are ready and awaiting your approval."

Leonard smiled, briskly entering the small office. Shaking his host's hand, he hesitated for a moment, his nose assaulted with a familiar smell. His eyes wandering nervously around the room he tried to pinpoint the location where the offending odour originated. Finally resting on four men eating greedily from brown paper bags, his senses reminded him the smell belonged to the Black Cat Inn. Shuddering, he reluctantly recalled his unsuccessful attempts to digest a similar repugnant curry.

"Coffee?" Maysoni glared at Reuccio, "We have much to discuss." He impatiently gestured the nervous historian to sit down. "I loved your blue prints, very good work for one person." Maysoni pulled heavily on his cigar, sitting back importantly. "However, Mr Small this is about teamwork." He beamed at his nervous guest. "So, we have put our heads together to make your show a little more exciting."

As Leonard sipped his coffee, Maysoni proudly heaped piles of paper onto a small table. Behind his bravado, he was more eager than the strange man sitting opposite him to get his project off the ground. His architects, he had been informed, had cleverly designed the proposed building to conceal fifteen stronghold rooms below. These would ultimately be used for storing ammunition, much needed for the coming wars. Certain drugs could also be concealed until needed. One room being ear-marked as a luxury underground apartment. This would be splendid to conceal wanted felons, especially Decesso when he made good his escape. Maysoni smirked contently surmising how safe his little fortresses would be. No one, not in their right minds anyway, would associate the potty historian and grossly illegal activities.

"Now we need to discuss some small details and I can let the work commence." Maysoni stood up unfolding a large sheet of paper. "This is the main diagram."

Leonard taking the paper casually glanced through its contents. It took a few moments until he started to choke on his coffee. "But this is a fair ride." Trying to stay calm, he desperately tried to stop his voice sounding like a farmyard animal.

"Yeah, it's great isn't it?" Maysoni looked for approval that was soon forthcoming from his four companions. "Your history-seeking people will have the thrill of a lifetime." He beamed at his guest. "Now let me explain how it will work." He took a pencil, pointing at the plans. "Firstly, as your, er, students walk through the entrance, a special host dressed up like a leaf will greet them." He rubbed his hands together. "And just for appearances, I thought he could have two red eyes, bloodshot through continuous beatings." He put his hands up to stop Leonard speaking. "That's to get people in the mood."

Glaring at Reuccio, he snapped his fingers, the small man quickly handed him a small tape recorder. Beaming broadly, he excitedly turned the contraption on.

Leonard nearly fell off his chair when the machine broadcast a noise that sounded like a cat being spayed without anaesthetic.

"Ha that made you jump." Maysoni was enjoying himself.

"Don't you think it might disturb people?" Leonard answered meekly.

"Well don't worry there will be plenty of signs, warning people with bad health to stay away." The big American paused, looking thoughtful. "We don't want any heart attacks."

Maysoni's companions chuckled with glee whilst Leonard shuffled nervously in his chair. He knew he should protest, but had no idea what to say.

"Now you will love this bit." Maysoni continued, excitedly. "Before anyone gets on their carriage they will be attacked by rats."

"Rats?" Leonard nearly choked.

"Yeah don't worry they are not real, its special effects." Maysoni paused thoughtfully. "But the punters will think they are."

Leonard, trying to utter some sort of protest, felt his jaw moving but without any sounds.

Maysoni thinking that this was a nod of approval continued. "Once we have them in their seats, we get them down a dark tunnel." He nodded at his companions smugly. "After a few moments they will think the ride has stopped and then wham." He turned on his tape recorder again, which emitted a hideous hissing sound followed by what Leonard deemed to be a lunatic screeching inaudibly.

"Bring the little evil creatures from Hell

This will give your village a story to tell

I will fly on my broomstick with my black cat

You will know it's me because of my hat."

As the noise droned on Leonard felt that he was going to be sick.

"Frogs, toads, and you people, why not?

Will go in my cauldron of a hot pot

I will curse you people and your land

My spell will turn you all to sand."

Leonard clung tightly to his chair in fear that he might collapse onto the floor.

"This is the story of the myth that must be told

To travel with us you must be bold

Sit back and enjoy your ride."

To Leonard's relief Maysoni turned off the tape and summoned Reuccio for more coffee. As the cup was placed into his shaking hand, a large wailing noise descended from the contraption causing him to spill black liquid over his battered trousers.

"That's the witch screeching." Maysoni beamed with pleasure.

To Leonard's horror, Maysoni spent the next ten minutes describing in graphic detail the atrocious things that their visitors would have to endure. They would be subject to all sorts of depraved creatures lunging at them from the dark. He proudly added that the faint-hearted would scream in distress. At last Leonard found his voice and started to protest.

"But this has nothing to do with the myth. The myth is to do with leaves."

"Ha ha", Maysoni croaked in delight. "A little surprise

for you." He took out another cigar, holding his conversation, until he was certain it was lit. "As the cars go through the black tunnel we are going to have luminous leaves jumping on them. They might even give a bite or two."

"You cannot do that." To his astonishment the historian felt his voice rise in anger.

"Well our technicians say we can." Maysoni sounded disappointed but soon grinned at his guest. Standing up he gently patted Leonard on the arm. "You must not worry about trivialities. I have this all under control."

"But this should be for children, children that require educating." Leonard was so incensed he felt the veins in his temple starting to protrude.

"Ha," Maysoni gestured to his companions, "we thought about that." He looked proudly over at Snakebite. "My colleague suggested having your Noddy and Big ears heads being decapitated." He ignored Leonard, who shook his head in disbelief. "But I thought, children like roundabouts, so we are going to send them dizzy on the largest corkscrew ride your country has ever seen." He passed another sheet of paper to his guest. "See, if that doesn't make them giddy nothing will and whilst they are looping about we will have your leaf things spiting blood all over them." Looking at Leonard for approval his face lit up with glee. "Now ask me how they are going to get clean again."

Leonard sat ridged in his chair. He tried to speak but could only muster a gurgling noise.

"We are going to have them driven in a river." Maysoni beamed with pride.

Leonard found his voice, determined to protest. Staring at the Americans intently, he fished for the right words. "But you see I intended for the children to take something away with them."

"Beat you to it again." Maysoni interrupted proudly. "They get their photograph taken whilst they are hanging upside down and the frame will be leafed shaped." Looking a little concerned at his ashen-faced guest he quickly opened a window, glaring at his companions,

"See, that disgusting food you eat has made the man ill."

Disturbed by the noise of angry voices, Maysoni's attention diverted to the outside of his office. Astounded that anyone would dare to interrupt one of his meetings, he ignored the now simpering historian and quickly made his way outside. His eyes taking in the perpetrators of the noise he nearly exploded.

Workers who he had hired to cut down the grotesque oak tree were being angrily restrained, the villagers shouting oaths at them. Maysoni stood silently for a moment watching the wind pull the leaves from the oak, slowly raising his hand, he gestured for quiet.

The incensed crowd stood silently for a brief moment and then defiantly directed their oaths against the angry American. Maysoni, surprised by the venomous insults, stepped back a little nervously. Immediately his henchmen surrounded him, glaring at the baying mob.

"What is going on here?" Maysoni shouted angrily, stepping back again to avoid a missile aimed at his head. Signalling for his bodyguards to keep their guns in their pockets he glared menacingly at the crowd who now stood awkwardly, mumbling amongst themselves.

Eventually an unelected spokesperson stepped forward, nervously watching the pockets of the now leering henchmen. Explaining in a muffled voice that the villagers were not trying to cause trouble he pointed anxiously at the old oak, its branches dancing to the beat of the wind. "Vandals," he mumbled, "were trying to cut down the cherished oak tree, it had to be protected, at all costs." Gaining confidence he added that the tree, an important part of Keys' history, was not going to be cut down at any time especially on Harvesting Leaf Day. He stressed that his fellow protesters would rather die than let this evil act transpire.

Maysoni, angrily musing that this could be easily

arranged, shook his head in disbelief. He could not understand the audacity of these people he had bent over backwards to please. His first instinct was to have his thugs beat the ringleaders of the uprising senseless. However, he knew this would involve a police presence so decided to act with diplomacy. Raising his hands in mock surrender, he mumbled about loyalty, instantly sacking the local workers from the village.

He had smashed unions in New York and he was certainly not going to bow down to a bunch of country hicks. He spoke slowly, spitting his words with venom. If the Keys residents wanted their new stadium to be built, he demanded they step aside and forget about some old lump of wood. Especially as that lump of wood now belonged to him. In the meantime, all the workers from the village were fired forthwith.

Assuming that was going to be the end of the matter, he turned on his heels, angrily making his way to his office. Before he could open his door, his ears were deafened by a chorus of boos, noisily infiltrating the cold air. Grunting angrily, his eyes smouldering with rage focused on the weedy representative, whom was now waving his hands frantically. Maysoni looked on speechless, amazed as each worker from outside the village, promptly downed their tools, trudging solemnly away from their posts to join the militants from the village. Within minutes the usually noisy arena was reduced to an eerie silence. Maysoni, shrugging his shoulders, turned to Leonard Small for some explanation, but the man had become a gibbering wreck, so he aimed his attention at the restless crowd.

Realising he was losing his grip with the situation he growled inaudibly, quickly thinking through the series of events. Perhaps he had jumped the gun, he mused warily. For sure, he had underestimated the hicks' determination to defend their tree. The tree had been mentioned numerous times, however he had mistakenly considered, the hicks seeing their new ground develop, would forget about it.

162

After all, it was only a bit of old wood, he pondered wearily. Now he was faced, unbelievably, with a site with no workers.

He angrily thrust a cigar to his lips, wondering why the outside workers had downed tools. Most of them were from miles away, some even from overseas and unable to speak English, so why they were interested in a scrawny tree he had no idea. Nevertheless, he considered slyly, if he pursued with the felling it might take him days if not weeks to replace them all. That might set his project back months. The bosses would not be happy. Contemplating the consequences, he realised the importance of immediate action. Forcing a smile he faced the defiant crowd, putting up his hands in capitulation. He stressed loudly, through gritted teeth, that the tree would be safe, he had made a mistake, and it would be fenced in. At his expense, of course. Getting no response from the silent crowd, he remonstrated that he had only joked about sacking his tried and trusted workers. They might not understand American humour. Crossing his fingers, he stated that he wanted to patch things up. The workers could finish early and celebrate Harvesting Leaf Day using the old football pitch, at his expense of course.

The sound of a lone pair of hands clapping frantically, quickly broke the strained silence, followed by many more. Each of the large crowd breathed a sigh of relief, clapping until their hands were sore. None of them had wanted any confrontation and now the genial American had seen their point of view they cheered him until their throats were sore. Everyone on the site cheering until his or her lungs hurt.

Maysoni, a little overwhelmed, felt an unusual embarrassment. He was not used to being cheered and decided to give the crowd a little bonus. He happily announced he would ask Cheryl from the Black Cat to supervise the catering. When the cheering changed to booing, he walked into his office, slamming the door.

John Goldsmith sat in his office idly watching his collection of gemstones embedded in his walls sparkle and continuously change colour. For a while he sat silently, his huge shoulders moving in time with the shimmering of the expensive gems. Trying to focus on his day's activities he reluctantly allowed his mind to dwell on the American gangsters, Decesso in particular. Involuntarily shuddering, he surmised what his life would be worth if the fat gangster was not permanently incarcerated. Certainly there would be no protection from the bosses any-more.

The big boss had let it be known that Goldsmith was now bad news, his eating-houses off limits. Again, shivering intensely, he recalled the strange evening with Mahodo and the eggs.

Until that fateful night, Jose Mahodo had always congratulated him on his fine cuisine. Which, Jose often reminded him, was a huge compliment coming from one with such a refined palate. He had been frequenting Goldsmith's eating establishments for many years, since his first visit. Suddenly appearing with his noisy entourage and demanding a table. Goldsmith had made every effort to impress, apprehensively watching the gangster devour his food. To his amazement, the ageing mobster was delighted with his meal and had insisted on generously tipping the catering staff with a thousand dollars each.

Ever since, the eccentric caterer and the infamous gangster's friendship had grown stronger and stronger with Jose and his vast entourage dining at a Goldsmith venue at every available opportunity.

Goldsmith took full opportunity, his ears alert for snippets of information, which regularly came his way. Another bonus for Goldsmith, Jose had awarded his favourite eatery with full protection, making it known, that many lives would be shortened if they interfered with his host in any way.

The big restaurateur shook his head despondently. The American, Maysoni, had put an end to that relationship.

Goldsmith chastised himself for not seeing it coming, He had to admit, it was a clever trick with the eggs.

When Mahodo furiously protested he had been proffered almost decaying food, all hell broke loose. The mobster immediately demanding a boycott whilst withdrawing all protection from Goldsmith's establishments.

He had a phobia about bad foodstuffs, emphasising that Goldsmith's blip would not be tolerated. The gangster's twin brother had died of food poisoning when young Mahodo had sworn revenge on all bacteria, becoming paranoid about food hygiene. It was well known in certain circles he had instigated sell by dates on consumable products, enlisting the help from his friends in the senate.

That fateful night Mahodo had muttered oaths in his native Italian, swearing never to darken any door belonging to one of John Goldsmith's restaurants ever again. The only reason that Goldsmith still lived was due to Jose's generosity,

Goldsmith shook his head violently, attempting to blot out those memories. Walking slowly to a wall safe nestling amongst the vast array of jewels, he fumbled in his pocket, producing a small silver key. For some reason, probably anxiety he mused, he needed to check on the safety of the recipe. Satisfied that the cherished document was safe, he closed the safe, moaning softly to himself. Fleetingly an unwelcome thought entered his head warning what could happen if Decesso were to get his hands on that important paper, it would most certainly cause distress to every living mortal. It was fortunate that the fat man was greedy and had not shared his discovery with the bosses. If that had been the case, Goldsmith and many others would have been dead long, long ago.

Staring at the lethal piece of paper for a while, he remembered that he must send a pot of honey to the witness. He deserved that, Goldsmith thought wistfully. The man had risked his life and the lives of his close dependants for a regular supply and Goldsmith was determined that he would get his reward. He wondered how long it would be before the bosses got to the witness.

Although on a police protection scheme and under twenty four-hour protection, he was on the top of the bosses' hit list and as sure as bees make honey, they would find their man. When that happened Decesso would be free. Goldsmith shuddered, reminding himself whose door the fat gangster would first grace. Placing the honey in some inconspicuous wrapping, he shouted to his young assistant to hurry to the post office.

The villagers, taking advantage of Maysoni's generosity, celebrated their coveted Harvesting Leaf Day in style. Relieved that the issue with the oak had been settled they happily drank, danced and ate. Those who had little energy sat around the massive bonfires, chatting noisily. Their children, who were allowed to stay up late on such an important occasion, played games, unconcernedly making a noise.

Leonard Small sat brooding, uncharacteristically drinking any alcohol he was offered. Downing each concoction he was jovially handed, his mood became depressed. The potent alcohol caused his fuzzy mind to recall how he had been let down. He could never have believed that the American would substitute his riveting exhibition for a vulgar funfair ride.

Solemnly watching the bonfires, he miserably considered his dreams were burning in them. His mind, playing tricks, led him to believe that he was asleep and suddenly due to awake. Then he would find his cherished exhibition splendidly on show, awash with crowds of adoring fans.

Looking groggily up to the dark sky he whistled softly, a sad whimper escaping through his teeth. At least the oak was now safe, he thought defiantly, if that had come tumbling down few could appreciate the repercussions. This sombre thought sent a shiver down his spine, his woozy

166

mind crammed with information he would dare not share. People were not ready for the whole story, not yet anyway, he thought warily.

Watching sparks from the nearby bonfire dance haphazardly he suddenly considered that he had failed in his duty, which was to educate unfortunates about the myth. Standing unsteadily, he deliberated that now was the perfect time for him to atone and deliver an important lecture. Reeling from one foot to the other, he clapped his hands, ordering the band to stop playing. Slurring at the tipsy revellers who were annoyed at his interruption, he stressed noisily that he had something important to say.

Everyone in the village thought Leonard a little odd, nevertheless they held an unspoken admiration for him. Whilst finding him strange, they grudgingly acknowledged his expertise concerning their beloved customs and myths. Alcohol contributing to their jovial mood, they cheered him loudly, calling him to make a speech.

"Men, woman and children." Leonard swayed in time to his slurred words. "Welcome to another Harvesting Leaf." Bending down he gulped his drink, holding out his glass to be replenished.

"Firstly let us thank Mr Maysoni for his hospitality."

The crowd, forgetting who had funded the evening, reluctantly clapped their hands, giving Leonard time to gulp another drink and request a refill.

"As you know Harvesting Leaf means to wash the field of leafs and that is what Mr Maysoni is doing, he is washing November Keys of its antiquated ways and building us a football club to be proud of."

Grinning foolishly, he pointed unsteadily at the ground. "But Mr Maysoni is not a witch like Isobel who cursed our leaves." Spotting a pile of leaves, he jumped back in mock terror. "Do you know what they are?" He addressed his question to a young girl, who had been watching him curiously. "Do you know what they are?"

The child shyly shaking her head, he waded amongst the

leaves kicking them everywhere. "Well I will tell you." He signalled for another drink. "They are demons, sent from Hell itself." He liked the sound of those words and the affect they had on his audience. Taking advantage of a now stunned crowd, he continued his rant, waving impatiently for his drink. "So very soon we will burn these demons just like we used to burn witches." He gestured to the roaring bonfires. "Then all these demons hiding in the leaves will be sent back to Hell." Nearly falling over he steadied himself, raising his voice. "But," he shouted at the same unfortunate child, "You must catch the leaves before they hit the floor."

The crowd sat mesmerised as he tottered from leg to leg pretending to catch imaginary leaves. Now breathless, he put his hand out for another drink, glaring at one particular man who he thought was not paying attention.

"Do you know why you must catch them?" He stared at the unfortunate man angrily. "Well do you?" Leonard's voice could be heard above the wood crackling in the fires.

Tom Doulby who had sat sulking looked up in alarm, glaring at his wife. It was one thing to have to spend the evening without a proper drink and quite another to be yelled at by a drunken lunatic. Staring hard at Leonard, wishing he were as intoxicated, he stood up, shouting as loudly as he could.

"So they don't walk around the tree throwing things."

If any of the crowd had heard Tom's reply, they did not show any concern. Indeed, they were far too busy trying to raise Leonard Small who had fallen flat onto his face.

Bridget Bluestone had sat watching the crowd for a while her eyes drifting from one to the other. She found it hard to believe that most of the people enjoying their celebrations had claimed to be friends with Jack and his family. Now, she thought angrily, they behaved as though he had not existed.

She felt a warm tear escape from her eye, splashing onto the coach ticket she was clutching. Desperately trying to stem the now flowing tears, she angrily pushed her fist into the bottom of her eye. These people, she thought testily, did not deserve tears. Standing up she carefully pulled her heavy rucksack onto her petite shoulders. Her tormented mind instantly questioned why the Carpets had not been in touch or even left a note. She shrugged her shoulders dejectedly, ready to proceed on her journey away from November Keys. As far as she was concerned, she hoped she never set eyes on the mouldy village ever again.

Tom Doulby, angry at being sober, smugly clasped the paper in his pocket. He kept it there for safety. He knew if his wife set eyes on it, she would immediately demand it be passed to bad mannered Bluestone. Well, he thought testily, he had seen it first. He knew it had Bluestone's name on the envelope but she had thrown his flask in the bush. Having read the note numerous times he had decided it was none of Bluestone's business where the Carpets had gone.

As the crowds fussed over the drunken historian, Snakebite, who considered himself Maysoni's top henchman, reluctantly decided he had better jump into action. Taking advantage of the commotion over the inebriated historian, he walked stealthily over to the oak muttering oaths every step of the way.

He had been happy sitting around the fire eating burgers and was not happy to be called away before he had had his fill. Being hungry made him angry. He supposed it was because of his abnormal appetite. That is what his mother had constantly told him. Definitely, over the years, it had got him into big trouble. Eating had made him big and being big made him eat. Food had been like an addictive drug and he had not been concerned how he got it. He would have happily killed for a lunch-box.

Shrugging his huge shoulders, he trudged towards the oak clasping a large petrol can and muttering under his breath. As chief henchman, the unsavoury job he had to perform should have been assigned to one of his inferiors, he mused moodily. However, the boss had told him what to do and he supposed he had better get on with it. Mr Maysoni had said it had to be done whilst the fires were burning brightly. That way people would think it was a jumping spark.

Looking behind him, happy that he was not being followed, he strode purposefully to the oak, quickly splashing it with the contents from his can. As the smell of the fuel met his nostrils, he stood for a moment wiping his nose on the back of his hand. Realising this was not going to wipe the smell away he carried on throwing the petrol, cursing under his breath. As soon as his job was completed, he could return to the party and engage in his favourite pastime again, he thought hungrily.

Looking up to the sky his eyes diverted to the peak of the oak. Two large eyes peering down at him made him jump back in alarm, his can dropping heavily. Muttering oaths at anyone who came to mind, he picked up the can and cautiously peered up into the doomed tree. The boss had told him the tree would be empty, It made him feel uncomfortable to be stared at. Wondering who would be stupid enough to sit on a branch in a tree that was just about to be ignited, his brow creased in to a frown It was not until the offending creature emitted a series of hoots that he realised his observer was only a dumb owl. Rebuking himself for being apprehensive, he strained his eyes to view the bird, allowing himself a noisy chuckle.

"Well Mr Owl, looks like you are going to have to find another house." He stared at the owl, laughing softly. "Or become a fried owl." Thinking his remark funny he fumbled in his pocket for the matches his boss had given him earlier. Pushing a match roughly along the side of the box he merrily watched it dance into flame. In a short while, he thought contently the tree would be ablaze then he could obtain another burger. Ready to toss the burning stick into the tree he furtively looked around, making certain he had no spectators. The boss had stipulated, the arson must look like an accident Content he was alone he flicked the match, watching a small ball of fire circle the base of the oak. Soon his job would be completed.

Leonard Small was laid down to rest for a while, as the band got into full swing inviting the celebrators to dance the night away. Even the not so energetic joined in, swaying along with the music.

Turning to walk away, Snakebite hesitated his ears filled with the sound of frightened giggling noises from above. Thinking as quick as his dull brain would allow, he deliberated that the tree contained more visitors. Straining his ears, listening to the weird sounds, he further deliberated that the visitors were children. His sister had kids who made the same types of sounds continuously.

Franticly dousing flames that had quickly spread, he stood clumsily, contemplating his next move. For sure, he thought gloomily, he could not fry the villagers' children.

He was pleased to hear the band playing on enthusiastically, its noise hopefully deafening the party-goers around the bonfires. He pondered that if he took advantage of the loud music he might coax the children down the tree and then finalise its destruction.

"Come down." Snakebite barked his orders in a husky voice. "Your folks want you at the party." Getting no response, he angrily kicked the offending tree that responded with a hideous giggling noise. "Come down." Snakebite was getting angry.

Again getting no response, he rested his hand on his chin staring solemnly up to the top of the tree. He knew that if he did not complete his mission Mr Maysoni would be quite mad with him. On the other hand, if he fried the villagers' children, they would be unimpressed as well.

Suddenly a rare event occurred, he had an idea. If the children would not come down, then he would bring them down, he thought angrily. Children had no right to disobey a command anyway, especially when he was trying to burn a tree down.

Gliding up the tree with the agility of a cat, he soon reached the peak, noiselessly he looked for the children. His probing eyes aided by the moonlit sky scanned the thick branches carefully, without success. Search as he may there was no trace of any children. Uttering every oath he could remember, he surmised the kids must have climbed down the other side of the tree whilst he had climbed up.

Whatever, he knew that the tree he was sitting in should now be on fire, Mr Maysoni would not be pleased. Starting to make his descent his ears were deafened by a hideous noise. Muttering oaths, he gripped a swaying branch with hands now dampened with sweat. The noise he had heard earlier seemed to be getting louder. His dull mind trying to locate where it originated, he made to descend the tree as quickly as he could.

There was no man on the planet that scared him, but spooky noises did. Before he could give his dilemma any further consideration, the haunting noise became louder. His face perspiring he was astonished to feel a cloud of leaves blowing frantically around his head. Aiming to get his feet on hard soil again, he clambered down as quickly as he could. Gripping the branches, he realised his hands were being bitten ferociously followed by bites to his reddened face. Screaming in terror, determined to reach the bottom, his distress increased when a floating leaf blew into his eye. Carefully holding on with one hand, he pulled at the offending obstacle amazed and terrified that it refused to budge. Certain that he was being attacked by the demons he had heard the villagers discuss, he screamed oaths. When another leaf lodged in his other eye, his oaths became louder. Panic stricken, his ears deafened by atrocious sounds, his fingers grabbed at the offending leaves prohibiting his sight. Realising his mistake he emitted a muffled cry and plummeted to the ground.

Snakebite would never crush the life out of anyone again. On hitting the floor his neck snapped in two, he lay very dead.

The Echo
American dies whilst frolicking in the big oak.
Mr Maysoni gives green light for biggest funfair ride
in England.
Historian Leonard Small found wandering naked
whilst under the influence of alcohol.

Chapter Twelve
Time Goes By (Ten Years Later)

Maysoni placed his phone down and grinned at his image in a polished mirror. "This is going to be big." He whispered to his reflection happily, aware if he pulled it off, it would put him in the super league of criminals. He had been residing in England for ten years and felt the bosses, although rewarding him well financially, had not fully appreciated his expertise. However, when they got to hear about his latest caper, they would have to sit up, take notice and finally bestow on him the adulation he was long overdue. He felt confident that quite soon he would be taking his place alongside the elite.

He poured himself a whisky, thrusting a cigar between his lips. Inhaling the thick smoke with extreme satisfaction, he strolled over to a window and peered out over his empire. It had taken some doing but he had achieved what others could only dream about.

The football stadium stood proud, its towers boasting of power and wealth. He had produced everything he had promised. A stadium worthy to host the world's elite, and a team that was virtually unbeatable. Binolitti, the club manager, had victoriously led the team through all the lower leagues guiding it to the peak of the Monster League. More importantly, much to the Keys' fans' delight, they were now competing in the World Super League.

Newspapers were full of his success stories, whilst television companies were falling over backwards for exclusive interviews. Moon TV regularly stated that Keys Football Club had the services of the best football manager in Europe, if arguably not the world.

Home fans and visitors would cluck in amazement, counting a vast amount of trophies sitting proudly in their glass cases. Over the last ten years the only trophy absent was the World Super League. Everyone knew that would soon be rectified.

Maysoni pulled on his cigar, making a mental note to allow Binolitti in on his deal. He liked a man who got on with his job, not asking too many questions. In addition, Maysoni was aware that numerous clubs were showing interest in his manager's amazing talent. As Maysoni did not intend to let him go anywhere, he thought a skeleton in his closet might help.

Pouring himself another drink he pondered for a moment why the bosses had not yet recognised his own vast achievements and rewarded him properly.

In one decade, as predicted, he had all but taken over the crime families in Europe. There had been some resistance but his aptitude for war with the backing of his armies had brought victory after victory. Utilising the stadium as a fortress they had swept the opposition aside. The bosses now controlled eighty percent of the narcotics trade and when he pulled off his next escapade that would likely increase to ninety-five. They would be able to implement charges whenever they wished, milking an ever-growing market. In addition, he had also been able to mete out the bosses' special justice to old foes and those who were too obstinate to see sense.

The Caterpillar Express had been built, becoming the highest newsworthy railway in history. Away from the public glare, the railway had conveyed much-needed weapons along with much-needed troops. Maysoni smirked, recalling the press heralding his benevolence.

Feeling the alcohol dim his senses, he stared angrily at the oak. He had lost that one little battle he thought testily.

When Snakebite had met his demise in bizarre circumstances, Maysoni had reluctantly decided it would be beneficial to protect the oak, as he had originally promised. He was not superstitious but reasoned sometimes it did not pay to mess about with folklore. For whatever reason, the hicks held the tree in high esteem and he had not wanted to cause any more animosity or risk his vast operations.

175

However, he also reasoned if it had not been for the inexcusable behaviour of the hicks, Snakebite would still be alive.

Watching a smoke ring floating aimlessly, he took in the vastness of the huge stadium. The huge towers now dominated the landscape that had once been farms. Newspapers all over the world marvelled at its architecture and precision building. The large domed walls with their glass effect brought a gasp of amazement from even the most reluctant away fan. Each wall would dramatically change colour, illuminating a series of small keys that represented past wins and trophies darting through each other. When the home-side scored the keys would link together giving the illusion of one gigantic gold key.

No money had been spared and consequently the bosses could launder millions of dollars allowing them to fund other important projects.

Peering at the tree again, he laughed aloud. He knew the hicks had thought they had one up on him and he was aware that some of them boasted about their small triumph, behind his back.

However, revenge was best served cold. This was absolutely what he intended to do. For their audacity, he had had his lawyers in New York transfer the ownership of Keys Football Club to every individual in the village, thus making them the legitimate owners. Consequently, when he had completed his mission and the bosses stopped funding the project, it would be they, the villagers, who would have to finance the ever-increasing running costs. His accountants had forecast that the only way such a club could survive would be to continually play in the World Super League.

The papers in England had screamed on front pages of his extreme generosity, not for one minute anticipating that if Keys ever faltered, the town of November Keys would go bankrupt.

Further to that, he had stipulated that the club could never be sold on until the death of the very last villager alive when he had originally took the club over. When Keys started to tumble there could be no reliance on outside benefactors. He laughed again. When the time came for him to depart, those tree-loving hicks were going to face big problems. However, that delight was for the future, in the meanwhile he had some pressing business to attend to.

Allowing himself one more drink, Maysoni prepared to get ready for his meeting. In a short while, he would have control of most of the crime trade from South America.

Decesso sat in his cell, squinting angrily at a well-read newspaper. Absorbing the headlines, it was apparent that he would be at liberty very soon. Nevertheless, he was angry. Ten years was a long time to be incarcerated and when he finally got his freedom, someone was going to pay dearly for his torment. The bosses had done their best for him he thought reluctantly, but that still did not replace ten years.

Indeed, they had made sure he dined from the best menus and drank the best wine but that did not suffice for freedom. They had also made many attempts to have him sprung. The authorities however had different plans, watching him like a hawk. Escape, however elaborate, had been out of the question.

He tried to contemplate how it had taken so long to catch up with the witness. With all the bosses' contacts, that matter should have been concluded years back. He had been pleased to hear of the spineless rat's grisly end though. He himself could not have thought up a better ending for the low-life dog that had him put away. Throwing the paper onto his bed, he recalled his earlier conversation with his attorney.

The witness, whilst being tortured, had apparently decided that the evidence he had given those years back had been false. Thinking that he might not live for long, he had helpfully stated this into a dictaphone, whilst kindly writing out a statement. The attorney had promised that in just a matter of days Decesso would be a free man.

The idea of being liberated cheered him up and he mused through his plans. After all the back slapping parties, he would get over to England. A certain Mr Goldsmith had something he required. If that certain Mr Goldsmith did not hand it over, he was going to feel the full brunt of Decesso's pent up frustration.

Maysoni glared at Reuccio and the two henchmen. They were arguing over a packet of crisps, he hissed at them to be quiet. He glared over at Binolitti who stood nervously trying to blend into the shadows.

When Maysoni had decided to include his football manager in on the action, it had not crossed his mind the man might object. Maysoni had taken that objection as a personal insult, forcibly demanding the man meet him later. He was offering the man a fortune out of the goodness of his heart and considered he was being ungrateful. He had to remind Binolitti they were all working for a criminal organisation. Because Binolitti was so successful with the team, Maysoni was prepared to ignore the man's unjustified protests.

Normally, he had informed him, Binolitti would be going for a last car ride. However, it had occurred to Maysoni that, had he shot his reluctant comrade, there would be no one to manage the team in the morning. However, if he ordered someone to do something, he expected it done without fail.

Standing quietly, the group could hear a large vehicle approaching. Maysoni rubbed his hands with glee. The lorry contained ten million pounds of narcotics. Earlier, Maysoni had pledged a fair price for the dubious cargo, not intending to pay one dollar.

After the merchandise had been checked for authenticity, the couriers would be executed and Maysoni would be richer. In case of any reprisals from the South American cartel, who were still very powerful, he had arranged a number of visits to their homes and clubs. In a short while, he thought happily, the bosses would take over the South American Empire.

John Goldsmith watched the flickering images on his television with great concern. If the reports were true, in just a few days Decesso would be free and that was going to cause him enormous problems. Listening sombrely to a confident attorney's enthusiastic words, he wrung his hands in nervous anticipation.

One thing for certain, he thought dismally, they had taken good care of the witness. Goldsmith winced, imagining the man's last few hours on planet earth. Certainly he had been brave and met a savage end because of his courage. Goldsmith felt pangs of guilt recalling how he had bribed the man with honey. Without doubt, if the man had not crossed his path, he would most certainly still be alive.

Shrugging his shoulders he pondered over his next move. It had crossed his mind to destroy the recipe but he knew he could not justifiably do that. It was there for a purpose and it was his responsibility to make sure that purpose was achieved. Further, if he did destroy the recipe, Decesso would have him tortured until he revealed its contents. Even worse, he might try to locate Jack Carpet and his family. Under no circumstances could Goldsmith let any harm come to them.

Opening a drawer, he pulled out a small automatic and placed it into his pocket. Laughing nervously he wondered how such a small piece of armoury was going to fend off a raving lunatic and his savage comrades.

Maysoni grinned like a Cheshire cat. His plan had gone perfectly. The unsuspecting couriers had pulled up in their vast lorry and actually jumped out to embrace him. He had done a marvellous job convincing their bosses of his good intentions and they wanted to pass on the respect they felt the American was entitled to.

Whilst Reuccio and the henchmen inspected the merchandise, he chatted to the couriers convincing them that the truck would be safely driven into the football club. Everything would be quite in order he had twilled. Nobody would turn a hair as they were used to deliveries to the club at almost any time of the day and night. Once the load was secured, he had said, his esteemed guests would spend the evening celebrating. They would then be paid and invited to enrich their lives in the company of Binolitti, the best football manager in the world.

At last, when Reuccio gave him the thumbs up, he raised his eyes upwards and the hapless men were dispatched into the next world.

Earlier, whilst driving the truck to the rendezvous, the hapless driver had rammed the old oak tree. Blaming the swirling mist for his lack of vision the cringing mobster had scratched his head, puzzled why his host had fallen into heaps of laughter. Although there was no damage to the vehicle the tree was now looking a bit sorry for itself. Maysoni chuckled loudly. He must be up early the next morning, he mused happily, to witness the hick's faces when finding the damage.

"Revenge served cold." He whistled happily.

Now all they had to do was get the vehicle under cover and his mission would be complete. Glaring at his comrades, who were now arguing over a packet of sweets they had found on one of the corpses, Maysoni swung the rear doors of the lorry open.

"Get those two in," he hissed "and be quick about it." He glared at Binolitti who was shaking like a leaf. "What you shaking about, ain't you ever seen a lorry before?" The poor man tried to reply but could only muster a gurgling noise, so Maysoni ignored him, climbing up into the cab of the lorry. Calling to the others, he turned the ignition causing the large engine to roar into life.

Having secured the lorry doors concealing its dubious cargo, Reuccio made to jump up into the cab with Maysoni. He was not superstitious, having witnessed many dead bodies, but felt it better if the others accompanied the two dispatched couriers, in the rear. He was feeling hungry and wanted to get back and find some dinner. The quicker he got the job completed the quicker he could eat.

Hurriedly gripping the handle of the passenger door, he felt a sensation like a needle pricking his hand. "Ouch," he moaned inwardly, "darned insects." Thinking it wiser to inspect his small wound later, he hoisted one of his feet onto the travelling rail. Again he was amazed when a series of sharp stabs penetrated his hand. Squinting into the dark night, he tried to distinguish what type of insect was attacking him. Soon his eyes nearly protruded, as he witnessed a batch of leaves circling around the front of the lorry.

"Reuccio, get in the dammed lorry." Maysoni hissed angrily.

Reuccio tried to reply but was rendered speechless. Looking up into the dark sky, even though the mist was thickening, he could distinguish thousands of leaves twirling around in the dark clouds. Trying to find his voice, he could only utter loud screams, pain surging through his body as sharp teeth continuously attacked him. Jerking the door of the lorry, he hoisted himself into the passenger seat, falling with a thud against Maysoni.

"What you doing, that's my suit you are pressing?" Maysoni reacted angrily.

"Boss, there are leaves and they bit me." Reuccio whimpered like a baby. "And there are thousands of them."

Convinced that his sidekick had been sampling the wares in the rear of the lorry Maysoni angrily threw the gear lever into first, attempting to drive the lorry away. Letting out the clutch impatiently, his ears were greeted with a strange giggling sound echoing to his rear. Cursing inwardly he promised himself that Reuccio and the other two would pay dearly for messing about with drugs when they were supposed to be working. Very soon, he promised himself, they would be on the next plane to New York.

Grunting angrily he revved the engine up loudly,

attempting to propel the besieged transport forward. Amazed that the vehicle refused to budge, he cursed again, smashing his hand heavily onto the steering wheel. Puzzled why the lorry refused to move, his eyes diverted to the windscreen where he was astounded to see a pile of leaves pressed up against the glass. Praying his eyes were deceiving him he gasped, aware that hundreds of yellow illuminated eyes were now staring at him from outside. Regaining his composure, he jumped from the cab, quickly shaking off his coat to use as a shield to lash out at the offending culprits.

His unexpected exertion made him hot, sweat starting to dribble down the side of his face. Realising the more he lashed out, more leaves appeared he uncharacteristically panicked, screaming franticly for Reuccio and Binolitti to attack the marauding foliage.

The three men, armed with their jackets, desperately stormed into the cloud of leaves scattering them everywhere. Maysoni, pleased with their progress, attempted to climb back into the cab. Placing his hand on to the door, he felt a searing pain shoot through his hand, causing him to shout out in distress Peering at his comrades, he was horrified to see them covered in the green and brown foliage, each screaming incoherently.

Frantically hissing at them to get into the vehicle, he determined to propel the lorry into the cluster of leaves, hoping the impact would render them motionless. Somehow he had stumbled into a nightmare and was determined to vacate it as soon as possible.

Police Constable Green sat for a while, meticulously checking his watch. Shaking his head sadly, he decided to investigate the erratic behaviour of the lorry driver he was observing. Watching the wheels of the lorry spin aimlessly he concluded the driver must be under the influence of alcohol or perhaps worse. Constable Green was aware of his duty. He was obliged to apprehend the driver before he caused an accident.

Maysoni was now beside himself with terror. The lorry refused to move whilst his two companions gibbered like lunatics. Desperately ramming the gear lever into first, he let out the clutch fiercely, urging the lorry to move forwards. Closing his eyes, he was relieved to feel the truck shudder forwards, on reopening them he was delighted to see that the offending leaves had disappeared.

Shaking his head vigorously, he tried to make sense of his situation. One thing for sure, he thought soberly, leaves do not normally attack lorries and bite the passengers. It must have been one of those unexplainable acts of nature. Satisfied with his own explanation and happy that he could now proceed, he moved the lorry forward.

What he encountered next caused his ruddy face to turn white. Standing in front of him, hands held high, was a tall figure dressed in a very familiar uniform. Maysoni cursed, his muddled brain accepting the police were now apprehending him. Thinking quickly, he soon decided the police officer would have to join the couriers in the rear. Hissing at the others to be quiet, he jumped down from the cab checking his gun was nearby.

"Evening sir," the police officer went through his usual routine, "you seemed to be having trouble."

"Yes officer, I was." Maysoni could feel beads of sweat running down the side of his face. "The driver left it here and I need to move it." He grinned at the police officer. "A bit out of practice I suppose."

"Okay," the police officer stood taking in the scene, "you all right now?"

"Yes," Maysoni felt his head was going to explode, "I had better get moving."

Constable Green realising that he was talking to the chairman of Keys Football Club decided to leave things as they were. He did not want to antagonise Maysoni and he certainly did not want to antagonise his inspector who strangely would always get very special treatment when he went to cheer on his football team.

Nodding to the relieved American, he went to walk away but was quickly stopped by an exploding noise forcing him to the floor. Hardly believing what had happened the officer took off his cap, now sporting a large bullet hole. Looking angrily at Maysoni he decided although the American was wealthy and influential, he should not go around shooting holes in people's hats. Indeed, his new uniform had only been issued two days earlier. Waving his hat in the air, he glared at Maysoni stating he intended to arrest him.

Maysoni stood trembling, staring at his revolver lying on the muddy grass. He could not for the life of him understand how it had fallen from his pocket, yet alone gone off. However, he reasoned, this was no time to ponder over things. He would have to shoot the police officer and bury him. Quickly picking up the gun he aimed it at the unfortunate man's chest and pulled the trigger. Both men stood in stunned silence, waiting for the blast. Maysoni shook the pistol pulling the trigger again. Once more, it refused to respond and he looked hopelessly up to the mist-filled sky.

The noise of police sirens was getting louder. Within seconds, the approaching police cars would be on top of him. He was caught bang to rights. Staring forlornly at his firearm he wondered why it had not fired. He always took good care of his weapons and could not understand why it had malfunctioned. Possibly, he thought, when it had fallen from his pocket it had fired its last bullet. As numerous police cars arrived, the gang of Americans put up their hands, weakly surrendering. It was apparent their assailants were heavily armed and they gave no resistance.

Maysoni stood despondently staring at his gun, which he had discarded back to the ground. As his hands were being cuffed, he heard a familiar noise. Glancing down, he cursed his eyes. He did not know if it was the mist causing him to hallucinate or something had snapped in his brain. Nevertheless, he stood horrified as he witnessed, descending from the guns barrel a leaf equipped with weird yellow eyes that glowed in the dark light. The vile creature moved with the aid of arms and legs resembling skinny twigs. Just to add to the horror, it emitted a hideous giggling noise.

The first thing he was going to do when he got to the police station, he thought grimly, was to ask to see a doctor.

Bridget Bluestone stood for a while looking at the proud branches of the oak drooping sadly. Trying to fathom what had happened, she tried to blot out the troubling thoughts that kept trying to penetrate her mind.

Fleetingly, her mind wandered back ten years. Those years had passed quickly. She guiltily acknowledged that while engrossed with her studies and subsequent travelling she had not given much consideration to Jack and his family. Now standing at the foot of the oak, peering through the swirling mist she promised herself she would make some enquiries and track her old friends down.

She had no idea what had made her return, reluctantly accepting that fate had played a part. Unaware of the circumstances she sensed there was some unfinished business that needed her attention. Something from the past was luring her, tormenting her thoughts. She cursed quietly at the gift nature had given her, a gift of clairvoyance. Shrugging her slim shoulders, she closed her eyes tightly, praying that everything would be all safe.

Everyone in Keys was soon talking about the events that had over shadowed their football club. While some grunted and reminded others of their distrust in the American, others genuinely were sorry to see him go. Cheryl at The Black Cat was missing them already. She had become considerably fond of Mr Maysoni's companions. They had always been courteous and obviously knew good food when it was presented. They were always complimenting her on her cooking. She smiled as she recalled the little one, waiting for leftover curry to take to work. As there was always a lot remaining, she would pack it into brown paper bags, smiling as she did so.

Standing at the bar looking miserable she realised she would never see them again. She beckoned everyone to be quiet when their defeated faces appeared on television. Everyone sat in deathly silence, listening intently to how Maysoni and his gang had instigated numerous murders and tortures. Apparently, the special branch had been observing the gang for months and a very high-ranking officer praised Constable Green for his bravery and quick thinking. He added that despite Maysoni and his gang claiming Binolitti, the Keys' manager, had misled them, they were being held in a high security prison.

An expert on law appeared next, stating that Maysoni's assets had been frozen. Regarded as a very high-risk prisoner, the authorities did not want his millions to buy him out of trouble. He added that because illegal earnings had funded Keys, its future looked bleak and was certain to be closed down.

Cheryl looked at three plates of uneaten curry and wept.

The Echo
The old oak is damaged whilst gangsters wage drug wars.
Mr Maysoni arrested and held on charges of murder, extortion, torture, drug trafficking and gun running, kidnapping, theft, grievous bodily harm, robbery and tax evasion. His appeal for bail has been turned down.
Future of Keys in doubt as Maysoni's assets frozen.
Club may go out of business warns the FA.
Real Madrid has stated they no longer have any interest in the services of Binolitti's management skills.

Chapter Thirteen
Top Dog, New Cat, Old Tricks

One month later.

John Gardner stared at his television for several minutes before leaping from his chair and jabbing its off button in utter disgust. After glaring at the now black screen for a while, he angrily banged his fist against the expensive wood adorning his huge desk. What did Van de Groot have to put his nose in for? He thought furiously. The man was Dutch, yet here he was maintaining that he wanted to liberate people in some outback in the middle of nowhere. Getting angrier by the moment, he questioned why the man had ventured to England in the first place.

Up until his arrival, Gardner's plans had been running as smoothly as clockwork. In fact, he had not had to do anything. Maysoni the American had taken care of that. Sometimes Gardner could not believe his own luck. When the American had been arrested the press had talked non-stop about the upcoming demise of November Keys. It would take a miracle, they lamented, to save the once timid farming village. November Keys would be sold to pay its massive debts. Gardner knew once that happened a lot of cheap land would be up for grabs. Once Keys bailed out of the World Super League, which they soon would without the supervision of the luckless Binolitti, the club, along with the whole village, was going to be bankrupt.

Gardner banged on his desk desperately. If Van de Groot had not come onto the scene, he mused miserably, he would have been home high and dry. The club would have drowned in its own debts. Then it would have been easy. John Gardner developments would sail to the rescue. At the right price of course. Within a year, what had once been a village, would be one of the biggest luxury housing estates known to man. The rich would be queuing up to live in such a remote area. The pampered elite he had in mind would

187

give their right hand to live in such an idyllic, isolated place. In addition, those who needed to commute had the Caterpillar Express sitting on their doorstep.

Pressing his buzzer, summoning his hapless secretary, he made a mental note to visit Van de Groot to investigate the man's loyalty. His credentials, without doubt, were faultless. Gardner knew that with his expertise and a little luck Van de Groot could keep Keys football team in business. That was not in Gardner's plans. Drumming his long fingers impatiently, he decided to visit Keys Football Club under the guise of offering some financial help. The fact that everyone in Keys who knew him could only mention his name in disgust did not deter him. Most of them were stupid anyway. He was going to get his empire one way or the other.

He pondered gloomily why the Dutchman would want to get involved with a club on the verge of liquidation when every club in Europe would queue for his services. They would pay handsomely as well. Yet here he was offering his services free. Gardner wondered if the man was all he pretended to be. Certainly he had arrived in a blaze of glory, shouting from the rooftops how he was going to save the club. However, that sort of talk cut no ice with Gardner. Experience had taught him everyone had their price. Well he would soon find out, he thought grimly. Feeling outraged, he shouted loudly into his intercom for his secretary.

Quickly heeding his request, she peered nervously through the oak doors guarding his office. He rudely ordered her to make an appointment for him to meet the famous Mr Van de Groot. Content at her nervousness, he barked for more coffee, making a mental note to replace the jittery woman as soon as possible. Her only useful purpose, he thought ruefully, was to make coffee. He would get one of those machines and that would be that.

Van de Groot sat at his desk carefully sifting through a mountain of paperwork. Things were looking very bleak for

Keys and he wanted to make sure they stayed that way. Standing up abruptly, he viewed himself in a full-length mirror, laughing loudly.

Arriving at the club a month previously he had wondered if he would get away with his scheme. He was sure at some stage he would be rumbled but to his astonishment, everyone had bent over backwards to accommodate him. His first press conference had been remarkable. He had talked confidently into flashing cameras, assuring those who wanted to listen that whilst he was at the helm Keys Football Club would only prosper. Walking majestically along the pitch, he saluted the air, thousands of cheering fans chanted his name. Every one of them was convinced he was some type of saviour. Whilst they cheered, he sneered inwardly, mentally plotting their club's downfall.

Trying to concentrate on his over-flowing paperwork, he gazed at the ugly animal sprawled across his office floor. When he had arrived at the club, the strange looking feline had made a beeline for him, refusing to leave his side. Not in the slightest bit flattered, he had had the cat ejected several times. Only for the pitiful creature to return repeatedly, purring its unconditional love. Eventually he had decided to take the cat to a feline re-homing centre. You could not be too careful he had thought cheerfully. Nevertheless, for some reason he had taken a sudden liking to the battered stray, subsequently allowing it to share his office. It had not been a bad move. Very quickly the press had noticed, and in true paparazzi fashion had splashed stories of Van de Groot's benevolence to dumb animals across the back pages of nearly every tabloid in the land. Wilfred, although an extremely ugly animal and devoid of any natural feline beauty, had become popular. He even had his own twitter page. It was extremely strange, Van de Groot mused how the hideous creature had the capacity to attract people to be fond of it.

Wrapped in a mass of dirty ginger hair it represented more of a health problem then a team mascot. Peering hungrily from two boss eyes, it was difficult to determine who it was looking at and where. Devoid of any energy, the only task it performed with any enthusiasm was to stuff food into its crooked mouth.

Van de Groot felt smugly pleased that the inhabitants of Keys had had such a horrible creature living in their village. It was proof of their inability to keep their village pure. However, a mangy cat was nothing compared to how they had allowed their proud village to be so soiled. Once they had had everything they needed, but their greed had brought their village to the point of extinction. Now they foolishly believed that Van de Groot was going to bail them out.

He grinned to himself, recalling the frenzied cheering when he had arrived at the club's gate. If only those fanatical morons knew his real purpose, they would be shaking in their filthy boots. To stand any chance of survival, the team had to progress in the World Super League. He was going to make sure it did not.

His press officer had unwittingly camouflaged his mission well. The whole world was soon to hear of the Dutch super manager giving his services free. John Goldsmith had even asked the village committee to give him freedom of the town.

Scanning his paperwork, he tried to work out exactly how much time Keys had left. When Maysoni had been arrested, all funds had been severed and debts were piling up. For his own reasons, Maysoni had stipulated, the club could not be sold. Although lawyers were working around the clock to try to find some loophole, the fact remained that, the club was now the responsibility of the village.

Many of the players were becoming restless with half the football clubs around the world paying extra attention. Very soon, when their wages were not forthcoming, the players would be even more disillusioned. They would be queuing up to get out of the place.

If he did his job properly, he thought happily, Keys would disappear in around five months' time.

Decesso strode down a shaky gangway grunting at the autumn sky. He fleetingly wondered where he would be dining later, shuddering as he suddenly remembered his last visit and the awful food he had to endure.

Whilst he had been incarcerated, he had often thought about on the dreadful place Maysoni had taken him to eat. He had been offered better food in prison. For a brief while he wondered what it was like to eat such food every day. Feeling his anger rise, he mused that Maysoni must have known what the food was like. Decesso tapped his gleaming boot angrily onto the tarmac. Maysoni had let him down. Nevertheless, despite the man's shortcomings, he liked Maysoni and made a mental note to pay him a visit.

He would also supervise some catering for the boys, he mused benevolently. While on remand they were allowed food from outside. He would make sure that they got the finest.

Glancing backwards he surveyed his new henchmen, who were carefully watching his every move. Each had their eyes trained for the unlikely. They were a good crew he thought contently. He would look after them when he had the recipe and make them comfortable.

For a brief moment he felt a lump in his throat, his thoughts turned to Stingray, Beesting and Snakebite. All three men had been loyal and had trusted him, now two of them were likely to be in prison for the best part of their lives and the other one was dead. Blowing his nose heavily he bowed his head, recalling Snakebite's quick demise. When the news had reached him, he had smashed up his cell. Now it was evident Stingray and Beesting were likely to be incarcerated for thirty years or more.

The bosses had tried, of course, to sort the witnesses but even they could not bend the strong arm of the English law. Muttering to himself, he quietly plotted his revenge on the people who had caused their demise. That was the least he could do, he thought charitably.

191

Shrugging his broad shoulders, he strode quickly forwards. When he returned to America, he thought contently, he was going to be the most powerful man in the world.

Watching Van de Groot feeding titbits to a grateful Wilfred, Bridget Bluestone felt a shudder of revulsion vibrate down her spine. Making a mental note to call in at the job centre, she stood silently, waiting for her boss' commands.

"Ah, Ms Bluestone," Van de Groot glanced at his spectator with unhidden disdain, "nice of you to call in."

"Yes I am sorry." Bridget stood clumsily, aware her words were nervously distorted, "The bus did not come."

"Ms Bluestone," Van de Groot was starting to enjoy himself, "football clubs do not run on bus timetables." Putting his hand up to finalise the one-sided conversation he pulled a large piece of paper from his desk. "Now you are here, take this to the appropriate departments." He snarled the rest of his words. "We are to have a health and safety check and I do not want any mishaps." Laughing inwardly at the girl's nervousness he nodded at his empty cup. "And get that refilled please." He made a point of looking at his watch. "Some of us have been here a while."

Bridget picked up the cup determined not to show her anguish. When her business took off, she thought grimly, she would tell Mr Van de Groot what to do with his job. She would be glad when the week was over and she could go back to the coffee bar. She had not asked to be his flipping dogsbody she thought ruefully. In fact, she was only helping until Mavis was better. Until then, she supposed, she would just have to put up with it. Turning to walk away, she shuddered, certain his loud voice would puncture her ears.

"And give this John Gardner a call and make an appointment."

Pulling a face behind Van de Groot's closed door Bridget cursed herself for accepting to be his personal assistant, even if it was only for a week. Mavis had never mentioned what a pig the new manager was. Nevertheless, she was quickly finding that out for herself. "Do this, get that." She spoke angrily wishing the man in the next room were a thousand miles away. She was going to love seeing his face when her business took off, then he could stick his job and his coffee bar. Pulling her slender frame upright, she sullenly crept along a bleak corridor.

When she had stood outside the ground selling beverages all those years ago she had never dreamt that one day she would be taking orders from one of the nastiest men in the world. She yearned for those days to return. Times were far happier then she thought sadly. Feeling a tear trickle down her cheek, it reminded her of her failure to trace the whereabouts of Jack and his family. Everyone she had asked had looked at her blankly before shrugging their shoulders. Well for sure, she thought angrily, she was going nowhere until she knew they were safe.

She hated working at the football club and, as soon as possible, she would make her exit. Unfortunately, due to the American Maysoni and the economic crisis he had caused, there was no other work to be found.

Fleetingly she wondered about JJ and what had become of him. She recalled an unusual conversation when they were young. He had maintained that if anyone harmed his father, he would hunt them down until the last breath had left their bodies. Well where was he now? She thought grimly. Perhaps, if he did show up, he might whack nasty Van de Groot for her. That thought made her feel breezier. She glared back at Van de Groot's office and skipped along the corridor.

Goldsmith tapped his pen nervously onto an ancient ink-pot, listening intently to the hollow metallic sound that echoed back to him. Strange, he thought idly, how different metals made different noises. Sitting upright, he tried to expel an unwelcome thought that had trespassed into his mind. When Decesso arrived on the scene, which was going to be soon, the next noise he heard might be his own bones breaking. Shaking his head vigorously to rid this unwanted thought, he sucked in his breath, forcing his mind to focus on other important issues.

Fortunately, he thought gravely, the Keys' committee had called on him to help them solve their impossible dilemma. He knew they had brought on their own problems due to greed and ambition, but he did not have the heart to refuse. After all, he was a Keys man himself, with his ancestors populating the village from its birth.

Thank goodness, he thought calmly, that he had obtained the services of Van de Groot. Fortunately the great manager's agent frequented his restaurants. Somehow the two men had procured his services, albeit, on a temporary basis. For sure, he was one of few men who could keep Keys in the World Super League. As long as they maintained that position, there was a glimmer of hope. If Keys went under he did not want to think about the consequences. Already the vultures were sitting, waiting.

He had tried to fund the club himself but Maysoni's lawyers had put a stop to that. The American's vindictiveness had led him to virtually destroy the club's finances. His attorneys had sealed a watertight set of conditions where only the native villagers still residing in Keys could make any funding to the club. He himself was excluded being that he had not lived in Keys for over ten years. Maysoni had planned the demise of November Keys very thoroughly. The only funding, other than the usual gate money, etc, had to come from the villagers themselves who in truth were in absolutely no position to fund anything. The only way to make sure those funds were adequate was to keep the tills clinking as the team progressed through the rounds of the most watched competition in the history of football.

Still tapping impatiently, he made a mental note to call his lawyers. There was a small hope he might be able to offer the club some short-term loans. If that was the case, and Keys were bundled out of the prestigious World Super League, they might be able to stay afloat a little longer. If that motion was disqualified and Van de Groot could not weave his magic, the whole of Keys would be obliterated from the map. The land that the villagers had cultivated for generations would be sold to repay debts. They would lose their homes and just about everything else.

He shuddered, knowing that the crooked entrepreneur Gardner was waiting like an over-sized spider in the wings. If he got his hands on the land, the first casualty without doubt would be the oak. Goldsmith rang his hands in nervous anticipation.

John Gardner made himself comfortable, his hawk-like eyes studying every detail in the illustrious football manager's office. For a short while he allowed his thin lips to curl into a rare smile. His day had been a lot easier than he could possibly have imagined. When he had apprehensively set about his journey earlier, he had no idea how his proposals would be met. In fact, only a mad man would have tried to engineer one of the greatest managers of all time into selling their club down the river. However, so far, everything he had proposed the Dutchman had smiled at and confirmed it could be done.

Accepting a cup of coffee, he congratulated himself on his cunning. He had known all along that the Dutchman was not right in his mind. Well that was the trademark of a professional businessperson, he thought gleefully, the art of reading people.

It crossed his mind to wonder why Van de Groot had come to the club in the first place. The press yelled every day of his benevolence but Gardner's intuition told him the Dutchman was more intent on ruining the club then saving it. Still, he thought that was of no concern to him. Very soon, he thought happily, he was going to become the millionaire that he deserved to be.

Gardner, happy that his business was concluded, was set

to make his rewarding return journey. For a while he sat silently, studying the Dutchman's face for any traces of insanity. For his act of betrayal, the manager had demanded ten thousand pounds up front and enough land to build a farm. Perhaps, Gardner thought wistfully, he might have saved his money. Anybody who thought you could mingle a farm with some of the richest properties in the country was not likely to succeed anyway.

Van de Groot sat aimlessly throwing peanuts at an overfull waste paper basket. Accepting his aim was not very good he soon became bored, diverting his attention to the ugly cat who sat watching him curiously.

"Why are you always so hungry Wilfred?" Without waiting for the cat to respond, he pulled a small piece of ham from his pocket, tossing it to the grateful feline.

Pouncing, as though it were a mouse, the cat devoured the meat in a flash of a second, before looking hopefully at its master for a repeat run. Realising the quick but appetising game was over, it gave it's donor a scowl, rolled over and went to sleep.

Van de Groot laughed aloud. "Go to sleep my hungry feline. You are plan two." Checking his watch, he hunched his shoulders. Very soon, he would be getting a visit from the health and safety inspectors and he knew exactly what needed to be done.

Knowing from experience how hot they were on fire fighting apparatus, he had conveniently removed two of the extinguishers from the main hall. When their absence was apparent, the club would be given a friendly warning in writing and another chance to secure their deployment. He grinned inwardly, if they were still missing on the second visit, negotiations would not be so amicable. The safety officer, becoming aggrieved at the club's flippant attitude, would withhold the required certificate. Although this would only be temporary whilst the club became organized, the damage caused could be devastating.

An already fragile club would be ridiculed in the press, whilst potential future advertisers, a financial necessity, would back away hurriedly. The longer the ridiculous scenario continued, the worse it would become. Keys' ground could be closed, meaning no home games or training. The team's moral, already at a low, would shatter into smithereens. Which would lead on comfortably to plan two. He felt like patting himself on the shoulders. However, there was still work to be done. On the coming Saturday they had a big league game. He would make sure they would win. He cackled manically, remembering one of his father's favourite sayings, watch for the calm before a storm.

The following Saturday Keys' ground, as usual, was packed to the rafters. Despite the financial gloom hanging over the club the numerous fans jostled happily, restless for the game to commence.

Long before the last fan had taken their seat, the far from friendly banter began. The opposing fans delighted in reminding their hosts what a precarious situation they were in. The faithful Keys fans responded by singing Van de Groot's name continuously, and loudly, throughout the game.

Ninety minutes later the Keys' players ran from the pitch amidst a thundering applause. Their win inspired a new confidence, which quickly buzzed around the ground. Van de Groot stood in front of the cameras cooing his love for the fans that had taken him into their hearts. Inwardly he sniggered. Very soon, he thought happily, Keys would be closed.

Bridget Bluestone raced along a bleak corridor as fast as her aching limbs would allow. Clutching the failure notice, she periodically checked her watch. She knew Van de Groot was not going to listen to any excuses and feared for her job and indeed any job with Keys It would be her own fault, she thought miserably.

Once she got into that library she was so carried away that time became unimportant. Cursing silently, she wished that Mavis was well again, which would mean she could return to the coffee bar. Half-running, half-skipping, she desperately tried to straighten her skirt which she was certain was creased. Her speed and posture made it an impossible task, causing her to tumble clumsily onto the cold floor.

"Damn," she muttered under her breath "not only am I late, I look a mess as well." Hurrying into Van de Groot's office she nervously placed the grey certificate onto his desk. For a while he said nothing, giving her the impression he had delayed shock. After a while, to her dismay, he found his voice, eyeing her up and down with disdain.

"Ms Bluestone," he let his words linger over the cold office, "it appears not only can you not respect punctuality but also you have problems with your attire."

Bridget started to protest but stopped in her tracks. She was horrified to see a cloud of dust trapped on the front of her blouse. Reluctantly trembling, she stood moodily, staring vacantly at the manager's large polished desk. Shaking his head, Van de Groot waved the buff paper in front of his face.

"Ms Bluestone, whilst you have spent your time deciding whether or not to grace our beautiful building with your presence, we have been given a temporary notice of closure." He spat his words at her, careful not to show his happiness. "In twenty-four hours our protagonist will return and if everything is not as it should be, he will close our club." He paused, allowing his words to sink in. "And then Ms Bluestone, we shall all be without employment." He passed her the certificate, speaking in a growl. "Make sure everyone reads this and is aware of the implications."

The following day Bridget ensured everything was in place. Although her week of being dogsbody was nearing completion, she wanted to prove that she was capable of more than just serving coffee. When her business took off, she thought proudly, she would have hundreds of people in her employment and she would treat them a whole lot nicer than her miserable boss treated her. Quickly dusting the Dutch manager's desk, she paused to speak to Van de Groot's ugly cat.

"It's all right for you Wilfred, sleeping all day." She smiled as the cat half-heartedly opened an eye. "But if the club closes, you will have to get a proper job." Laughing again, the over-nourished cat scowling at her, she bent down to pick up some loose papers. "When my business takes off I will adopt you and take you to The Isle of Dogs."

The cat suddenly arching its back, made her laugh again. "I was only joking pussy cat." Chuckling happily to herself, she placed the loose papers onto Van de Groot's desk. Pleased with her efforts she made to leave the office, delayed by a sheet of paper falling onto the floor.

Snatching the offending paper her eyes scanned its contents and she jumped back, biting into her lip. A cheque for ten thousand pounds made directly payable to Van de Groot stared back at her. Looking closely, she was able to see a Mr Gardner had signed the cheque. Standing awkwardly, she tried to weigh up the situation. She was aware, as were many people, that Mr Gardner had his eyes on the club but why was he writing cheques to Van de Groot?

"Ah Ms Bluestone, now going through my personal papers?"

Bridget jumped back in alarm, her mind recognising the angry voice booming behind her. "I was just clearing up." She could feel her face turning scarlet. "Anyway you should not creep up on people." To her surprise, on hearing her angry retort Van de Groot burst into laughter. Looking at the cheque in her hand he quietly took it, placing it into his top pocket.

"It's for advertising space, Ms Bluestone." He grinned at his ugly cat. "We have to feed the pets." Without waiting for a reply, his expression quickly changed. "Now in about half an hour." He looked down at his watch. "Our chap will come back and check us out for safety." He motioned with his hand. "And we do not want any mishaps, do we?" Bridget could feel his eyes penetrate her whole mind. "Have you checked the extinguishers?"

Bridget nodded silently.

"Good, then you may go."

Looking alarmed, Bridget glanced at her watch. Van de Groot laughed again. "Ms Bluestone, do not look a gift horse in the mouth, go and enjoy your afternoon." As Bridget hesitated, not sure how to take her manager's command, Van de Groot looked up with a sneer on his face. "You can spend the rest of the afternoon in your second home." Aware of his employee's discomfort he continued. A mocking tone in his voice. "Why do you spend so much time in the library Ms Bluestone?"

Bridget, still not sure of Van de Groot's intentions, replied cautiously. "I am researching my business plans." As she uttered her words, she felt her face starting to redden.

"Business plans, I say how very grand." Van de Groot's eyes looked towards Bridget in curiosity. "And what business do you propose to have plans for?"

Still not sure if her boss was genuinely interested, Bridget stammered her answer. "It's… its good luck mottoes for shoes and boots."

"Good luck mottoes?" Van de Groot looked up enthusiastically. "Tell me more Ms Bluestone, please."

Bridget, pleased that her boss was eyeing her curiously rather then scowling at her, continued enthusiastically. "The mottoes are sewn into the bottom of the shoes." She looked at the manager proudly. "They bring the wearer good luck."

Heeding the girl's enthusiasm, Van de Groot stared at her thoughtfully. "So if we were to sew these mottoes into the players' boots." He tapped on his desk playfully. "Do you think we might win a few more games?"

Delighted that she was receiving some well-earned attention Bridget smiled, nervously rubbing her cheek. "Yes, and I can organise them for you, if you wanted."

"And Keys will never lose again?" Van de Groot sat back, bellowing with laughter, the noise making Wilfred sit up in alarm. "Oh dear Ms Bluestone, I have never heard of anything so funny." His prolonged laughter caused his eyes to water and he daubed at them with his handkerchief. "Oh dear, oh dear. Ms Bluestone go and enjoy your afternoon. Good luck mottoes indeed."

Watching Bridget slouch off, her ears burning, Van de Groot sat back in his chair scowling at Wilfred. "Tell me my furry friend, why does it have to be like this?" Not waiting for a response he threw the grateful cat a piece of fish. "I can possibly understand the others but not her, I thought she was much more loyal."

After a while he got up and strolled down the corridor. Making sure that Bridget had vacated the building, he approached two red fire extinguishers. Manhandling them along the now dark corridor, he placed them in his office, carefully locking the door. Smiling, he took his mobile phone from his pocket. "Jones," he spoke abruptly, "I need to go out." He grinned again, listening to the muffled reply. "Health and safety will be here soon. I have Ms Bluestone's word everything is in shipshape condition."

Snapping his phone shut, he strode quickly along the deserted corridor. He wanted to be out of the way when the inspection took place. He whistled softly in what he considered a happy tune. Very shortly, Keys would be closed. Plan one completed.

Bridget unwrapped her sandwich whilst pouting at the old oak. She had wanted to spend her unexpected free afternoon in the library but to her dismay found it was half-day closing.

Despite ridicule from various people, she felt her business idea was a winner and was determined to implement it as soon as possible. When she had sufficient funds, she intended to locate the Carpets and if necessary fund a new farm for them.

Slowly chewing her sandwich, her thoughts were interrupted by a strange noise, seemingly coming from the top of the tree. Sitting still, she strained her ears, attempting to identify the noise that was getting louder. Without doubt, she thought while listening intently, the noise resembled that of young children giggling excitedly. Fully aware that no child from the village would dare scale the forbidden oak she stood up, whispering for whoever was in the tree to come down. Adding that the tree was a prohibited place to be and its invaders might be eaten by the owl.

Getting no response, she shrugged her shoulders, continuing to eat her lunch. If children wanted to climb the oak, it was none of her business, she thought angrily. She only wished it were her boss up there, being attacked by the creatures from Hell. Rebuking herself for having nasty thoughts she watched in amazement as two glossy brochures fluttered down towards her. Quickly inspecting the un-requested literature, she was amazed to read about the importance of fire extinguishers especially within a football club.

Suddenly, her mind moved reluctantly to the editor of The Echo, Lionel Bains and the rest of the villagers who had sold their birthplace. None one of them were bad people she mused sadly, but greed and personal ambitions had blurred their reasoning. However, although she was angry with them, she did not want them to lose their village and she was positive that, despite the way he had been treated, Jack Carpet would not want that to happen either.

Trying to rid her unwanted thoughts, she gasped, a gust of wind catching her unexpectedly and forcing her backwards. Muttering under her breath, she sat mortified, nervously witnessing hundreds of leaves floating aimlessly at the peak of the oak.

Covering her ears, she recognised the strange noise she

had heard previously. Now trembling she stared at the blowing leaves forming a cloud similar to a group of angry starlings, propelling themselves towards Keys Football Club.

Returning to the building, Van de Groot was surprised that no one had waylaid him. The safety officer would have been and gone and he had anticipated a frenzied chaos. Striding purposely into his office he was taken aback, his eyes narrowing at the sight of Bridget seated in his chair, grinning contentedly. Watching him enter she jumped up, excitedly waving a buff coloured certificate near to his nose. He did not have to be told what the paper contained. Keys had passed the inspection.

"What do you think you are doing?" He spat his words angrily. "How did you get in to this office?" He fumbled inside his pocket for his keys. Realising they were safely in his possession he stared accusingly at a startled Bridget.

"Mr Jones has a spare set." Bridget's face crumbled. "The library was closed so he asked me to let the inspector in." Her voice trembled, quickly explaining that the club had a pass. She was frightened she was going to burst into tears. Expecting Van de Groot to be pleased with the outcome of the officer's visit she had expected a minor bit of praise. Instead, her horrible boss just glared at her. She tried to speak, only finding her words sticking to the back of her throat.

Van de Groot stared angrily at Bridget, then to his phone. That would be ringing off the hook in the morning, he thought grimly. When Gardner realised the club was still open there would be hell to pay. His eyes darted to the side of his office, not surprised to see the extinguishers he had earlier procured were not where he had left them. He pondered how the slightly built girl had manhandled them both on her own. He wondered if she had mentioned their absence to anyone else. If that was the case, he might be in trouble.

"Well done Ms Bluestone." He felt his congratulatory words clogging his mouth. "I am so pleased you noticed the extinguishers." Waiting for her reaction, he was surprised to see a puzzled expression etched on her face. Shrugging his shoulders, he strolled out into the corridor. He would have to resort to plan two.

Passing two fire extinguishers, he muttered angrily under his breath. They were covered in leaves. He made a mental note to complain to the cleaners the next morning. Feeling that he needed a strong drink, he decided to stop for the day, conserving his energy to implement his next tactics. Gardner would have to wait a little longer. Looking along the grey corridor, he mouthed his words silently but furiously towards the ceiling.

"You will close Keys." His silent words not echoing back to him, he jumped back nervously. He was sure he could hear a sound of giggling, similar to the noise young children might make.

The Echo
Super manager Van de Groot set to lead Keys to Safety.
John Goldsmith unsuccessfully tries to buy out Keys Football Club.
Reports that Mr Maysoni has had a breakdown whilst in custody.

Chapter Fourteen
Sleepy Players, Naughty Refs And Dubious Coffee

Bridget Bluestone watched Wilfred in fascinated disdain. She knew he was a strange cat but his eccentricity still made her bewildered. Recently, much to her mirth and completely out of character, he had taken to guarding one of the goal posts. Furthermore, he had taken his new role seriously. Everyone connected to the club had great fun watching the strange feline, who would sit for hours staring intently at the goal post, a strange look on his face, eventually pouncing on absolutely nothing. Renowned for being an exceptionally lazy animal, Bridget could not fathom out his new energy. Perhaps he was catching mice, she thought breezily.

Anyway, she thought seriously, chasing shadows was better than sitting in Van de Groot's office. She wondered for a while why the dumb animal had made a beeline for the horrible manager in the first place. It certainly could not have been for his charisma. In truth, the nasty Dutchman had had the ugly cat evicted on numerous occasions. That was until a reporter had run an article on Van de Groot's love of animals.

Of course, nasty Van de Groot had milked the situation, misleading the whole country to think he was the nicest man on the planet. Well, she thought intently, when her business took off, she would write to the papers from afar, and tell them the truth.

Getting bored watching Wilfred, she stood up, resignedly placing her hands across her face for protection against the icy wind. Pulling her drab, woollen, company-issue jumper nearer to her slender frame, she muttered under her breath. A girl should not have to be out in this sort of weather she moaned sourly. It was only because of his lord-ship's vindictive attitude.

Jumping up reluctantly, she checked her watch in a panic, quickly changing her thoughts towards the burger bar. In a very short while, grumpy Van de Groot would want his regular cheeseburger and coffee and it was her awful duty to deliver it to his office. At one time she had thought she had seen the last of him, at close range anyway. When Mavis returned she had sighed with relief, wondering how the poor girl, continuously endured his nasty ways. However, that was not to be. Suddenly, he had this thing about burgers and chips, and worse he had insisted Bridget carry his meal to him every day. His harsh warnings still rang in her mind about the importance of getting it to him promptly.

She had begged her supervisor for another role but her pleas had been ignored. For the time being she was stuck with the obnoxious manager, deciding it wisest to give him the best service possible. She knew he was less than impressed with her and she delighted in thinking, when her business took off, she would tell him what to do with his job and his burger too.

Playing with her necklace for some comfort, she wondered if her ingenious idea would ever take off. Personally, she thought it was brilliant, but every time she confided in one of her friends, they would just burst into laughter. The idea of putting good luck mottoes in to shoes was very original, so she put their behaviour down to envy. One day she would show them all.

Realising the hands of her watch were turning fast, she hastened towards the large burger bar. Although she could not care less about the Dutchman's stomach, she thought it advisable to hang onto her job. Her get rich scheme was light years away and she had been warned once too often about her tardiness. As she hurried away, she turned abruptly, putting her hand up to say goodbye to strange Wilfred. However, if she had expected any response, she was to be disappointed.

The strange feline had a leaf in his mouth and was walking around in circles, oblivious to the outside world. He was certainly behaving like the cat that got the cream. Although she risked being late, she could not resist watching the dumb animal, staring proudly as he paraded his catch, behaving as though he had caught a giant mouse or something. Shaking her head she went to go on her way, amused by her interruption. Until again interrupted, this time by a hideous screeching noise. Looking up abruptly she noticed the hair on Wilfred's back standing erect, as though it had been starched. The cat appeared terrified.

A gust of icy wind did no favours to the felines cause. Now smothered in leaves propelled by the angry wind, he dropped his dubious prey, screeching hideously as though on fire. Shaking himself furiously, he scampered towards the grey building that housed his basket. Bridget shook her head, now running towards the burger bar. What a dump, she thought, a mad manager with a mad cat that was spooked by dead leaves.

Van de Groot slammed down his phone, scowling at the unkempt cat sitting forlornly at his feet. He wondered what had caused it to flounce into his office in such a panic. He was glad it had returned though. It was time for another piece of Wilfred's special meat. He was not sure if continuously knocking out the cat was a good idea. However, the angry words from Gardner still vibrating in his ears, he decided he had better resort to plan two very quickly.

He grinned at the cat, then scowled, remembering how plan one had failed so dismally. Somehow, two large fire extinguishers had vacated his office, finding their way back to their rightful place. For sure, somebody was poking his or her nose into his affairs and he was determined to find out who it was. He had scanned the CCTV footage for hours, but found no evidence of anyone moving the extinguishers. The only sign of any activity was a cloud of dead leaves blowing along the corridor. Briefly he mused over the design of the state of the art building. The overpaid architects had not even made it draught proof.

Forcing his mind to focus on coming events, he smashed his fist angrily onto the innocent desk in front of him. Someone was interfering in his business he shouted at the now trembling Wilfred, and when he found that someone, they would wish they had never been born.

Wanting to daydream about his revenge, his thoughts were stopped short by a timid knock on his door. How strange, he thought grimly. He had just been surmising who might be messing around with his plans and Bridget Bluestone was standing right outside. Exaggeratedly checking his watch, he gestured for her to enter and place his meal onto his desk.

"Well, I get my meal on time." He nodded towards a tray of food. "Ms Bluestone, have you turned over a new leaf?"

At the mention of leaves, Wilfred jumped up emitting a large meow. Bridget surprised at the cat's unexpected outburst, burst out laughing. Realising her mistake she quickly made to leave the office.

Van de Groot, idly studying the girl, reluctantly acknowledged how pretty she had become. In different circumstances he might have even asked her out for a drink. He grinned as her face reddened. Pretending not to notice he picked up his food, waved her away and ate hungrily. Opening his drawer, he took out a small phial, carefully placing some bluish coloured liquid on to a small piece of meat. "Wilfred." He called the cat fondly.

Realising it was time for one of its favourite games, the dejected cat forgot about its miseries, jumping up abruptly to take a piece of meat. Within seconds, it was fast asleep. Van de Groot slapped his thigh, laughing merrily.

During his team talk, Van de Groot watched each player intently. It had been no problem administering a little of the liquid in their orange juice and he sat back waiting for results.

Too much and he would have the drugs squad on his

back, not enough and his plans would be in vain.

Delighted, he sensed his plans were going to perfection. The players were already looking stifled with another ten minutes to kick off. One of the lads was even yawning.

They were playing bottom of the league Redford, who the experts predicted would suffer another humiliating loss. Van de Groot had other ideas. It was now a good time to get the Keys' fans used to losing.

Ninety minutes later, the players sat bewildered and humiliated. They had been played off the park, losing five nil. Their fans had booed them from the pitch.

The drug now wearing off, they turned on each other in their frustration. For a while, Van de Groot let them argue, and then interrupted to administer one of his soothing speeches. He personally had been jeered off the pitch and he was feeling content to the pit of his stomach.

Van de Groot arrived at his office in a determined mood. Summoning all the players to train on their day off, he wanted to be certain his spin-doctors informed the whole of Fleet Street about his plans. Reading his paper in delight, he took a large piece of fish, tossing it to a delighted Wilfred.

"This one is clean my furry friend." He patted the cat fondly. "Sorry that you had to be my guinea pig." Watching the cat eat hungrily, he picked up his paper, devouring the words that described the debacle of the day before.

The Echo
SKELETON KEYS
Despite the crowd trying to get behind them, the normally resplendent Keys were very far from being on their best form. They were not just beaten but humiliated by a far less superior team.

From the kick of the first ball, each Keys' player made it painfully aware that they did not intend to play football. At half-time, being two nil down, they were booed from the pitch with spectators commenting they

looked like they had taken sleeping drugs.

What super manager Van de Groot told them during the break we have no idea but one thing is for sure – his pep talk did not wake them up. In the second half, they played with no purpose and without any formation.

Most of them would have been pleased to hear the final whistle when they left the pitch five goals worse off amid catcalls from the angry crowd.

Van de Groot is said to be furious and summoned his players to explain their uncharacteristic behaviour.

Throwing the paper happily onto his desk, he picked up his phone. If he was going to be here for the day, he thought greedily, he would need plenty of coffee. He would keep that Bluestone girl busy. After ordering his beverage, he stood by his window. His coaches were putting the unfortunate players through their paces and he felt confident he could leave them to it and move on to plan three.

The referee who was officiating at the next home match was a chap named Ian Baird. Van de Groot had found out accidentally that the man was a chronic gambler. Apparently he was in debt to some bad people, for some very large sums of money. Grinning at his phone, Van de Groot decided he would help the man out. For a few favours of course.

Bridget Bluestone took the tray offered to her, balancing it on one hand. She glared at her supervisor, reluctantly proceeding to Van de Groot's office. Feeling the icy wind kiss her cheeks as she stepped outside, she muttered curses under her breath. She did not like working Sunday and the weather was not making her feel any better.

The previous day she had rushed into the library, wanting to borrow a book to help with her business venture. Somehow she had mistakenly picked up a book on black magic. Not realising her mistake until she had returned home she groaned loudly. She had been hoping for some free time to study and now all she had was a silly book of spells.

To make matters worse her supervisor had called, insisting she work the following day. Van de Groot had stipulated everyone must be at the ground and her supervisor was not going to be held responsible for her slacking off, just because she was too lazy.

Still muttering under her breath, she ambled across the pitch, hoping to save time. The players, training hard on the grounds nearby, met her with a chorus of catcalls. Pretending not to notice she stood watching Wilfred. The stupid cat was guarding the goal post again. However, it was not doing a very good job. She laughed loudly. It had obviously tucked into a big meal because now sleep had taken it over and it was lying ridged covered in leaves.

Decesso relaxed, staring at the light reflecting from his gleaming gold teeth. A large mirror gave him ample view of his grotesque features and he grinned happily at the evil face staring at him from the polished glass.

Very shortly, he thought contently, he would be able to let loose his smouldering anger, venting misery on the world and its peoples. Furthermore, once his gang located Goldsmith he would have the pleasure of sharing his anger while he slowly took the restaurateur to pieces, little by little. Rubbing his hands in anticipation, he eyed his reflection, watching an evil smile form around his crooked mouth. Goldsmith having lost his protection from the bosses had made his soon-to-be demise easier than Decesso could ever have imagined.

He lazily watched his smile disappear, replaced by a distorted line that covered his face. He owed a lot to Maysoni, he mused humbly, and once he ruled the world he would have the now lunatic gangster, released to become his number two. The pair of them would attend the best operas and eat the finest meatballs. Fleetingly he pondered over his good fortune, raising his hand, saluting the grotesque face peering from his mirror. Very soon, he thought proudly, he would have his prize. Adjusting his enormous frame, he allowed himself a rare smile, contemplating his illustrious future.

Once he had the recipe, which few knew existed, he would rule the world. He had waited a long time for his reward and intended to savour every moment of his new life.

His mind wandered back to the time he had been a young enforcer for the bosses. One of his assignments had been collecting overdue payments from one of the numerous hot dog vendors protected by the gangsters. Locating the terrified man, he had been amazed when, instead of being given the obligatory protection dues, he had been offered a pot of honey in lieu of payment. His victim screamed that the honey was special and could change his aggressor's life. Having beaten the man within an inch of his life, Decesso finally conceded that his victim might be telling the truth. After all, no man in the universe could have taken such a severe beating on the pretence of such a bizarre story.

Taking the honey, he had investigated its origins and been astounded at his findings. Whoever had conjured the strange concoction had developed a drug more powerful and habit forming then man could visualise.

He discovered that it originated from the United Kingdom. Manufactured by monks using a recipe hundreds of years old. Initially it was intended to accompany herbal remedies given to young children. As the children mostly refused to take their medication, their parents would administer it with a spoonful of succulent honey. Medicine time was no longer a chore. The honey, being highly addictive, meant children would queue up screaming for more.

As time progressed the honey was administered to livestock, which revelled in its high protein. Chicken farmers could produce much larger eggs while their beasts of burden could sustain another three or four hours of work a day.

Demand on the honey increased dramatically, the fowls and animals becoming addicted to their new medicines. The monks quickly turned their small brewery into a lucrative business. Experimenting, they found they could employ the honey to brew a popular and potent beer. Adults now became interested, rapidly increasing sales. However, the monks could not keep up with demand, causing their disappointed and addicted customers to rob and even kill for the ale that took over their lives.

Decesso had spent years tracking the recipe back to a strange village in England known as November Keys. Consequently, he had influenced the bosses to set up an overseas operation, which necessitated purchasing the village's run-down football club. The bosses, convinced the club could be employed as a fortress along with other dubious activities, listened intently. Promised that their foes from across the channel would have their severed heads presented to them on plates, they had nodded in agreement.

Very soon his plans were implemented, aided by a reluctant but very capable Maysoni. Now with the club on the verge of ruin, it was time to collect his prize. He intended to produce the honey at its strongest and most addictive state. He would then have it packaged in cereals, spreads and drinks. Every man woman and child would become addicted, begging for more. Politicians, heads of armed forces and the world's top bankers would lie down at his feet. Even the bosses would have to kneel in his presence. Eventually he would rule the world. Moreover, it would be ruled on his terms and conditions.

Decesso smashed his hand angrily into his large mirror, his reflection disappearing as the splintered glass fell at his feet. His subsequent arrest and incarceration had delayed his plans. However, those plans would soon be fruitful and he intended to have his revenge.

Van de Groot snarled into his phone. "You give The Giraffes a penalty in the first ten minutes. Any goals scored by Keys are to be disallowed." He sat quietly whilst the man on the other end of the line grovelled. "Well you do have a choice. Find ten thousand pounds by tomorrow evening." Van de Groot, knowing the referee's predicament, forced his point home. He was becoming impatient, drumming his fingers angrily on his desk. "Do you know what happens to a man that owes that kind of money?" At last getting the response he required, he snarled, banging his phone hard on to the table. Sitting back with satisfaction, his head jolted upwards, realising he was not alone. Standing in front of him, nervously clutching a tray was Bridget Bluestone.

"How dare you enter my office without knocking?" He glared at the trembling girl fearful at what she had overheard.

Bridget jumped back in alarm. She had been certain grumpy Van de Groot would be outside on the training ground and had intended to deliver his coffee in his absence. The less she saw of him the better. Now, she thought moodily, here she was, doing as she was told only for him to be criticising her again. Feeling a tear well up in her eye, she glared at the obnoxious manager before placing his coffee onto his desk as hard as she could. Watching the liquid spill onto a sheet of paper, she grinned inwardly. Normally she would have recoiled in fear but her anger had the better of her. "Don't think you can talk to me how you want." She was angry, feeling a tear now trickling down her cheek. "I am a human being too."

Van de Groot sat back, amazed, his mind racing ten to the dozen, genuinely sorry he had upset the girl. However, delighted she had not overheard his conversation. Picking up his coffee, he sipped it gratefully, trying to disguise his embarrassment. Lost in his own thoughts for a moment, he raised his hand and apologised for his unacceptable behaviour. Blaming his temper on the team's sudden loss of form, he acknowledged Bridget's distress, telling her to have the rest of the day off, with full pay of course.

Bridget left the office grinning from ear to ear. She was going to spend her recreational time wisely, she thought happily. There must be a spell somewhere in her book on how to punish a very nasty man.

Van de Groot sat drinking his coffee jovially. Picking up a copy of the Echo, he laughed loudly. Baird, as planned, had been brilliant with his dodgy decisions causing Keys to lose their first game in the group stages of The World Super League.

The following week they would be travelling to play on-form Moscow F. No one would be surprised to see Keys lose that game which would leave them hanging precariously at the bottom of their table. The Dutchman would shoulder the blame for that one. After all, he thought happily, even the best managers make mistakes. Humming softly, he embraced life with utter joy.

The Echo
COME ON REF

The Keys were left fuming after losing the first round of their World Super League venture due to horrific refereeing decisions. Van de Groot must be wondering how he can win anything with such blundering officials in charge of important games like this.

You would not have to have the keenest of eyes to see such a blatant foul by the Cape Town Giraffe's forward on hapless goalie Mickey Gum. However, Ian Baird must have left his glasses behind. Despite his linesman flagging the foul, he awarded a penalty to The Giraffes.

In the second half, Terry Downs for Keys glanced a perfect header past Giraffe's goalkeeper. Baird disallowed the goal. It would take the whole of this newspaper to highlight this bumbling official's mistakes. He was a disgrace and rightfully booed from the pitch. Van de Groot for his efforts, was booked for arguing

**and dispatched to the stands, if there was any better case
for electronic refereeing, we have yet to hear about it.
Next week Keys travel to Moscow F where a defeat
could see them in precarious trouble.**

Van de Groot writhed in agony, rushing again to the small
toilet cubical. Pausing for a second, he tried to remember
what he had eaten that had upset him so violently. Whatever
it was he thought glumly, the doctors had banned him from
travelling to Moscow and he was not happy. He was sure
the team would still lose but would have liked to make sure.
Sitting back with a groan, he contemplated Keys soon going
out of business, which brought a bit of colour back to his
pale face.

Bridget Bluestone sat fumbling with her necklace. She
wondered how long you could go to prison for
administering something unpleasant to someone's food. She
grinned at the book lying in front of her. You did not need a
special spell to keep someone on the loo, she thought
contently. She had not managed to turn a pig into a frog but
she had managed to stop a pig being a pig.

The Echo
KICKING KEYS
**Despite the absence of marvel manager Van de Groot,
the Keys put on a wondrous display of football. Assistant
manager, Mick Jones, could not have done a better job
and the Keys left Moscow with a vital point.
Although the whole team played with adventure and
flair, a special mention must be made of Gum and
Downs. Both players were magnificent in their
respective roles and left Keys clinging on to some hope.**

Chapter Fifteen
Managers That Go Bump In The Night

Van de Groot gazed through the window of his office, watching his new empire carefully. Allowing himself a rare smile, he contemplated a successful future. Despite people meddling in his affairs, all was going to plan. The game in Moscow was just a setback, he thought dismissively. November Keys was going to reap its just desserts.

For a while, his eyes rested on Bridget, who had appeared from nowhere, walking seductively across the gravel pathway opposite the training pitches. Wearing a tight fitting cat suit that showed off her curves, she was attracting a lot of attention. Van de Groot, letting his eyes wander over her body, reluctantly acknowledged her beauty, forcing his mind to concentrate on his activities for the coming day.

Feeling nervous that he might be distracted from what he had to do, he picked up a crumpled newspaper cutting. Sitting quietly, he sullenly read an article testifying of a farm being sold ten years previously. The crumpled paper explained the details of a certain Mr Maysoni purchasing Jack Carpet's farm for a substantial amount of money. Van de Groot read the cutting carefully, angrily aware that a bead of sweat was trickling down his pale face. It was amazing, he thought aloud, how the press could be so easily manipulated to print a load of rubbish. Wiping the unwelcome moisture from his face, his eyes rested on a fading photograph attached to the cutting of Jack and his wife April. They both smiled happily, slightly the worse for wear, with no idea what was to befall them. Shaking his head, he placed the cutting into the top drawer of his desk. As soon as Keys were put out of business the better, he thought wearily.

Bridget Bluestone whistled loudly, exaggerating her best wiggle, noisily prancing through the doors of the burger bar.

Earlier she had felt conspicuous, reluctant to leave her flat. Squeezing into a tight suit had made her breathless, painfully aware of every flaw in her body. It was not until she had started to paint whiskers, her face resembling a cat that she managed to get into the swing of things. Not that she had been given much choice. Van de Groot had insisted everyone should dress for the occasion. He stipulated that November Keys Football Club, despite its precarious situation, was still in the entertainment industry. The long-suffering fans deserved some entertainment. It was Halloween and such a day should be fun.

However, it was not until she made her way, still reluctant, across the gravel paths amid a chorus of catcalls that she really started to feel comfortable and quietly confident. If she was honest, she was enjoying the attention. Stopping for a moment, she eyed her reflection in the glass of the burger shop's door. "Goodness Bridget," she giggled to herself, "what do you think you are on?"

Shyly looking around the crowded eating-house, she was soon aware of appreciative eyes, quickly changing direction when she glanced at their owners. She giggled again. "Well you can look, but don't touch." Still giggling, she bounded through the door of the small office situated at the rear of the bar's counter.

James Book looked up appreciably, ginning at Bridget. He had been looking forward to this day for weeks. Bridget was to be acting manager, which meant he would be spending a lot of time in her company. Pretending to investigate the chrome cooking appliances, his eyes slyly diverted to the beautiful figure in front of him. His face reddening, he wished he were a few years older.

Impatiently watching the hands on his watch, Van de Groot stood up angrily striding purposely over to the burger bar. He had allowed enough time, he thought impatiently, for Bluestone to make her presence felt and he needed to be sure his guinea pigs were in place for his forthcoming extravaganza. Chuckling contentedly, he tried to recall the proverb about the skinning of two cats.

Striding into the small office, he could not help feeling a pang of jealousy seeing the young boy and Bridget laughing together. Although he would rather have his finger nails removed then admit it, the girl still made him feel jealous. Especially when she was with someone else.

"Right we do not have time to mess around." He snarled his words at the startled pair. Pointing at Bridget, he gestured angrily with his hand. "Against my better judgement I have allowed you to be acting manager for the day." He tossed his head back. "You have been given some responsibility at last." Tapping his fingers on the palm of his hand, he stared hard at Bridget. "I suggest you use it wisely."

Leonard Small watched happy customers descending from the myth ride, moaning to himself sadly. To his amazement, everyone seemed to be having great fun. He mourned woefully of his exhibition that never happened, only to be replaced by a crude fun fair ride. The ride in fairness, he thought reluctantly, had proved to be a success. Today, because the management had reduced the entrance fee, it was at its busiest ever.

He watched a wide-eyed young lad proudly showing to an older couple Leonard presumed were his equally proud grandparents, a photograph he had had taken on the ride. Some young girls giggled amongst themselves, brushing past him, tripping clumsily as they raced to beat each other to the long queue.

Whilst he was pleased that the crowd were enjoying themselves, he could not hide his pain in having his pride and joy turned into a crude ghost train. The winding queue should be looking forward to a pulsating lecture on the Keys' myth, not having their stomachs and minds upset by a vulgar fun fair ride, he mused miserably.

Fleetingly he recalled his past conversations with Jack,

vowing that if he were to ever clasp eyes on his old companion again, he would shake his hand whilst telling him how correct he had been.

Turning his gaze towards the burger bar he cocked his head angrily. They had stationed a young lad outside, made up to look like a vampire. He watched intently as small children wandered over to the youth, quickly running away, screaming in mock terror, the youth hissing at them in true vampire fashion. Shrugging his shoulders he acknowledged the boy's acting expertise and enthusiasm but was appalled that such a special day could be turned into little more than a circus.

James Book tossed another burger, his mind conscious of the day's fading time. In two hours the burger bar would be closing which would mean the end of a perfect day. He had enjoyed working with Bridget immensely, not wanting his shift to finish.

Standing upright, he adjusted the devil horns drooping over his forehead, allowing his eyes to roam around the busy eating-house. They had certainly done the place proud, he thought contently. Imitation cobwebs and plastic spiders mingled with witches and scarecrows. James looked on fascinated. He loved horror films and felt that his surroundings matched those of any film he had enjoyed. Sensing a pair of eyes scanning the back of his neck he turned swiftly, startled that Bridget was smiling fondly at him. Feeling his face redden he tried to reciprocate her smile only for his face blush to get deeper with embarrassment.

"James," Bridget giggled teasingly, "you look like one of those wizard things." Without waiting for a reply, she mused for a moment, what a wizard-thing looked like. Satisfied she had the right picture in her mind, she pointed towards the hot plates, grinning at the red-faced youth.

"Now because you are so wicked." James puzzled expression made her giggle, nodding mischievously she

220

pointed at his plastic horns. "You are not to have any rest." She pointed towards Van de Groots's office. "Sir says that all the players and substitutes may sample one of your delicious Double Deckers." She grinned as the youth stood open-mouthed. "That is twenty in all." Laughing inwardly at the lad's apparent embarrassment, she purred the rest of her words. "Are you up to that James?"

James jumped back in amazement his face full of pride. He could hardly believe his luck. Not only had he spent the day with lovely Bridget, now he was being commanded to cook dinner for the entire Keys' players. He stood silently for a moment, pinching his arm to ensure he was awake. Just a few weeks previously he had been unemployed with very little prospects. Now he was standing alongside one of the most beautiful women in the world and was about to cook burgers for his heroes. Just wait until he told his mates, he thought proudly.

"Well daydreamer, are we going to get those meals?" Bridget giggled, sensing James elation and nudging him playfully.

Feeling his face redden again, James tried to put on an act of bravado, smiling nervously at his tormentor. "Yeah, coming up Bridget." He tried to talk without stammering. "No problem Bridget."

Bridget hummed happily, her eyes weighing up her unexpected customer. Quickly serving him a burger she turned her attention to helping James get ready the order for the football team. Finding a little confidence, he tried to flirt with her, the pair of them collapsed in laughter.

"Have you got those meals for the players yet?"

Van de Groot's loud voice made James jump back in alarm causing his plastic horns to drop down onto his face. Shaking his head in disdain Van de Groot glared at the youth, his eyes turning to the pile of burgers ready for cooking. "Am I to take it you are going to feed my multinational players that garbage?" Jumping forward

221

angrily, he swept the burgers from their plates, each falling to the polished floor.

James jumping back terrified, tried to say something but could only imitate a gargling noise.

"Bridget," Van de Groot shouted angrily, "those burgers have been sitting there for hours." He put his fingers to his nose exaggerating a shudder. "How much bacteria do you think they have accumulated?" Nodding his head angrily, not waiting for a reply, he glared again at his startled employees. "Now the pair of you, go to the freezer and get some more." Watching them slink unhappily to the back of the diner, he grinned whilst mouthing a silent thank you to the cobweb-infested ceiling.

After searching in vain for the freezer keys, Bridget decided to let James cook the burgers Van de Groot had earlier demoted to the floor. There was nothing wrong with them she thought stubbornly. Besides, they had been feeding them to customers all day long. In fact, the November Double-Deckers at half the usual price had been flying off the shelf.

Later, making her way to the training ground, Bridget practised her wiggle ready to meet the players. Delighted to be greeted with a chorus of catcalls she grinned, gesturing at her laden tray and was soon surrounded by appreciative young men

"Cor, I wish I were a mouse." One of the players inched closer to Bridget whispering into her ear seductively. "You could catch me all day long."

Bridget laughed loudly, handing out burgers to her noisy customers. "Mr Van de Groot says you can have one each."

"And are you for dessert?" The player nudged closer whilst the others laughed naughtily. Laughing amongst themselves, they set their minds on tormenting Bridget until interrupted by a booming voice.

"So you think you have all day to take your meal break?"

Van de Groot waved a newspaper angrily. "If any of you can read I suggest you read this cutting and memorise its contents." He opened the paper and pointed to the headlines at the inside back page.

KEYS ARE NOT FITTING.

"For those who can't read." Van de Groot spat out his words venomously. "It is saying that if we lose our next game we are all but out of the World Super League." He pointed the paper aggressively at his startled players. "Do you know what that means?" Without waiting for a reply he shook his head angrily. "No more inflated wage packets." Realising he had picked on a subject close to his players' hearts, he again waved his paper. "I suggest you eat and get back to training." He spoke quietly but menacingly. "Or perhaps you will prove our inspired journalist correct."

Happy that he had made his point he went to walk away. Stopping momentarily, he glared at his unhappy players whilst pointing a finger at Bridget. "And you Ms Bluestone, please remember we pay you for your catering skills." He nodded at the burgers disdainfully. "Not your entertainment virtues."

Watching their manager stride away, the players ate quietly, their mood despondent. They all felt they were playing their part and did not take kindly to being ridiculed. Many did not like the way their manager spoke to Bridget either.

Wilfred, whose steep slumber had been disturbed by an appetising smell, wandered amongst them rubbing himself along their legs. Now they had woken him so rudely, he reasoned, he was entitled to be fed.

Relieved that Van de Groot had disappeared for a while the players relaxed, chatting happily amongst themselves, tossing pieces of burger to a very happy feline.

John Goldsmith wearily placed a wad of papers onto his

desk, dejectedly reaching out for more coffee. Sipping gratefully, he propped his chin onto his hand. He had been scanning his paperwork for two days and was feeling the strain of having no sleep.

Despite his tiredness he had scanned the papers several times, digesting each word, praying his discoveries were wrong. If his prediction was correct, he muttered to himself, the whole of Keys and worse, the whole of humanity, could be turned on its head. For a while he sat motionless, savouring his drink whilst trying to absorb information, hoping it might sink into his tired brain. He chastised himself for not realising earlier, but then who would have, he thought grimly.

The first real clue had stared him in the face, Maysoni's name flashing repeatedly onto his small screen. The news channels had not stopped broadcasting. Maysoni, apparently, had suffered a serious mental breakdown. Continuously claiming that dead leaves had attacked him, he forcibly elaborated, that the offending leaves had stared at him through luminous eyes whilst moving with the aid of spindly arms and legs. The press explained the gangster's weird behaviour was part of an elaborate scheme, a disguise of madness to attract a lenient sentence at his forthcoming trial. However, Goldsmith had different opinions. He was certain that no man could have put on such a gifted display of acting. Especially the brash American, who would have preferred the death sentence rather than let the world think he was insane.

He had investigated further, astounded at his discoveries. If he was correct, it was apparent that the Keys' myth was a lot nearer to the truth then people would like to have imagined. Further sinister overtones suggested the Devil himself was involved.

He had commenced his strange investigation by sifting through past archives of The Echo. Without any shadow of doubt, mysterious leaf-like creatures had suddenly appeared, aiding anyone in the village in times of trouble.

Open mouthed, he read report after report of these strange creatures rescuing the day in the most bizarre circumstances.

Most notably was the time when old Charlie Simpkin's horse took fright, bolting frantically through the village, discarding anything that interfered with its new found, albeit unasked for, freedom. Cascading along narrow lanes, it approached local infants being led along a nature trail. Spectators could only scream and pray as the maddened horse neared the terrified children who fled desperately in all directions. The Echo would have been printing news about death and mayhem had not a sudden gust of wind blown hundreds of leaves in front of the equine, causing it to stop in its tracks and sullenly await its distraught owner. Witnesses had joyfully testified to an act of nature that had mysteriously saved the day and the children.

When out of town thieves had called at the Black Cat, outside of licensing hours, to gather their own takeaway, it had been wet leaves that had caused the intruders to slip and injure their bodies to the point of unconsciousness. Although the would be thieves had ranted about strange manifestations attacking and harming them, no such beings were found and it was attributed to the amateur thieves' profound imaginations whilst under the influence of whatever they indulged in.

After reading countless similar tales Goldsmith had emailed a friend at the British Museum, asking for information, however trivial, to be sent ASAP. When his friend hastily replied, he had nearly fallen out of his chair. His mouth agape as he learned of insects existing prior to the Stone Age. His friend having kindly attached photographic evidence made Goldsmith heave his weary body erect in his chair.

The photographs showed that the insects had a strong resemblance to common leaves with frog-like luminous eyes protruding from a triangular body. Equipped with what appeared to be spindly arms and legs, aided by a strange triangular mouth and nose their appearance was akin to a horror film monster. Further, the strange beings would nosily make an odd giggling sound when excited. The report added that the insects had been extinct for several centuries with no further sightings of them.

When he had phoned his friend and asked whether it was possible that some of the insects had escaped extinction, the answer was a resounding no. Although the insects could easily camouflage themselves, his friend had stressed that they could not possibly survive in the modern climate.

Perplexed, he had continuously studied the papers he had borrowed from Leonard Small concerning the myth. After hours of study he was convinced that the insects had played a part in the formation of November Keys.

Perhaps, he thought furtively, it was possible that Isobel had manifested them back to life from some sort of frozen coma. Indeed, many witnesses claimed Isobel had constantly called to something from her makeshift prison. Doubtlessly, they had certainly tried to protect her. The occasion she had jumped from a tree was testimony to that. Perhaps again, that had been a sign of their gratitude. Which would mean, Goldsmith thought curiously, they were able to think in the same way as a human being

Ignoring the tiredness gnawing at his body, he had sat up for another night trying to piece his strange jigsaw puzzle together. As night quickly turned into day, he ignored his hygiene and hunger continuously studying the evidence he had at hand.

He was convinced, despite his friend's protests, that the insects had somehow evaded nature and were populating part of November Keys. His next objective was to find out how and more importantly, why?

There comes a time in everyone's life that they discover facts that are way beyond their comprehension. John Goldsmith grudgingly was soon going to visit his time. His father had warned him continuously, only to use the gem when it was absolutely imperative. When he or he thought other people were in grave danger

Wringing his sweating palms in nervous anticipation Goldsmith felt that time had arrived. Forcing his mind back hundreds of years he tried to imagine how Isobel and Alfred must have felt, harbouring such a dangerous secret.

Following his father's instructions he procured a large candle, quickly firing its flimsy wick. Placing the half opalescent above the flame whilst roughly turning it's blue body he sat back hurriedly as a mass of vivid writing flashed across his wall.

After twenty minutes, he screwed up his tired eyes and slumped forward in his chair. For a moment he silently prayed that his eyes had deceived him. If not, without doubt the whole world was at risk from something that no human being could even start to imagine.

Gaining his composure, he knew he had to act fast. If his theories were correct, someone in Novembers Keys, probably without knowing it, had an affinity with the insects. In fact that person, whoever they were, was the reason for the creatures' prolonged existence. Burying his troubled head in another pile of books he trembled violently. For sure, whoever it was, their life was at great risk.

Bridget crashed through her front door cursing softly to herself. Although tired she had, despite grumpy Van de Groot, enjoyed her day. Shy James had been good to work with and flirting with the players had cheered her up. Every girl needs their ego boosting she thought happily. What better way to boost it then having some of the most handsome men in the world trying to flirt with you?

Checking her watch, she deliberated whether to join her friends for the evening's celebrations. Studying her tired face in a polished mirror, she decided to stay at home. Not only was she extremely tired, she also wanted to experiment with her business plans.

Mouldy Van de Groot had played his last card as far as she was concerned. He was never happy, she thought angrily. She had worked her fingers to the bone running his rotten old burger bar and all he could do was moan because one or two of the players chose to speak to her. It was he who had made her dress up in a skimpy cat suit in the first place, she thought testily, and then he got annoyed because his precious players paid her attention.

Anyway, she thought determinedly, she was not going out and enjoying herself, she would stay home and get her business off the ground. Then she could tell stingy Van de Groot what to do with his rotten old job.

Kicking her shoes across the room, she gratefully remembered a bottle of wine in her fridge. Muttering silently, she tried to locate her one and only corkscrew. Eventually clutching a large glass of wine, which rapidly helped her relax, she half-heartedly scanned the pile of papers in front of her. Quickly becoming bored her eyes rested on a paragraph, expounding the merits of enamel paint. Gulping her wine thirstily, she tried to concentrate on the mass of long words, wishing that she had gone out after all.

She was surprised to learn it was advised to heat enamel paint before use, making it more pliable. This idea fresh in her mind, she decided to experiment. Giggling she poured her paint into a small saucepan shaped like a witch's cauldron. She had spotted it in the market and could not resist buying it. She giggled again, the strong wine now starting to take effect.

If anyone came calling, she thought mischievously, they might think she was a witch brewing up a spell. Happy that everything was in order she gulped down her wine and lay down on her bed. Funny, she thought wearily, how a little responsibility made you tired.

Deciding to watch some television whilst her paint heated, she aimed her remote control, delighted to find one of her favourite horror films loom onto the screen. Draining another glass, she felt her eyes droop while she desperately tried to pay attention to the flickering screen. Aware the film was scary she hugged her knees for comfort. She knew her paint needed attention but fatigue prevented her from moving. Considering it was best to rest a while, she made herself comfortable, lying back with a sigh.

Feeling tiredness overtake her body, she fiddled with her necklace, attempting to stop herself falling into a sleep. Yawning exuberantly, she had allowed her eyes to rest on the beams of a full moon shining through the room, illuminating objects hidden in corners. She felt unusually comforted by the moon's strong light.

Suddenly, she had no idea why, she remembered JJ and his incessant teasing, sadly wishing she could see him again. Peering around the moon lit room, her eyes rested on her collection of hippy paraphernalia, wondering what a farmer's son would make of her obsessions. Shrugging her shoulders, she felt a tear trickle down her face. She had loved the Carpets and wished she could have helped them some more. However, she mused hazily, when she was rich she would find them, and everyone would live happily ever after.

Happily engaged in her new thoughts, she was crudely distracted by a strange noise which she likened to the sound of children giggling. Swivelling her head towards her television, she quickly determined the weird noise was not coming from that area. Hardly daring to breathe, she screwed her eyes up trying to identify the cause of the strange sounds that appeared to be getting louder. Warily, she allowed her eyes to wander to her window, observing the richly coloured moon hovering low in the darkened sky. Stifling a scream, her body stiffened, the light of the moon silhouetting hundreds of leaves floating in the mild air. To her horror, the patchy coloured foliage appeared to have faces, with yellow frog like eyes that glowed in the dark night.

Hypnotised by fear, she sat motionless, surprised the noise that she could hear appeared to be transmitted from the floating leaves. To her horror, she was convinced they were giggling at her. Shaking her head, she looked apprehensively into her now empty glass. "Wow that is strong stuff." Rebuking herself for drinking too much and watching silly films, she closed her eyes hoping that when they reopened the apparitions outside her window would have disappeared. Feeling a little braver, she glimpsed at her window and was relieved that the leafy intruders had now vanished.

Vowing not to drink so much again, she remembered the simmering paint and rose quickly to inspect any damage she might have caused allowing the liquid too much time on the hob.

Muttering silently, she stepped back violently, astounded that her window was now open, aided by the force of hundreds of strange looking leaves, which quickly entered her room, hovering haphazardly around her head. Putting her fingers into her ears, she desperately tried to suppress her intruder's clamour, which seemed to be getting louder. Terrified, she fleetingly hoped she was asleep. Soon to awake.

"Bridget, Bridget, are you in there?"

A familiar voice brought Bridget back to her senses. Rubbing her eyes furiously, Bridget assumed that she had had a very bad dream. Still afraid to open her eyes properly, she squinted at her empty wine glass and again vowed to give up drinking. Looking carefully around the room, with the aid of her flickering television, she was relieved that her window was shut tight with not one leaf to be seen.

She had read in her magazine about nightmares and their causes and vowed to rest and eat proper food.

"Ms Bluestone, open up immediately."

Van de Groot's impatient voice interrupted her thoughts, causing her to curse. Mouldy Van de Groot was real and not part of a nightmare that would go away. Reluctantly opening her door, her mind raced trying to surmise what her obnoxious manger could possibly want so late at night.

"Ah Ms Bluestone." Van de Groot glared at Bridget, "I

thought you were going to keep me outside all night."

Bridget started to apologise until realising her miserable boss was now on her property. "And what gives you the right to bang on my door so late at night?" She spoke defiantly. "This is against my human rights." She was now getting into the swing of things. "I shall call my MP, he knows what to do with people like you." Putting her fingers onto her lips, she wished she could keep her thoughts to herself. Nevertheless, her words gushed out involuntary. "You are just a bully."

"Very admirable Ms Bluestone." Van de Groot's harsh tone rendered Bridget silent. "And I am sure your MP will be delighted to hear from you." He gave Bridget a sickly grin. "You can write from your prison cell."

Bridget stepped back trying to regain her composure, pinching her nose tightly. The smell from her unwelcome visitor's breath was very unpleasant. "Prison cell, what do you mean prison cell?" She felt her throat tightening, hoping that Van de Groot would laugh telling her he was playing a Halloween joke.

Instead he stormed past her, wrenching a mobile phone from his pocket while busily taking pictures of her paint still in its strange saucepan. Bridget did not have to guess the cause of his erratic behaviour, the smell of stale whisky filling the room. It was evident her illustrious manager was very drunk.

"What do you think you are doing?" Although she was in awe of the strange man stumbling around her apartment, she was determined not to tolerate his bizarre behaviour. Staring at Van de Groot with a mixed emotion of fear and anger, she defiantly waited for an answer.

"Further evidence Ms Bluestone, not that I really need it."

Certain her boss had gone mad Bridget stepped back nervously, watching him curse incoherently whilst trying to keep his balance. After what seemed to her ages, he pointed a finger, swaying from side to side.

"You Ms Bluestone cannot go around poisoning my players and hope to get away with it." His words slurred, he gestured towards her novelty saucepan. "I was trying to work out your motives, now I know." His next words made Bridget step further back, feeling a hard wall pressing into her back. "You are a witch." Without waiting for a reply, he aimed his phone for more photographs, occasionally turning his head to hiss at her. "And witches go to prison for a long time."

Pinned up against the wall Bridget had no alternative but to listen to Van de Groot who gleefully told her that all of his players were under medication for food poisoning. He added that food experts had found evidence that the players had been poisoned from burgers that she had liberally given them earlier that day, despite him warning her of the possible consequences.

Not pausing for breath he ranted, that because of her cruel behaviour, his entire first team was seriously ill and unable to participate in one of Keys' most important matches. Because of her callousness, he would have to field his second team, almost certainly to cause Keys to be relegated from the coveted World Super League. Eyeing her smugly, he stressed loudly that she would become the most hated person in November Keys' history.

Bridget tried to reply but could not force any words from her tightened throat. Her stomach was starting to churn and she felt sick. Clutching her necklace for support she prayed that she was still asleep, soon to wake up. However, her drunken manager's words flowed violently.

"This will teach you to meddle in my affairs and move my fire extinguishers."

Bridget, despite her fear eyed Van de Groot in amazement. Somehow the most proclaimed manager in Europe seemed to be going mad and he seemed to be doing it in her apartment. Screwing up her eyes, she could feel a rush of anger surge through her body. Angrily remembering the insults she had to endure from the horrible man standing

232

in front of her, she found her voice.

"Now I don't know what you are going on about." Feeling adrenalin flood her body, she spat out her words confidently. "Those burgers did not poison anyone." Sensing alarm on her manager's face, she continued loudly. "Just before you came earlier, criticising as usual me and James for serving bad food, Chief Inspector Roberts purchased a burger and enjoyed it." Aware that her obnoxious manager was extremely drunk she decided she should choose her words carefully. "So if the players are not well nor will he be."

Watching the colour drain from Van de Groot's face, she pouted angrily, pointing towards her door. "I think if anyone is going to prison it will be you. The police will investigate and see what a horrible man you are."

"How dare you behave with such insolence?" Van de Groot slurred his words, his face turning crimson. "I can prove you are a witch." Picking up Bridget's paint, he sniffed at it suspiciously. "You have put a curse on my football team." His eyes protruding like stalks he waved the cauldron at Bridget, hot paint spilling everywhere. "Everyone can see you are a witch." He grunted his words menacingly. "You would have been burnt at the stake."

Bridget feared that she was going to burst into laughter. However, she knew this was not the right time. Eyeing Van de Groot carefully, she decided he was either demented or drunk, probably both. She wanted him out of her flat and knew she would need assistance.

Fumbling for her mobile phone, she watched Van de Groot warily. She had learnt from her collection of magazines that maniacs could be unpredictable. Trembling violently, she suddenly remembered she had not charged her phone's battery. "The police will be here in a minute." She prayed her bluff would work. "You will be on the news tomorrow."

Now ashen faced, Van de Groot stood silently, staring at the petite girl. Shaking his head vigorously, he desperately tried to free his brain from the effects of the whisky he had earlier consumed.

Weighing up his situation, he decided his foolish plan had been derailed. Evasive action would have to be taken. Lashing out at Bridget, he grabbed her phone tossing it to the other side of the room. "You are not going to stop me getting my farm." Van de Groots's eyes bulged with anger. Lurching forward, he grabbed hold of Bridget's shoulders. "It is my farm, mine and dad's."

Bridget, shaking like a leaf, realised she had made the wrong decision. Muttering silently she wished she had tried to appease Van de Groot, instead of confronting him. She knew, far too late, she had fuelled his anger. Appreciating she had no means of escape, she decided to plead with the lunatic, hoping he would see reason. "Who has got your farm?" She spoke softly surprised to hear her words uttered calmly.

Without replying, Van de Groot, eyes bulging, produced some cord from his pocket, pointing it at the girl menacingly he muttered incoherently. "I am going to get my farm."

Bridget eyed her tormentor terrified. Trying to stay on her feet, she felt waves of nausea moving along her body right to the centre of her head. Her body seemed to weigh like a ton of lead. She tottered forward involuntarily. Before she fainted, she could hear her own words echoing around her room.

"This Halloween is turning out to be a right horror show."

The Echo
KEYS LOCK IN
Everyone in November Keys is holding their breath in anticipation as Keys prepare to take on The Mighty Samba's from Brazil's Rio de Janeiro in tomorrow's crucial leg of The World Super League. A win for Keys would put them in pole position to continue in this

prestigious tournament. A defeat would take the result out of their hands.

Rumours from the Keys camp are indicating that many of the players have fallen prey to a mysterious virus. Mr Van de Groot was not available to comment.

Halloween celebrated in style at November Keys Football Club.

Chapter Sixteen
The Truth And Nothing But The Truth

Bridget cursed, feeling the tight cord pressing into her sore wrists and aware that every movement made her predicament worse. Desperately trying to fend off the fatigue that gripped her body, she willed herself to stay awake, knowing that if she succumbed to sleep precious minutes would be lost. However, despite her best endeavours, she felt the lids of her eyes shutting like iron gates. Cursing the wine she had consumed earlier, she fell into a reluctant stupor.

Soon, although exhausted, the tight rope cutting into her wrists caused her to awake violently. Realising she was back in her living hell, she contemplated her dubious future. Struggling against her bonds, she cursed the day she had decided to move into the complexes accommodation. Indeed, she cursed having taken employment at the football club. Jack, had he been around, would never have condoned it in a thousand years, she thought miserably.

She wondered what had sent Van de Groot mad. She had read in a magazine that work pressure could send people over the top and presumed he had met the same fate.

Franticly pulling at the cord biting relentlessly into her wrists, she felt a tear roll down her cheek. She knew it was not a time for crying but she had no idea what Van de Groot's intentions were. However, she knew that this was not a girl guides' outing. Crouching in the faint light that the now hidden moon afforded her, her ears picked up the sound of footsteps followed by a loud crash from a door being violently flung open. Sitting upright she screamed loudly, a high-pitched squeal that echoed around the room. Despite being in darkness, she could recognise the silhouette of her demented manager, skulking into the room.

"You can't keep me here for ever." Dismayed to hear her words resemble a whimper rather than a roar she

236

nevertheless decided to carry on protesting. "The police will be here soon." Eyeing Van de Groot warily, she continued her protests. "I had a date with James." She studied her captor's face, as she lied. "When I don't show he will call the authorities."

"Ms Bluestone, kindly be quiet." Van de Groot's angry voice made Bridget sit back with a thud. "You have only yourself to blame for getting in this situation." Van de Groot paused for a moment. "I had no wish to harm you." He looked at the girl sternly. "But you had to interfere, didn't you?" Glancing out of a window, he nodded his head in satisfaction. "Nevertheless, very soon you will be no trouble to me at all."

Disturbed by the clinical sound of his voice, Bridget resorted to omitting a howling noise deep from her throat, hoping that someone might hear.

"Bridget, please be quiet." Van de Groot spoke softly, his lips quivering. "I only wanted to get our farm back." He looked pathetically at the girl. "I want things the way they used to be." Taking a roll of paper from his pocket, he gestured for Bridget to look. "These are the plans that I had drawn up." Without waiting for a reply he unfolded the paper, pointing at a juvenile drawing of a house. "This will be mine and dad's new farm." His eyes bulging, he poked the drawing with a dirty fingernail. "You could have come to visit, like you used to."

Bridget recoiled in fear, making out even in the dim light that her captor's face had taken on a vivid red hue. He had also decided to impersonate a werewolf, a hideous howling tunnelling from his throat.

"But you had to interfere." Delighted at Bridget's fear, he dropped his voice to a hoarse whisper. "Anyway, I want you to meet my friend." Producing a glass fish tank he looked on triumphantly.

Bridget's eyes bulged with fear. Sitting in the centre of the tank was the biggest spider she had ever seen in her life.

Watching her cringe, Van de Groot sneered, placing the

tank a foot away from his captive's legs. Opening it casually he grinned like a man possessed. "I think Rose is hungry."

Bridget trembled with fright. "Rose?"

"Yes, she is named after a dog I knew."

Van de Groot reminded Bridget of one of the villains in the horror films she loved to watch.

"And she does not like meddlers."

Shaking her head, Bridget sensed that words were going to be a waste of time. The spider was produced for one reason only. "Look I did not meddle." She hoped she sounded persuasive. "You need to see a doctor. He could help you."

Van de Groot responded by putting his head back, expounding a noise which resembled an injured hyena. "Too late for words Ms Bluestone." Kicking the dodgy container gently, he eyed Bridget triumphantly.

Bridget, trembling, desperately tried to remain calm, watching the spider intently, crudely stumbling inside its makeshift home. Suddenly, sensing food, it raised its ugly head and walked clumsily towards its prey. Bridget tried to scream but could only hear a muffled sound coming from her throat. Her eyes started to water, her face flushed red.

Van de Groot watched the spider with the glee of a curious child, rolling his bulging eyes at the dimming moon. "You were always afraid of spiders, Bridget." Glaring through drunken eyes, his mouth uttered a torturous scream.

Bridget feeling a familiar dizziness revolve around her head realised that pleading eyes and countless words were not going to get her anywhere. Unless she wanted to imitate a fly, she had to act fast. Summoning the last of her strength, pain searing through her bruised arms she managed to stand upright.

"Sit down Bridget." Van de Groot, incensed at his captive's audacity, lunged at her, pushing her roughly back into her seat. Stumbling backwards, her hand caught her necklace exposing it to the ebbing moon.

Both captor and captive were rendered silent, the

darkened room suddenly glowing a golden yellow. Speechless, both were frozen to the spot, horrified that the bright glow was being transmitted from hundreds of small eyes. For an instant, they became reluctant allies, both as terrified as each other. Hundreds of leaves, dancing frenziedly, circled the room omitting a terrifying giggling noise. Van de Groot was the first to recover, hurling abuse at his young prisoner.

"You are a witch, you have created beings from Hell." Astounded that his earlier accusations were in fact proving to be correct, he feared for his own life.

Suddenly his numb brain managed to reason that the evil creatures should be fought with fire. His eyes alerted to an old paraffin lamp, he stumbled across the room, fumbling with a lighter buried in his pocket. Quickly helping the lamp's wick to burst into flame, he set about setting light to the curtains adorning the small window of the makeshift prison. Screaming obscenities at Bridget, he watched the curtains burst into flame, his mouth falling open in amazement at the strange creatures, now screaming hideously, whilst flying frantically around the small room. Van de Groot ready to hurl more abuse, suddenly reaped the results of his earlier drinking binge and collapsed into a drunken heap.

Bridget, though relived that the unconscious manager could now not harm her, could hear her own screams of panic echoing around the room. Surprisingly, she had felt a vague protectiveness whilst Van de Groot was awake, now it was just her and the creatures from Hell.

Squinting her eyes, she could determine the leaves had multiplied in numbers, now hovering precariously close to her weary body. Screaming loudly, she pulled violently at the cords biting into her arms. Although close to collapsing she felt a surge of energy vibrate through her body, her bonds dropping loosely to the floor. Astounded at her sudden liberation she decided to follow Van de Groot's example and fight the evil invaders with fire. Remembering hairspray in her bag, she quickly retrieved it aiming the nozzle at the now blazing curtains. Watching the flames expand, she forced her fingers into her ears, deafened by the creature's incessant screaming.

She had never heard sounds like it in her life and the pitiful wailing, despite her fear, made her burst into tears. Distressed, she hung her head in relief, her invaders disappearing as quickly as they had arrived.

Still mortified with fear, she knew she had to prevent the blazing curtains spreading to the rest of the room.

The familiar noise of her door crashing open caused another involuntary scream from her parched throat. Wide eyed she watched as a portly figure sprayed the curtains from a red fire extinguisher. Screwing her eyes up in the now darkening room she recognised her rescuer as John Goldsmith. Trying to find some words, she sat back startled, the normal jovial eccentric staring at her angrily.

"You might have frightened them away for good." His voice softened, acknowledging Bridget's distress. "But you were not to know." Getting to his knees, he gently tapped Van de Groot now sitting up, wide-eyed. Mumbling to the intoxicated manager while he checked his pulse. "He will live." He smiled kindly at Bridget, Peering over the edge of his large gold-rimmed glasses, he reminded Bridget of a headmaster.

"Mr Goldsmith, it is so nice to see you." She wrinkled her face in mock horror. "But you should know that Mr Van de Groot is a madman." She glared at Van de Groot, happy in the realisation he was unable to retaliate. "He tied me up and tried to poison me with a big spider." She pointed at the guilty tank, relieved that her hairy assailant had climbed back into its prison. "And he was rude to me all the time." She could feel herself getting in the swing of complaining.

"Yes my dear, I know." Goldsmith patted Bridget's shoulder. "But he was not himself." He stared grimly at the now shame-faced manager. "Is that not correct JJ?"

"JJ?"

Bridget, aware her voice resembled an incoherent gurgling stared unbelievably at her one-time friend. "How could you?" Not wanting or expecting a reply, she rushed towards her assailant who now stood unsteadily on his feet. Although feeling drained, she managed to make a fist, striking the unsteady man with all of her might.

JJ, white-faced, reeled backwards, grateful to feel Bridget's bed take his weight. Suddenly he felt different as although he had been locked away in someone else's body. Staring at Bridget, he wondered how he could have intended to hurt her. Half listening to her complaining about his harsh treatment, he sat silent, taking in her beauty.

"JJ, goodness knows what damage you have done." Goldsmith's voice boomed across the room. "But it is the future we have to worry about now." He smiled sympathetically at the young man. "You are not to blame entirely, it is evident you have suffered a great deal of stress."

Putting his fingers to his lips, he gestured Bridget to cease complaining. "This young man has been very ill." He looked hard at Bridget, willing her to understand. "He was not responsible for his actions."

Bridget, intending to start another tirade of abuse, bit her tongue, trying to force a smile. She had heard of mental illness, aware of its repercussions. Deep down she felt great sympathy for the crushed man, wondering what Jack would think if he was around.

Suddenly, she recalled the occasion JJ had presented her with a brand new pair of shoes, hers being just about to fall apart. Smiling, he had never mentioned that he had spent the last of his money. Although bewildered and humiliated by his actions over the last few weeks, she could never really hate him. Besides, she thought generously, he had been ill.

JJ, shaking his head, wondered what miracle had snapped him out of his insanity. He knew he had many consequences to face, but was pleased to be back to JJ again.

His thoughts wandered to when he had booked a ferry across to France. After a while of watching grey waves dancing majestically, he had walked to the stern of the ship. Here he had encountered another man who could have passed as an identical twin. They had both laughed about the uncanny resemblance. The man had introduced himself as Van de Groot, a football manager whose name was on the lips of every football fan in Europe, JJ professing his love of the game, locked them in conversation for a considerable time. Eventually, they decided to play a joke on Van de Groot's entourage.

Swapping jackets, it was decided JJ would impersonate Van de Groot, wagering how long their innocent espionage could last without him being discovered. However, their game was never bought to a conclusion. A freak wave sweeping across the ship caused both men to tumble into the angry sea. JJ made it somehow to the shore. Van de Groot was never seen again.

During his time in the sea, the cold conditions took their toll and he was hospitalised. Initially suffering amnesia, he was amazed on his recovery to be referred to as Van de Groot. Recalling the switch of jackets and the intended hoax, he had kept quiet about his identity.

Suddenly a plan formed in his mind where he could take revenge on the villagers who had stood by watching his parents being run out of their property. If people thought he was Van de Groot then he would be Van de Groot. It had taken no effort to bestow his services on Keys.

Being desperate for leadership after the incarceration of their manager, the club were delighted to have the services of someone as famous as the Dutchman was. Arriving back at November Keys he had no concerns with people guessing his identity. A change of haircut with an exaggerated gait had concealed the young farmer.

The villagers could only recognise their new hero as the illustrious football manager from Holland, cheering him every step of the way. Quickly he was plotting Keys demise, determined that every villager would have a taste of what his parents had to endure.

What he had not foreseen however, was the insanity that took over his mind. At first, he had tried to fight it but as it gained control he submitted to its terrors.

"It is in the past now."

JJ's mind was brought back to reality, Goldsmith's voice puncturing the room.

"The police will decide your fate if there is to be one." The chubby man spoke nervously and quickly. "Am I to assume that Keys will lose tomorrow?" Goldsmith looked sternly at JJ who hung his head trying to sidestep his stare.

"Yes and he tried to blame the poisoning on me." Bridget's voice was getting back to normal and she wanted to make it heard.

"Yes, yes my dear." Goldsmith looked soothingly at the tired girl. "And he will be dealt with in due course."

Goldsmith and Bridget fell in to a sudden silence, interrupted by the sound of muffled crying.

"I am so sorry." JJ dabbed at the tears streaming down his cheeks. "I have been so stupid." Shaking his head, he looked accusingly at Goldsmith. "I thought my family were friendless."

"I know JJ and I can only apologise." Goldsmith uttered his words with sadness and compassion. "But I had to get you all from that farm. Your lives were at great risk."

"Like mine with the spider?" Bridget piped up again.

"Worse than that my dear." Goldsmith looked concerned. "I had known for some time that a certain Mr Decesso had been trying to locate your father's honey ale recipe." He turned quickly, placing his hands on JJ's shoulders. "JJ, if he does get his hands on that recipe, the whole of mankind will wish it was never created."

"But what did that have to do with dad's farm?" JJ shook his head puzzled.

Goldsmith gave a frenzied laugh. "This man is completely evil." He looked sympathetically at the young

243

couple. "He would have thought nothing of torture or anything else." His eyes penetrated through JJ's anger. "I had to get you all to safety."

JJ and Bridget sat spellbound, listening to how Goldsmith had become involved with the Carpets' farm. How, masquerading as an eccentric connoisseur, he had persuaded Jack to leave his recipe for his honey ale in the custody of Goldsmith's safe.

The restaurateur explained how at the time he had had protection from the bosses. However, it was evident that Decesso was in pursuit. The American, aware that Jack knew the recipe back to front, intended to have him tortured until he parted with his valuable information. Worse, if Jack had managed to last through such an ordeal, the attention would have turned to April.

He stressed the importance of the protection from far over the sea. Whilst that protection was in place, no mob member would have dared lay a finger on Goldsmith, who had endeavoured to have the same protection afforded to the Carpets.

The American Maysoni had put an end to that whilst also turning Jack's friends against him. He cleverly replaced the honey bees with a variety that could kill. This fact, a man paid dearly with his life, to find out.

The villagers were outraged in case their precious club along with their own interests did not expand as expected, and they turned their hostilities towards Jack. Fuel was added to the fire when it became apparent a batch of eggs from the Carpet farm was identified as being contaminated. Another clever trick from Maysoni, who was intent on grabbing the farm.

Goldsmith squirmed with embarrassment, recalling how he had poured oil over troubled water, publicly denouncing Jack and his farm. He stressed how essential it had been to keep the bosses on his side. However, that had not been the case and the rest was history. It had been fortunate Decesso had found himself incarcerated.

JJ, having sat motionless devouring every word, rose quickly, offering his hand to Goldsmith. Thanking him for his endeavours he begged the chubby man to forgive him, promising that he would do everything to put matters right again.

Urging Bridget to make some coffee, Goldsmith proposed that the past should be forgotten whilst they concentrated on Keys' bleak future. Invigorated by the caffeine, he rose to his feet, ready to discuss his plans.

Whilst accepting Keys were going to lose their next game, he maintained they still had a chance to qualify for the next rounds of The World Super League. JJ, keeping up his pretence as manager, would have to make sure of that. Failure, he stressed in a strained voice, was not an option.

Maysoni had cleverly sold off the club to the villagers. The gangster would not have done this through any benevolence, it was simply to avoid taxation and scrutiny from the authorities. Consequently, November Keys owned Keys. A club about to go bankrupt. Quite simply, if Keys failed to qualify everyone in the village would lose their homes, businesses, land and much worse.

JJ looked on in shame, embarrassed as he recalled his conversations with Gardner, who was waiting in the wings ready to pounce. It was his fault that Keys were balancing on a tight rope. If Keys disappeared, his father would have been destroyed.

"He is safe with your mother in Portugal." Goldsmith spoke softly appearing to have read the young man's mind. "More than can be said for me." He looked at his two companions desolately. "By now Decesso's spies would have informed him of my location." He drummed his fingers nervously on the table, causing some of the coffee to spill. "Believe me, he will not stop until he gets his prize."

Bridget, who had been sitting quietly, peered softly at the kind man in the gold suit. "But what is so important about a recipe that makes a honey drink, Mr Goldsmith?"

"Well my dear, we have to go back a long way to answer

that one." He spoke patiently. "Back to the start of time in fact."

JJ and Bridget sat speechless again, whilst Goldsmith unfolded his strange story. Their mouths fell open as he explained the creatures that so many had sighted, especially young Bridget, were in fact descended from prehistoric insects. In the age of dinosaurs, they had existed in their thousands, if not millions.

Over the course of time, however, they had become nearly extinct. Making a tasty meal for hungry animals along with the uprooting of their homes had caused many of the problems. Their inability to breed in their new surroundings had caused their numbers to dwindle considerably.

He detailed how Isobel had played an important part in Keys future. Perceived to be an old crone concocting spells and involved in witchcraft, her neighbours eyed her suspiciously. However, Isobel, despite her dubious reputation was a very astute woman.

Her friendship with Alfred the monk had given her access to the recipe he used to lovingly brew his ale. After a few experiments she quickly realised, with the aid of her potions, the recipe could be used to produce an addictive drug. It was only after wrongly intensifying the ingredients that she realised how addictive the honey could be.

Although it has been widely acclaimed that it was monks who originally concocted the brew, it was Isobel who produced it to its full strength.

Goldsmith, sensing his companions were becoming impatient, tapped his spectacles and proceeded with his strange tale.

"Although from vastly different backgrounds, Isobel and Alfred shared many common interests. Stories of Alfred's love for God's creatures were abundant. A trait that Isobel admired and tried to emulate. Whilst on one of her daily jaunts she encountered our strange insects. One had flown into a spider's web, whose inhabitant was more than ready for lunch. Entangled in the web, the doomed insect could only cry out to its companions. A cry that resembled a strange giggling noise. Isobel, distressed by the pitiful noise, quickly disentangled the insect and placed it gently onto a leaf in a nearby bush. It was now she noticed how the creature appeared invisible. To all intents and purposes, it looked like a common leaf from any tree. Not having witnessed such a creature before, she studied it intently, until disturbed by a hideous noise above her head. Circling above her, were hundreds of the same creatures, calling in a strange tune."

Goldsmith studied Bridget and JJ's reactions. He knew he was getting to the part of his tale that would most interest them. He proceeded, speaking quickly.

"The creatures, indebted for the saving of their comrade's life, befriended Isobel, wishing to make hers' and the inhabitants' of Keys lives safer. Isobel quickly realised the insects were far from normal. They seemed to have powers far greater then could be imagined. Harnessing these powers, they worked relentlessly to protect the villagers from all types of danger."

JJ whistled softly to himself recalling the time he had fell from the oak. There was no question that they had saved his life.

Goldsmith, reaching out gratefully for more coffee, proceeded with his tale, whispering to his stunned audience

"If the creatures or Isobel considered that the villagers were to be grateful they were very disappointed. Because of their ignorance of such matters, it did not take long for these people to abuse their rescuers and accuse Isobel of calling them up from Hell. Stories were rife of her strange behaviour and they wanted her executed as a witch. Now this is where our story takes a far more sinister turn. Many tales have been told of Isobel's behaviour and subsequent imprisonment. However, it was not made clear."

Goldsmith took a deep breath, his face taking on a pale hue. "That there was one being in the whole of the universe that was afraid of these strange insects. It is not understood why, but these creatures put fear through the Devil himself. Unbeknown to the residents, whilst the insects populated November Keys, he stayed at arm's length vowing to have them destroyed. Further, promising that when the last one had expired he would wreck carnage on Keys and the rest of the world, a wrath that no one had witnessed before. All the years of his humiliation would be avenged."

Goldsmith poured more coffee, eyeing the other two sympathetically. He knew this was a story that they should not have to endure, but there was no time for pussyfooting, time was of the essence. Gulping his drink greedily, he carried on with his strange tale.

"Now onto the scene, came Mario Decesso. Willing to serve any master for the right price, it was said he made a pact with Lucifer to rid the village of the insects. His reward was to be made immortal with riches beyond all expectations. He would also sit with the Devil, in his next world.

Again, many stories have been told of his murdering and torturing innocent women right up to his subsequent execution. Although he had not rid the world of Isobel, his legacy did accomplish something of great importance.

Everyone is aware of Harvesting Leaf Day. A celebration instigated by the evil Decesso. This presumed innocent celebration over the coming years resulted in many of the insects losing their lives to fire, thus explaining to this day their morbid dread of flames."

JJ whistled softly whilst Bridget squirmed, both remembering their involvements earlier.

"Back to Isobel. Now imprisoned with no future in November Keys, her only solace was Alfred. They would sit for hours praying and discussing their future. Alfred cooked up a successful plan, helping them both to escape, but neither one would be able to set foot in Keys again. In addition, the creatures themselves were planning an exodus.

Heartbroken by Isobel's treatment they had no wish to

offer any further protection to the ruthless and uncharitable residents of Keys. Isobel, fully aware of the implications of their departure, pleaded for them to remain. Explaining that during one of her liaisons with Alfred she was now pregnant which meant that there would be a future heir of Isobel's to protect. After much discussion, it was agreed the creatures would remain, only to offer protection to the one who wore Isobel's necklace.

Isobel planned to plant an oak tree where they would live undisturbed. Therefore, to this day, these creatures have inhabited the old oak, unwittingly giving protection from the foulest creature in the universe. They reside inconspicuous until anyone ventures near their habitat or attempts to interfere with their surroundings."

Goldsmith recalled the demise of the American gangster who had been ordered to burn down the oak.

"Of course, over the years, incidents and sightings of the insects have been recorded. When the one with the necklace was near, the creatures, offered her their protection extending it to her friends and the village as a whole."

Looking at Bridget sadly, he lowered his eyes.

"Mr Goldsmith," Bridget gestured to the big man, "why did the leaves want to save me?"

"Ha, Bridget my dear, you have a great deal to learn." Goldsmith smiled unbuttoning the top of his red shirt, exposing a beautiful looking necklace.

Bridget trembling, examined the identical jewel hanging around her own neck. Sitting silently, she tearfully recalled how she had chased her benefactors away with fire. The one dread they had in their tiny lives. They had tried to save her life and she had tried to destroy theirs.

She knew now, what her necklace meant. Her mind wandered back to her infancy. Her mother pleading for her to guard the heirloom with her life. She had been entrusted with the world's future. Suddenly, as though a bolt had hit her she forced a smile, turning to face John Goldsmith.

"You mean," she uttered her words meekly, "me and

you?"

Goldsmith laughed aloud. "Now my dear it's not that bad." He looked at the young girl seriously. "You're down the line from Isobel and I'm down the line from Alfred."

JJ, ashen faced, tried to comprehend the implications of his own actions. Bridget, the youngster he had teased, was related to Isobel, and Goldsmith to Alfred the monk. Shaking his head vigorously, he tried to rid his unwanted thoughts.

"It is serious JJ." Goldsmith interrupted his splintered thoughts. "When you masqueraded as Van de Groot, you thought you were Van de Groot." The restaurateur eyed the young man sympathetically. "Let's say your mind was not your own."

Gesturing with his podgy hands, he pointed towards the Keys' playing pitch. "When Decesso arrives his mind will not be his either. He believes he is coming to steal a recipe, Lucifer has other ideas." Goldsmith shuddered involuntarily. "The repercussions of the recipe falling into his hands would rock humanity."

Looking at JJ intently, he spoke his words slowly. "However, if November Keys goes bankrupt, it will mean the subsequent felling of the oak, the leaves will disappear. The Devil will then inhabit November Keys fulfilling his promises to wreak carnage. All humanity will cease to exist.

If Keys do survive and don't go bankrupt, he will demand that the wearer of the necklace be destroyed." He tried not to look at Bridget. "One way or the other," he eyed the youngsters miserably, "if that has not happened already, the creatures will be doomed."

The Echo
LOST KEYS
Although The Keys were a shadow of their normal team, the brave youngsters battled the talented Brazilians for ninety minutes. However, the superiority of the opposition showed and the Keys walked back

down the tunnel pointless. With other results favouring Keys, they now must win their next game or it is probably goodbye once and for all. Van de Groot had little to say, pointing out nine first team players were absent due to sickness. It is not over to the fat person sings, was his final words as he promised Keys would be safe.

Residents of Keys, prepare for Harvesting Leaf Day.

Chapter Seventeen
Remember, Remember,
The 13th Of November

Goldsmith attempted to pass the time fiddling nervously with stress balls clenched tightly in his podgy fist. Hearing the voices of excited fans beginning to enter the stadium, he shivered with expectation. Very soon, he thought dismally, those same fans would either be dancing triumphantly or mourning the loss of their proud village. If only the team could overcome their defeats and win their points. His thoughts trailed off, shrugging his broad shoulders he shook his head sadly, not wanting to contemplate the disasters that awaited failure.

Catching sight of his large bulk reflected from a polished case of drawers, he allowed himself a rare smile. He looked every inch the eccentric millionaire that he liked to portray. If only people knew his real purpose, he thought sadly.

Trying to concentrate on the day ahead he fleetingly wondered where Decesso might be hiding. Without doubt, the cunning gangster would not be far away.

Tapping his gold pen noisily on his neat desk, he mused whether his foe had had his mind taken yet by the Evil One. Shuddering, his own mind was not able to deal with his unwanted thoughts. The gangster was formidable enough without assistance from supernatural powers, he thought gravely. Whilst Decesso's mission was to secure the recipe and wreak carnage in revenge for his friends, there was no doubt that his supernatural master had different aims.

He pondered over a possible Keys defeat and its awful consequences Goldsmith reflected on crisis talks with his lawyers. If Keys managed to keep their position in the World Super League, it could be plausible that he might just be able to donate necessary funds in the form of advertising.

Pressing his hands together, his mind wandered to the

plight of the creatures living in the oak. It was also possible, he thought grimly, that JJ and Bridget might have accomplished what the Devil himself could never do, expel the insects from Keys. Forcing his mind to suppress this dreaded thought, he considered whether the authorities should have been told the whole truth.

For a while, he tried to picture the strange police inspector's face changing colour while Goldsmith explained about the Devil and curses. For sure the man would have him locked up as a lunatic.

Disgruntled, he walked over to a well-stocked drinks cabinet, pouring himself a large whisky. Sipping his drink quietly, he wondered how JJ was going to cope. Although the stupid young man had made his bed, so to speak, he had not realised what he had been getting into. To expect him to take charge of the forthcoming game was a huge responsibility to put on such young shoulders. Nevertheless, if he did manage a victory, it might just alleviate some of the consequences heading his way.

JJ was not a bad lad he thought kindly and if he pulled off a sensational win, many would soon forgive his previous transgressions. It would be pointless for Goldsmith to testify that the young farmer had been under the influence of evil. No one would want to believe such dangerous talk.

Refilling his glass, his thoughts wandered to Bridget. It was almost impossible to contemplate the terrible danger the feisty girl was in. Especially if Decesso got hold of her. Without any protection from the creatures in the oak, her future looked bleak. Swallowing his drink, he stood up briskly. Not all the worrying in the world was going to change things, he reprimanded himself. Firstly, he had to steer Keys to their much-needed victory and then worry about the girl.

The fans swept through the gates, frantically grabbing piles of floating leaves, essential for their superstitious making of wishes. Many did not fully realise the implications if Keys failed to win, treating the day like a carnival. Excited children donned Wilfred masks, laughing happily as they clutched their parents' hands without any understanding of what the day's events might lead to.

Others, who were too much aware, peered nervously. Many had spent the last few days protesting at the injustices suddenly bestowed upon them. Some had sent petitions to Downing Street. They protested that gangsters, especially incarcerated gangsters, had no right to dictate to them the future of their beloved club. Desperately they chanted the name of John Goldsmith, the only man they felt could save them. Knowing if Keys failed to win, they could be without jobs, homes and a village, however, none had any idea of the real terrors, which only a fiction writer could describe, that awaited them.

The large police consignment, mostly sympathetic to their cause, supervised patiently and kindly. Police officers geared themselves up for the aftermath if Keys did not get their vital points. The inspector's message to the nervous crowd was simple. Despite their concerns, act sensibly, get behind your team and cheer them to victory.

John Gardner bandaged his battered face, deciding that a housing complex in November Keys was not a good idea. Not if he wanted to stay healthy, anyway. He flinched violently. Not so much at his pain but of the memory of events that had taken place in his office earlier. Delighted that November Keys was just one game away from falling into his hands, he had contemplated a very bright future. That was until he had visitors.

The big American had very impolitely advised him to get out of the picture. Rather foolishly he had argued. He now realised it was not a good idea to disapprove of another man's intentions. Especially a maniac. Tenderly touching his bruised face, he shrugged his shoulders, musing over the plans for his next project.

Decesso checked his reflection in a polished mirror, chuckling loudly. He had learnt that his ugly features looked more fearful when he laughed so decided to ponder on coming events that were going to make him happy. However, his grotesque features were not the only ugly part of him. His mood was ugly too.

Just a few days earlier he had visited his friend Maysoni. The man had been a gibbering wreck. It had distressed him immensely. Today he and his friends were going to exact a large slice of revenge.

He had fixed the coming game. Keys were going to be knocked out of the World Super League, causing the inhabitants to face ruin. Then, while they contemplated their demise, he was going to blow their beloved stadium (and most of them) high into the sky. That was the least he could do, he thought benevolently, for his friend in prison. Before this happened, he was going to have the detested Goldsmith apprehended. An early death was far too good for him.

Studying his face in his mirror, he was reminded that it was Goldsmith who had instigated his time in prison. Before he had the fat restaurateur tortured, he thought maliciously, he would lay on a cabaret for him. Whilst awaiting his own fate, Goldsmith would witness the very unpleasant death of the girl and the chicken farmer's son. Isobel's death was going to be an overdue reward for Decesso. The chicken farmer's son would be a favour for Maysoni who had detested his father.

He laughed happily, watching the corners of his mouth curl into a cruel sneer. A nagging thought in his head told him he must destroy the oak also. That too would be a pleasure.

JJ approached the manager's dug out, shyly acknowledging the fans' applause. Trying to divert his eyes from the vast crowd, he stared steadily ahead. The same people would be baying for his blood, he thought timidly, when they got to know his real identity. Especially when news of his activities over the previous weeks was broadcast.

Shrugging his shoulders, his eyes wandered to Bridget. He grinned, watching her as she sipped one of her favourite milk shakes, apparently carefree. Staring hard at her slight frame he realised how fragile she was and in need of protection. He shuddered, screwing his eyes tightly shut, remembering the ordeal he had put her through. Still, he thought grimly, there was no time for such thoughts now, he had a game, a very big game, of football to win.

Despite various distractions, the fans remained restless. Many sitting silently waiting apprehensively for the official in black to blow his whistle. Cheers rang around the stadium when Wilfred appeared.

Ignoring the attention he usually craved, the unhappy feline crept towards the pitch, eyes down, refusing to acknowledge his admirers. The last time he had participated in fun and games he had been rendered seriously ill. Helping those people eat their burgers had brought on very serious consequences. He screwed his eyes dejectedly, remembering the vet demand he be put on a water only diet for three days for a severe case of food poisoning.

Listening to his name being chanted he stood up reluctantly, glaring at the noisy crowd. Turning his back rudely on those he perceived as the perpetrators of his misery. When the cheers became louder, he closed his eyes, rolled over and went to sleep.

Mike Matthews paced his newsroom, chattering nervously. Aware as a professional reporter he had to remain impartial, was not making his day any easier. Despite his supposed neutrality, he was hoping for a Keys victory. The hardest part for him was going to be commenting on the coming game without giving that away.

Being a professional reporter, he was aware that both teams deserved equal respect. Nevertheless, he knew what a defeat for Keys would mean and did not relish the thought of having to tell over one million listeners, in a short while, that Keys were to go into liquidation. Over the years he had, like many others, fallen in love with the club and had great sympathy for their predicament. Shrugging his shoulders, he resigned himself to the afternoon ahead and picked up his microphone.

At last the time came. A nervous referee blowing his whistle for the much-awaited game to commence. Both teams were cautious from the outset, playing defensively and causing both sets of fans to groan and boo their own players.

Resigning themselves to a half-time draw and an unpleasant second half, the Keys' fans were rendered silent. Torments by opposing fans, reminding them of the consequences if their team did not score a goal, made them check their watches, longing for the first half to finish. They reasoned that after Van de Groot had conducted his dressing room team talk and the team regrouped, the second half would be much more prosperous.

They remained silent when a perfectly timed ball fell onto the boot of Jimmy Evans who wore the number seven shirt. Their silence changing to groans when he dispatched the ball straight into the hands of the opposing goalkeeper. Their moans changed to gasps when the normally reliable goalie threw the ball back to the boot of Jimmy Evans. Their gasps changed to cheers when Jimmy, not looking a gift horse in the mouth, took his second chance and floated the ball perfectly into the corner of the net. Their cheers changed to boos when the referee tried to disallow the goal. Overruled by his defiant linesman, urged on by an angry crowd, the goal stood.

The Keys' players kissed and cuddled. The Keys' fans screamed with delight. The referee, peering fearfully into the crowd, blew his whistle to end the first half.

Bridget, although happy with the first half outcome, sat quietly, apprehensively looking into the crowd. The strange police inspector had promised her safety. Leering, he had also promised to buy her dinner to celebrate later. However, as hard as she looked, she could not spot one single police officer. Supposing they must be in plain-clothes, she picked up her bag, peering into it for the umpteenth time.

Fondly caressing a battered Valentines card, she hoped JJ's punishment would not be severe. She chuckled, rolling back the years. The card arriving anonymously, the familiar writing pointing to JJ's guilty pen. Fiddling with her necklace, she wished the old days could return. Things had been so much happier, she thought wearily. Her time spent with the Carpets, squabbles with JJ, everything had seemed forever.

She wondered sadly, what would happen to JJ. Although he had been despicable whilst masquerading as Van de Groot, she was ready to forgive. Anyway, as Mr Goldsmith had explained, sinister forces had been at work. She knew, however, that he was in serious trouble.

Trembling she contemplated the impact on Jack and April. Jack, having suffered enough, would have the indignity of his son incarcerated in some dingy prison. Shuddering, she felt a tear trickle slowly down her cheek. Dabbing at her eye shadow and causing a dark blue smudge, she promised quietly that she would do everything to help. John Goldsmith had promised that he would help her with her business. The proceeds would at least help the Carpets in the future months. That is, if there were to be future months.

Her thoughts concentrated on the dangers that lay ahead. It was possible that she and JJ had unwittingly caused the leaf creatures to flee November Keys. If that was correct, she shuddered nervously, as Mr Goldsmith had said, the Devil might take his revenge. Biting her lip, she tried to stop more tears trickling down her pale face.

It had not helped learning of her ancestry to Isobel the witch. All those years ago, she thought miserably, the creatures had saved Isobel and when the time came, they tried to save her as well. For their reward, she had chased them with fire, the one thing they feared the most. Whilst pleased that Keys were winning, she wished that by some miracle the little leaves would reappear making their strange noise. She could then tell them how sorry she was.

"Looking good Bridget." Her thoughts were interrupted by the kindly voice of Goldsmith.

"Thank you Mr Goldsmith, I try to look my best." Bridget's face reddened at the chubby man's compliment.

Goldsmith's face also coloured, realising Bridget supposed his remark was aimed at her. "Well, I did mean the team." He paused a little embarrassed. "But you look very nice as well Bridget."

Bridget acknowledged her mistake by blushing violently. Making her excuses, she hurried to the burger bar.

JJ, his mind in turmoil, tried to sound positive as he gave the jubilant players his half-time talk. His earlier, unexpected, visitor had added extra tension to his dire situation. Especially when he had been forced to come clean about his dubious activities. Trying to concentrate on the difficult second half, he demanded each player give more than one-hundred-percent commitment. Reminding them that one lapse of concentration could lead to the loss of the homes and livelihoods of thousands of decent hard working people. Happy that he had made his point he prepared to lead his team back to the pitch.

Despite the fans calling his name, Wilfred slept through the interval. He was fed up with people and in future was only going to give attention to his owner. The last time he had been friendly and partook of a few morsels from people he trusted he had been very ill. You could not trust anyone, he thought testily, so from now on he was going to keep himself to himself.

The game resumed, thousands of nervous fans watched

quietly. It was obvious, to those who had any inkling of tactics that Van de Groot had reverted to defending their solitary goal. As their watches slowly ticked away the seconds, each said silent prayers, willing the final whistle to end their misery.

JJ, in his dugout, shouted furiously. Checking his watch, he knew that if Keys held out for another ten minutes they were safe. Barking endless orders, the shrill of his mobile phone momentarily rendered him speechless. Angry with himself for leaving it switched on, he irritably pressed it to his ear, astounded that someone could be so stupid as to interrupt him during such an important match.

"Ah Mr Van de Groot, or should I say Jack Carpet Junior?" The voice on the phone sounded hostile, making JJ stand rigid. "No questions, be in your office in the next minute."

JJ perplexed, at his unwanted call, quickly tried to weigh up his options. Obviously, the caller knew his identity. This realisation sent goose pimples running down his spine. Frantically trying to decide his next course of action, he sucked in cold air, resigning himself to his coming fate. Whispering in the ear of his assistant coach, he quickly ran to his office.

During the short journey he envisaged the sight of burly police officers waiting with handcuffs. Headlines would appear the next day, telling the world of his heinous crimes.

Breathing deeply, he quietly opened the door of his office. His eyes rested on three smartly dressed men slouching across his desk. His eyes darted from one to the other and he felt a mix of emotions from fear to relief. The men staring menacingly at him were certainly not police. His confused mind identified that fact. However, his confused mind also identified that they could be a lot worse.

"Ah JJ," Decesso sneered at the young man standing in front of him "nice of you to join us." Putting up a podgy hand to prevent JJ answering he sneered, pointing to the roof. "In about eight minutes your beloved football club is going to be blown out of existence." He spoke slowly and chillingly. "That is unless you cooperate fully."

JJ shook his head violently, praying that he was asleep. Fleetingly closing his eyes, he imagined the stadium in turmoil, people screaming. Wondering, angrily, how people could make such threats, he eyed his trespassers defiantly.

"Now when you get back you are going to make some substitutions." Decesso growled his words, taking no heed of his victim's defiance.

The American's growl forced JJ's mind back many years before. The American gangster, Maysoni, had used the same tactics on his father. Recollecting the misery steeped on his family, he stepped forward angrily, his mouth uttering as many abusive words as he could remember. Before he could utter another word he felt a blow to his jaw, propelling him backwards until he lay in a heap.

"There's more where that came from." Decesso chuckled happily, eyes bulging, daring his victim to retaliate. "But we don't have time to mess around and nor do you."

JJ, back on his feet, stood like an awkward schoolchild, his mind desperately seeking some inspiration. It was evident, he thought wearily, that the American was mad. Every time he mentioned bombs he would take a detonator from his pocket, mimicking exploding sounds through a twisted mouth. In between his abnormal behaviour he demanded that JJ substitute the Keys' goalkeeper and a striker, replacing them with defenders. Gleefully reminding JJ that it would need a thousand ambulances to clear the carnage if his instructions were not followed, he nodded, indicating their conversation was at an end.

Hurrying back to his dug out, JJ ran a finger along his swollen face. Trying to unscramble his mind he desperately figured what was going to happen over the next half hour. For sure, if he made the substitutions Keys would lose the game. Even if he did not make the ridiculous substitutions Decesso had gleefully informed him the referee had been paid to alter the scores.

He shuddered, recalling the fat American sneering whilst describing a dubious penalty that was going to be awarded. If John Goldsmith had been correct, the whole world was at risk.

Peering timidly into the stands he spotted Goldsmith, a smile etched across his ruddy face. For a while, he deliberated whether to obey the fat American or disobey and face the consequences. Sucking in the winter air through clenched teeth, he instructed his coach to make the substitutions.

The sombre mood in the stadium soon changed to a noisy angry cauldron of hate. Keys' fans shouted obscenities at their ashen faced manager.

Goldsmith witnessing the events unfolding below him angrily smashed a fist into the palm of his hand. What a fool he had been, he thought dismally. He had given JJ the benefit of the doubt and now the young upstart was wrecking the football club again.

He had thought long and hard about letting Jack's son continue but concluded it was the right thing to do. If the players had known about his dubious activities just before an important match, all hell would have broken lose.

Pleased that the Keys' goalkeeper Mickey Gum was refusing to leave the pitch he decided to take advantage of the mayhem and rush to the dugout. Jumping to his feet he ran as fast as his large frame would allow, joining a trembling JJ.

"What on earth do you think you are doing?" Goldsmith's squeaky voice had changed to a growl.

JJ sprung around, surprised the normally mild-mannered man could sound so angry. He knew explanations would not suffice so quietly handed Goldsmith his mobile phone. Fortunately, he had been able to record his earlier conversation with the American.

Goldsmith, feeling the colour drain from his face, could only make a mumbling noise. His instincts were to summon the emergency services, however the American had made it clear that such an act would necessitate the waiting detonator to be plunged early.

His own mobile phone, now screaming for his attention, interrupted his worried thoughts. The caller's voice was harsh and to the point. Goldsmith must be at a rendezvous or else. They already had the girl. His eyes swivelling around the vast stadium came to rest on Bridget's VIP seat. Goldsmith could not contain the unwelcome scream that forced itself through his mouth. The seat was empty.

Each Keys' player pushed their bodies through the pain barrier, knowing it was just minutes before they could celebrate their most famous victory. None of them could fathom Van de Groot's strange substitutions, but put it down to some weird mind game he was playing. Their job was not to challenge their manager's authority, it was to challenge for the ball. With the crowd screaming with excitement, they called on every ounce of energy, willing the next few minutes away.

As the clock ticked around to the last two minutes of added time, The Mississippi Bards played a wonderful high cross, causing the Keys' fans to gasp in admiration and nervousness.

The Keys' defender and club captain Steve Brown, having defended similar balls through the entire game, read the situation well and put in a well-timed tackle, hooking the ball over the side-line and away from danger. These balls were bread and butter to him, smiling contentedly, he placed himself to defend the subsequent throw in. Watching the referee blow at his whistle constantly, whilst waving his arms aimlessly, did not warn him of events to follow. Only the noisy complaints from the crowd and his colleagues, forced his mind to realise that the referee was pointing to the penalty spot whilst brandishing a red card.

The violent protests that followed never changed anything. A penalty was awarded, the offending defender trudged to the dressing room perplexed and mortified.

Mike Matthews sitting up in his control room, despite his supposed neutrality, screamed angrily. Knowing that the referee had made the wrong decision, he wanted to show the replay as quickly as possible. The referee was a buffoon and he wanted to prove it to his millions of viewers.

However, to his dismay, the studio technicians had lost the picture and not all the shouting in the world could restore it. Here was an epic in the history of football taking place and he could not relay it to his viewers. Looking down over the pitch he watched dumbfounded whilst shouting obscenities.

Now a burly man, dressed in a smart blue suit, approached the penalty taker, roughly handing him a note. The player, who had been standing mockingly by the ball, read the note, all colour draining from his face. Walking uncertainly to the ball, hands together as although praying, he smashed it in to the back of the net.

"The referee is crooked."

JJ whispered out of the corner of his mouth. Listening to the complaints of the crowd, he faced the pitch forlornly cursing himself for his past actions, making up his mind to hand himself into the police straight after the match. If it had not been for his madness, Keys might still be in their lucrative tournament. Instead, here they were on the brink of disaster. He shuddered, contemplating what his father would think when the news got back to him.

Wilfred, unceremoniously woken up, shook his head disdainfully, glaring at the noisy football pitch. Now his rest had been interrupted, he meant to pursue his favourite pastime – eating. His pleasant slumber had made his stomach better, so now he had to fill it. Recognising many of the people standing around the pitch, his attention diverted to a solitary figure dressed in black. His feline instincts told him the man would have something tasty for him.

To a thunderous applause from the crowd he walked clumsily onto the pitch. Siding up to the referee, he nuzzled up to his leg, eyeing him expectantly. The official hardly able to believe his eyes, aware that he was on national television, gently pushed the ugly feline with the toe of his boot. Wilfred surprised, ran to the back of his supposed benefactor, gently nudging his calf. This was a bonus, a game and then some food. The referee, slightly forgetting he was on national television, called for assistance before lunging angrily at the frisky feline. Wilfred, now basking in the lime light, attacked the referee's boot mischievously, quickly jumping back. Repeating the episode several times, spurred on by both sets of supporters, he stood staring expectantly at the man in black. Although he was enjoying his game, hunger was now getting the better of him. He wanted his treat. Swiftly moving behind the irate official, he managed to sink his teeth into the back of his calf. A playful peck to remind him about supper. The outraged referee, jumping back in pain, completely forgot he was on national television and aimed his boot angrily at the naughty cat. Missing completely, he lost his balance, fell backwards with his head hitting the floor with great force.

It took the cheering crowd several moments to realise he was out cold.

Decesso, sneering triumphantly at his reluctant guests, ordered his driver to proceed. Hugging his prized detonator tightly, he periodically threatened to push its plunger, indicating that very soon the stadium was going up in flames.

Goldsmith, aware that his captor's mind had been taken, felt it fruitless to utter any words. Placing an arm around a terrified Bridget, he prayed that her ordeal was not going to be as horrific as he surmised it would be.

The technical staff, above in the control room, darted from one place to another. There was history happening on the field below and yet they could still not get a picture. If the non-existent penalty was hot news, what about a cat that had just taken out the referee? As much as Mike Matthews shouted obscenities, the picture did not appear and millions joined him, swearing at their television sets.

On the pitch the substitute referee studied his watch, placing his whistle in his mouth to blow for time. His two minutes of fame had gone quick. Hoping that his family were watching his first televised match, he tried to locate one of the many cameras to give a knowing smile.

The Bards' defender, sensing the official was about to call time, gently rolled the ball, unhindered, to his goalkeeper. He had looked for an attacking player but as suspected, Keys had run out of steam. Their missing man had taken its toll. Smiling, satisfied, he fleetingly wondered how his colleagues were going to celebrate progressing to the next stages of the competition.

Around the stadium, the sound of groans from the crowd became deafening, quickly turning to jeers, many noisily complaining they had been robbed. A few cheered Wilfred for injuring the hated referee, who they saw as the perpetrator of their coming miseries. Unhappily acknowledging their failure to take the three points, their minds diverted to their miserable futures, causing a sullen quietness amongst them.

The happy Bards' fans, as though commiserating for their rival's demise, stopped cheering and taunting, eyeing the Keys' fans with sympathy.

Soon the ground was rendered into an eerie silence. No one uttered a sound when the floodlights flickered off and on, their dim lights casting shadows to fall over the pitch. A few murmurs could be heard, cursing a light wind picking up empty wrappers, tossing them at the crowd.

Few had previously heard the strange giggling noise that penetrated the silence in the sombre stadium. Every fan stood mesmerised, watching the pitch fill with leaves dancing frantically, aided by a fierce wind. No one could muster one word, as though hypnotised by the cloud of vegetation now circling the discarded football. Hardly able to believe their eyes, they bellowed in fear and astonishment. The green and brown foliage seemingly picking the ball three feet into the air, hurling it into the back of the Bards' net.

The stadium descended into darkness, the floodlights altogether failing. The Keys' players locked in a celebratory huddle, stood motionless surrounded by hundreds of yellow luminous eyes.

Tom Doulby had screamed himself hoarse, hurling oaths at the referee's decision. He had then laughed until it hurt, watching him carried from the pitch. Fuelled on by the vast intake from his flask he had hurled abuse at the substitute referee who he deemed was blowing his whistle too early. Watching the ball float into the enemies net, he shouted obscenities at his fellow fans. Sharing his oaths amongst the Bards' players and fans, he gestured insults with his fingers.

Not considering his rudeness might cause others to take offence, he suddenly became silent. An object, he presumed thrown from the Bards' rabble, landing onto the crown of his head. Uttering oaths at anyone who might be unfortunate to hear, he raised his hands to dislodge his unwanted parcel, intending to hurl it amongst the Bards' fans. Gingerly touching his balding head, beads of sweat trickled down his face. He realised something was rubbing against his fingers. It was something extremely furry and it was moving. Mortified, his body stiffened, feeling the furry bundle start to crawl down his face, its hairy legs now touching his quivering chin. His eyes were wide open with fear. Although dark, he was certain he could glimpse thousands of small hairs.

"Goodness me, goodness me." He spoke through clenched teeth, similar to a ventriloquist, terrified the creature might crawl into his mouth.

As quickly as the lights had failed, they flickered back to life, illuminating the stunned faces of the spectators. Dancing gold keys on the glass interior walls were enthusing the fans to celebrate their goal.

When the penny finally dropped, the Keys' fans found their voices, their cheers shaking the rafters. The referee, whistle still clenched between his teeth, could only muster a faint murmur. Whilst the opposing players, dumbstruck, screamed for the goal not to stand. They reasoned that the goal was an act of nature. Complaining that leaves, blown from a nearby tree, had hindered their goalkeeper. However, try as they might, not one player could produce one leaf. They had completely disappeared.

Mike Matthews screamed even louder at his back room staff. His crew had only the feeblest of excuses about leaves clogging up their equipment. He insisted vocally, that there would be more then equipment clogged with leaves if he did not get his picture back.

On the pitch each player stood quietly whist the referee deliberated with his linesman. The crowd, their fingers crossed, hissed and booed. After what seemed hours, the referee waved his hands, acknowledging that the goal was to stand. Waving away objections from the opposing team, he put his whistle into his mouth, blowing for full time. The eruptions from the crowd were explosive.

Tom Doulby now seeing no evidence of anything hairy groaned incessantly. Taking his cherished flask, mumbling inaudibly, he tossed it into the crowd.

JJ, paralysed at the touchline, tried to avoid the ecstatic coaches and players determined to hug and dance with him. Looking apprehensively around the vast stadium, he tried to identify any signs of a bomb erupting. Certain that an explosion was inevitable, his mind prompted him that he must alert the emergency services to the carnage that was to follow. Frantically tapping his keypad, he was rendered motionless by the sound of loud bangs echoing from the top of the stadium. Hardly able to breathe he stared foolishly. A thick blanket of smoke drifting above the proud arena.

Decesso eyed his captives triumphantly whilst waving his prized detonator wildly. "I thought we will all have a ride on the ghost train." His voice reached a high pitch, reminding Bridget of a banshee. "But don't worry I am not going to charge the fare." The American gangster, finding his remark funny, bent forward in raucous laughter, saliva dribbling from the corner of his mouth. "But first things first." Lifting the detonator to chest level, eyes bulging, he firmly gripped its plunger, intent on blowing Novembers Keys to oblivion.

"Wait," Goldsmith's voice sounded far from squeaky, "your quarrel is with me, not with them." Whilst he spoke, he wrestled with the tight cord binding his wrists, praying his voice did not betray his anxiety.

Decesso, mistaking Goldsmith's words as a plea of mercy, hopped from one foot to the other. Twisting his mouth in to a cruel sneer his eyes swivelled from Goldsmith to Bridget in turn. "They will all die." He spat saliva, his words screeching from his throat. "It is the master's wish."

Bridget cried out loudly, fearfully watching the American's face take on a sickly green pallor.

Sensing her distress, Decesso grunted with delight and plunged the detonator as hard as his podgy hands would allow. Goldsmith shook with trepidation, thinking of the thousands that were going to perish He wished he had gone against his instincts and warned the emergency services. At least some would have had a chance.

Wrapped up in his pitiful thoughts, he waited for the noise of the coming massacre to commence. After strained moments of silence, realisation hit his mind hard. For whatever reasons, the bombs had failed to explode. Nearly sobbing with relief, he glanced at a now livid Decesso, whose face had changed from sickly green to a vivid red.

Decesso, glaring at his subordinates, screamed oaths, constantly pushing the plunger on his defunct detonator. Hardly able to speak through his anger, he gestured for Goldsmith and Bridget to be thrown into the carriages of the ghost train.

The two captives, hardly daring to breathe, stared ahead, reluctantly listening to the loudspeakers above their heads transmitting their awful noises, which seemed to mock their predicament. Their compartment thrust forward slowly, taking them to their fate.

"Ah Isobel, we meet again." Decesso leered at a frightened Bridget. "However, this time you will not escape my punishment." Sitting behind his captives, he leant forward, his sickly breath causing Bridget to retch, coughing violently.

"When I have the recipe I will rule the world." His voice reached a high crescendo. "Everyone will bow at my feet."

Both Bridget and Goldsmith realised they were dealing with a lunatic, his voice resembling a hysterical woman.

"My master will rule the universe."

Goldsmith, ignoring the noises droning through a darkened tunnel, twisted around to stare at his captor. "Decesso, you can have the recipe, just leave the girl alone." Quickly he slouched forward, trying to remain conscious. Before he fell into a sleep, his last recollection was of a brightly coloured bar.

"Please have the courtesy to address me by my real title." Decesso smashed the iron bar angrily again onto Goldsmith's head. "My name is Mario."

Bridget, terrified, pulled hard at her wrists, praying her bonds would loosen. Her actions making her arms throb with pain she emitted a pitiful whine. Sitting back dejectedly, she trembled at the thought of her fate in the hands of the demented American. Straining her ears, she was relieved that Goldsmith was still breathing. The sudden halt of the carriages brought her senses back. Feeling a large pair of hands around her shoulders, she was manhandled from her seat and thrown to a cold floor.

JJ blinked nervously, desperately relieved that the thick smoke dancing above him was caused by cheap fireworks let off by the happy fans. Not understanding why the bombs had not exploded, he felt it a priority to find Bridget and Goldsmith. Racking his brains to where the mad American might be holding them, his mind suddenly recollected the story of the myth. It dawned on him that the ghost train was a perfect place for a lunatic to hold hostages. Gasping, he started to run.

Fighting the exhaustion that was persuading her body to faint Bridget battled to keep her eyes open. Squinting through the dark, reluctantly listening to the words from the ghost trains loud speakers demanding the witch be burnt.

Shuddering, she quickly closed her eyes, suddenly aware that the once darkened area was now glowing, reflecting flames of raging bonfires. Dense smoke attacked her nostrils causing her to cough violently. Relieved that Goldsmith, lying close by, was still breathing she tried to sit up, the bonds on her wrists hampering her actions. Hearing footsteps, she laid back feigning sleep.

"Another one for the fire."

Merriment could be heard through the gruff voice. Feeling a weight drop beside her, she half opened her eyes, horrified to see a beaten JJ.

" It is time for your punishment."

Bridget trembled, the half-audible voice of Decesso puncturing the room. Straining her eyes she made out a pyre, neatly assembled, a pole erect through the centre.

"Come Isobel, time for you to go."

Bridget screamed hysterically, huge hands grabbing her tired body, manhandling her towards the crude pyre.

"Your friends can't help."

Decesso, as though reading the terrified girl's mind, joyously explained there was no chance of history repeating itself. Her insect friends would not go anywhere near fire.

He happily continued that after she was burnt at the stake, the creatures would be obliterated. The oak would be destroyed and he would own the Carpets' honey ale recipe and rule the world. A gift from his grateful master, who would subsequently wreak havoc on the whole of humanity.

"Don't you see, you are being used?" Bridget was surprised at the defiance in her voice. "How can you rule a world that will cease to exist?" She knew she had only words as weapons and intended to use them wisely. "Once you have exterminated the leaves, your master will exterminate you as well. He just wants you to get rid of the creatures he is so terrified of." Staring straight at the bloated face of her captor, she forced a strained laugh. "You will then become his slave."

Decesso, showing no sign that Bridget's words hurt him, leapt forward, slapping her hard across the face. "Quiet Isobel, time for your destiny." Mumbling incoherently, he placed a piece of wood in one of the fires, chuckling menacingly as he watched the tip burst in to flame.

Bridget, feeling cold liquid, which she recognised as petrol, splashed over her, clasped her hands and prayed.

Decesso dancing with glee, waved his torch, igniting the petrol drenched firewood.

Goldsmith, knowing it was useless to fight his bonds, rolled over attempting to console an ashen faced JJ.

Above the noise of hissing flames, Bridget's screams echoed around the room. Suddenly a noise far louder than Bridget's screams filled the room causing the captives to shake with terror. The red flames of the fire changed to green casting eerie shadows to dance along the surrounding walls. Goldsmith and JJ retched violently, a hideous odour penetrating their nostrils. Both could not prevent strangled screams escaping from their throats. Hovering above them, swaying in time to the movement of the flames a monster stared hideously at them. Its two horns reflecting an eerie green light.

Decesso, dropping to his knees, pointed humbly at the fire now starting to curl up to Bridget's limp body.

JJ, tears running down his face, tore desperately at his bonds.

"Bridget, I love you."

Decesso, his green pallor matching the flames from the fires, hissed manically. "Goodbye, Isobel." Grabbing an old parchment and scanning it fleetingly, he looked knowingly at the visitor with the two horns. "On November 13th, Isobel will be destroyed." He jabbered excitingly. "Afterwards the village will be washed of the leaves."

Throwing the parchment aside, he grabbed a large can of petrol. Staring at his perceived master who was now smiling broadly, he made to throw the contents of his can over the terrified girl.

The sudden hissing noise that filled the air rendered the room into silence. Captors and captives alike stared foolishly at numerous red fire extinguishers blowing a steady stream of white foam.

Jack Carpet, stern-faced, watched the flames die around Bridget before diverting his attention to the other bonfires. Leonard Small, Lionel Bains and the other villagers whooped in triumph, their own firefighting skills overcoming the flames.

Jack shook his head in disbelief, taking in the scene in front of him. It had been hard to digest his son's story earlier in the day, but now he could witness it with his own eyes. Trembling, he gestured for his comrades to free Bridget and the two men. Pleased that he had followed his instincts, he bellowed out a scream, relieved that he had arrived on time.

Earlier, after an agitated discussion with his son, he had seriously considered having JJ sectioned. The boy's behaviour and subsequent babbling about the Devil had persuaded him his offspring needed help. However, standing by the beloved oak his mind had been warned not to discard his son's strange tale so readily. Fortunately, he had followed his thoughts. Wiping a sweaty hand across his face, he shuddered at the thought of what would have happened if he had not.

Decesso, speechless with rage, squinted his eyes whilst prompting a huge torch into action. Establishing that his men were ready for action he gave orders to fire. In seconds, several machine guns were ready to discharge their lethal cargo. The podgy American, although furious at not having his victim overcome by fire, was now determined to destroy everyone with bullets. Peering nervously at his two-horned friend he gave the order to fire.

The giggling noise, which filled the room, caused everyone to clasp their hands over their ears. The whole area was awash with luminous yellow eyes, rendering everybody motionless, except the two-horned creature that trembled with fright.

Alphonso, finding his nerve, desperately tried to reignite the fires, beckoning his cronies to follow suit. This was a good time to destroy the creatures from the oak, he thought madly. Right in front of his beloved master. Fumbling with matches, he too shook with fear, witnessing a foreboding creature walking straight towards him.

Everyone stared ahead, speechless. A witch glowing bright green, resplendent with customary broomstick, pointed menacingly at the now gibbering American. Behind her, glowing bright yellow, an ancient executioner resplendent with axe also pointed at Decesso menacingly.

Although they tried to move, the onlookers were rooted to the spot. The bright yellow executioner swung his axe at the fat American whilst hissing loudly, a pillar of smoke pouring from its mouth.

As quickly as they had appeared the witch and executioner vanished leaving behind them a swarm of creatures emitting noisy sounds resembling that of a child giggling. Quickly they formed a banner that glowed through the dark. BRIDGET WE LOVE YOU. WE LOVE NOVEMBER KEYS, BECAUSE OF YOU.

Decesso shaking with rage demanded his henchmen stay and fight the supernatural visitors. The American's cronies had different ideas. Terrified by the apparitions, they dropped their guns and scrambled to a prearranged exit. They were well aware what had happened to Maysoni and had no wish to follow his fate.

Alphonso's two-horned guest shimmered with anger. Its green eyes now glowing red stared hard at Bridget.

Decesso, himself realising the folly of attempting to defeat the leaves alone, screamed incoherent oaths, his fat body lumbering behind his comrades.

A mass of yellow eyes diverted their attention to the two-horned monster that now jiggled with fear. Forming a shape of an umbrella, they hovered above its two horns, giggling incessantly. The umbrella turned upside down, a cloud of yellow dust spraying over the unwanted guest. The bellowing noises it emitted caused everyone to push their fingers into their ears. Suddenly it disappeared, leaving an awful odour that enveloped the quiet room.

Every one jumped involuntarily, a stubborn cork noisily dispatched from an innocent champagne bottle shattering the silence. Although now on safe soil in Portugal, memories were still full of past events. As the popular drink flowed, the group became relaxed, recalling the amazing events over the last years.

Goldsmith related his story how ten years previously he had helped Jack and April to flee to Portugal, where Jack had set up a new farm for his beloved bees and chickens. Looking sympathetically at Bridget he hastily explained it was essential to keep the Carpets whereabouts absolutely secret Jack and April's lives had been in great danger .He added, that although falling foul of the bosses he intended to resurrect his restaurants whilst overseeing finances in the football club.

Jack, to every ones amazement, maintained that despite missing November Keys he loved his new life style and had no wish to return to England. Although not having any issues with his old friends who had pleaded with him to return, surprisingly, he loved his new home in the sun and so did a much-tanned April.

The judge had been lenient, bestowing, on a very relieved JJ, a suspended sentence, every resident of Keys providing glowing testimonials. His barrister, puffing noisily, had pleaded for mercy, emphasising, in true barrister fashion, that JJ's mind had been temporarily stolen. That it would be a travesty to put the genial young man behind bars.

Both JJ and Bridget stressed they would be returning to November Keys. Bridget proclaimed that she now regarded herself as the protector of the oak. Maintaining that the creatures, hopefully residing there forever, having saved her life, now needed her protection.

JJ wanted to be with her, whilst spoiling a very popular Wilfred. Jack, pleased that the feisty girl would have his son's protections, winked knowingly, promising he and April would attend the wedding. Much too every ones amusement, Bridget had stamped her feet in customary fashion, glaring at JJ, Jack and April in turn.

Although Decesso was certain to make another assault on the oak, it was deemed that some of the past events should remain hushed up. One day the whole story would be told. However, it was wildly felt that in the meanwhile the residents of November Keys still had many obstacles to climb without enduring stories of addictive honey, giggling leaves and a mad American gangster who befriended the Devil.

The Echo
THE KEYS OPEN THE DOOR.
Despite leaving it to the last second, the Keys progress to the next round of The World Super League.

Given a goal that will be discussed for years, the players will be forgiven in thinking that Harvesting Leaf Day played a part in their victory. A game full of incidents saw a penalty that never was, a cat KO the referee and a goal scored by leaves.

Police are investigating several unexploded bombs placed around November Keys stadium. Experts have maintained that many lives would have been lost had it not been for the mechanisms of the explosives being clogged with wet leaves.

John Goldsmith has announced he will be sponsoring Keys Football Club.

The British Police have requested the assistance of USA authorities in apprehending Alphonso Decesso. He is wanted for questioning for a number of crimes, including murder, attempted murder, arson, and kidnapping. His whereabouts are yet unknown.

The End.

Lightning Source UK Ltd.
Milton Keynes UK
UKOW03f0147161014
240157UK00001B/4/P